The Merchants of Health

The Merchants of Health
and Other Fantastic Stories

by
Pierre Véron

translated, annotated and introduced by
Brian Stableford

A Black Coat Press Book

ISBN 978-1-61227-372-3. First Printing. March 2015. Published by Black Coat Press, an imprint of Hollywood Comics.com, LLC, P.O. Box 17270, Encino, CA 91416. All rights reserved. Except for review purposes, no part of this book may be reproduced or transmitted in any form or by any means, electronic or mechanical, including photocopying, recording, or by any information storage and retrieval system, without permission in writing from the publisher. The stories and characters depicted in this novel are entirely fictional. Printed in the United States of America.

TABLE OF CONTENTS

Introduction

Les Marchands de Santé by Pierre Véron, here translated as "The Merchants of Health," was initially published by Dentu in 1862. The second novella in the collection, *Monsieur Personne*, here translated as "Monsieur Nobody," followed from the same publisher in 1864; it was reprinted in 1878 by Calmann-Lévy as *En 1900*—misleadingly, since it is deliberately set in 1901, that being the first year of the twentieth century. The two short stories preceding the first novella, "Le Déluge en Paris" (tr. a "The Paris Deluge") and "Le Journal de la dernière Robinson" (tr. as "The Journal of the Last Crusoe") were both published in book form in the collection *Les Marionettes de Paris* in 1862, but if they follow the common convention of setting futuristic fantasies a precise number of centuries in the future after the date of writing, the former must have been written in 1859 and the latter in 1860.

The four items following the second novella appeared in book form in four further Dentu collections: "L'Omnus aérien" (tr. as "The Aerial Omnibus") is from *Comédie en plein vent* (1867); "La Double vue" (tr. as "Second Sight") from *Paris à tous les diables* (1874); "Le Raccommodeur des cervelles" (tr. as "the Brain-Mender") from *La Vie Galante* (1888); and "Encore la fin du monde" (tr. as "The End of the World Again") from *Propos d'un boulevardier* (1888). The last-named is not a story but a brief exercise in speculative whimsy; its inclusion is not out of place, however, as it humbly takes its place within the history of speculative fiction as a kind of pocket manifesto for far-futuristic fiction. The original publication dates of all four of the later pieces are likely to have been the year previous to their collection in book form.

When he began to carve out a successful career as a journalist in the early 1860s, Pierre Véron (1833-1900) swiftly became a frequent contributor to two of the most popular Parisian humorous papers, both founded by Charles Philipon, *Le Charivari*—the satirical magazine which served as the model for the English magazine *Punch*—and the more broadly humorous *Journal Amusant*. Most of his contributions to the periodicals were made during the editorial reign of Charles' son and heir, Eugène Philipon, which began in 1862, and Véron succeeded Eugène in his turn as editor-in-chief of both periodicals in 1874, retaining that position until his retirement, only a few months before his death. Once he had taken over the editorial chairs, his own contributions to the magazines became considerably less prolific, and somewhat less mordant. It is arguable that he did his best satirical work in the early 1860s, and that his work became steadily more relaxed and amiable thereafter, as his sarcasm gradually smoothed out the aggressive edge contained in the two novellas featured in the present collection.

Apart from an early collection of poetry and the published versions of some of his plays (which were mostly written in collaboration with Edmond Gondinet), the contents of Véron's many books, including his patchwork novellas, were derived from his writings from those humorous periodicals, almost all of which was done in the form of vignettes that rarely ran to much more than a thousand words. Almost all of his prose pieces, whether fictional or non-fictional, were ironic reflections on Parisian life, and his work for the theater, including librettos for operettas with music by Robert Planquette, is in the same vein. Although *Les Marchands de Santé* is an interplanetary romance set on the Planet Fantasia, Fantasia is, essentially, Paris writ large—even larger that the immense future Paris featured in *Monsieur Personne*. All of his speculative works were stimulated by his interest in the manner in which Paris was evolving, both physically and socially.

The dates of the two novellas straddle the publication date of Jules Verne's first novel, so Véron's speculative fiction is mostly contemporary with the birth and early development of Vernian *roman scientifique*, reacting to the same social stimuli, albeit in a markedly different fashion. Life in Paris during the Second Empire was dominated by the metamorphosis of the city directed by the Prefect of the Seine, Baron Haussmann, who supervised the total demolition of many of the old cramped districts and the planning of the network of boulevards and squares, complemented by parks, fountains and an elaborate system of sewers. Details of the work were always controversial, and even those sympathetic to the overall plan often wondered whether the Baron's demolitions might not be a little too extreme and his reconstructions more than a little too "vulgar." The social changes represented and embodied by the physical alterations were bound to occasion satirical reaction, and also to stimulate curiosity as to where the city, and the society to which it played host, were headed in response to scientific and technological advance and the inexorable forces of commercialization.

In tackling those questions in his two novellas and various shorter pieces, Véron was picking up a satirical tradition initiated by Emile Souvestre's *Le Monde tel qu'il sera* (1846; tr. as *The World As It Shall Be*) and continued by several other writers—including Jules Verne, although nobody knew it at the time, because his publisher. Pierre-Jules Hetzel, refused to publish his visionary account of *Paris au XXᵉ siècle* (written 1863; published 1994; tr. as *Paris in the Twentieth Century*). Véron's work is a significant precursor of Albert Robida's more elaborate series of humorous accounts of twentieth-century life, begun with *Le Vingtième siècle* (1883; tr. as *The Twentieth Century*), and of the speculative works of such humorists as Eugène Mouton, Alphonse Allais and Paul Vibert. The technological innovations featured in Véron's works are very modest by comparison with Robida's, but that reflects the relative limitation of the technological advancements of the early 1860s, compared to those of the 1880s, when electrical technology had begun a rapid and spectacular proliferation. Véron was, in any case, more interested in "social innovations" and the evolution of commercial quackery in an era when medicine was yet to begin its serious scientific reformation.

Véron's narrative methods are modest too, by comparison with what came later, but *Les Marchands de Santé* was published at a time when interplanetary fiction was only just beginning the revival that would replace the calculatedly absurd devices of transportation favored by such satirists as Cyrano de Bergerac and the tokenistic ones employed in 18th century *contes philosophiques* featuring trips to the Moon with devices of a more robust nature, and its tokenism is forgivable. *Monsieur Personne* is more "advanced" in employing an immersive fantasy strategy, equipped with the prefatory essay still obligatory at the time; its futuristic narrative is unusually straightforward and casual for its era, cultivating a laconism that adds significantly to the blithe surrealism of some of its imagery and commentary. Although the novella is an uneven text, as all patchwork texts tend to be, it has an overall coherency that makes it more than the sum of its parts, and it is one of the more remarkable works of its transitional era.

Le Charivari had run into serious trouble with Napoléon III's censors in the first decade of the Second Empire, and had been forced to adapt in order to survive; by the time Véron began publishing in its pages it had become a more diplomatic and somewhat chastened periodical. Although the censors were easing up by then in the pressure they put on the more general themes tackled by novelists, they were still very sensitive about anything resembling direct political criticism of the Empire and the Emperor, and that helps to explain the near-total absence in Véron's work from any direct political argument and any reference to the political order of the Planet Fantasia or the Paris of the year 1901 featured in *Monsieur Personne*. While that absence might be regrettable, it nevertheless leaves plenty of scope for Véron to turn his satirical lens on features of contemporary life whose consideration was not likely to get him or the periodical into hot water. His satire is undoubtedly weak-kneed by today's savage standards, but if it had attempted more it might well have ended up achieving nothing at all. Robida, operating in the era of the Third Republic, had a much greater freedom, but even he tended to be careful about treading too hard on political toes.

Fashions in humor change, of course, and many of Véron's jokes inevitably fall flat today, compounding the fact that many of his satirical targets are long out of date. On the other hand, in spite of the fact that modern medicine is immeasurably more competent and better organized than the medicine of 1862, it is slightly disturbing to see how many of his observations regarding the psychology of patients and some of the tendencies of the "merchants of health" still ring a bell today. The dramatic sophistication of scientific medicine has, in fact, allowed us to become far more obsessive about our health than was even possible in 1862, and there is a sense in which "Argan's descendants" are far more numerous today than any direct progeniture could ever have produced. Molière would surely have been greatly amused by that, and perhaps a little saddened—and so, undoubtedly, would Pierre Véron.

All of the following translations were made from the copies of the relevant Dentu texts reproduced on the Bibliothèque National's *gallica* website.

Brian Stableford

THE PARIS DELUGE

The newspapers, large and small, have all recently made a meal of the certainty of a new Deluge resulting from a rupture of equilibrium between the various seas.

The due date of that scheduled inundation is, in truth, distant by a number of years that guarantees our generation against any non-Duval *bouillon*.[1] However, a day will come—*dies irae*—when the impotent Parisians will see themselves submerged beneath the umbrellas of the *Medusa*. It is that day and its consequences that we ask your permission to envisage, transporting ourselves in anticipation into the remote future.

Before

The year 4859 is reaching its end, but for ten years already the most alarming news has been circulating. Every day, in fact, the seas have been gaining ground in the north and retreating in the south; a scientist beloved by Parisians, Monsieur Babinet LXIV,[2] charged with monitoring the scourge, has declared that the equilibrium will be broken within a week. That was six days ago.

---

[1] The new restaurant chain created by Pierre-Louis Duval and vastly expanded by his son Alexandre, the largest of which was *La Belle Bouille* [Lovely Stew], the rest becoming known as *Bouillons Duval* in consequence, seemed to many observers to be a key feature of the New Paris in the process of creation by Baron Haussmann.

[2] Undoubtedly a descendant of the physicist and meteorologist Jacques Babinet (1794-1872), whose public lectures were famous for wit and accessibility; one of them might well have been the stimulus for this piece.

Thus, the physiognomy of the great city is unrecognizable; the theaters have stopped opening, the boulevard cafes are devoid of customers.

All the vices have suddenly disappeared; all the good qualities are the order of the day. Everywhere fees are being offered to agents who can procure some poor individual with whom a rich one can share his fortune. Shopkeepers are advertising their merchandise at below cost price. Proprietors are stopping passers-by in the street and begging them to accept gratuitous hospitality.

The columns of all the critics are devoted to defaming their own works and praising those of their colleagues. Three novelists have taken abnegation so far as to returning to all the purchasers the money from three novels which, they admit in a circular, is not worth two sous.

Such is the enthusiasm for virtue that has gripped the population that the Académie has been obliged to renounce judging the Prix Montyon, seventeen million, nine hundred and seventy-seven thousand people having been deemed worthy *ex aequo*.

On the site formerly occupied by the Bréda quarter, three gigantic houses of retreat have been built; each of them contains three thousand penitents and is directed by a former dancer at the Opéra.

After virtue, the unique occupation of Parisians is constructing balloons, dirigible or otherwise, in order to escape the scourge. Monsieur Godard CXI[3] has made a profit in that operation of twenty-three millions, which he has generously donated to the Association of Ruined Stockbrokers.

---

[3] The Godard family, headed by Louis Godard and his brother Jules, although their fame was exceeded by one of Louis' three sons, the daring aeronaut Eugène Godard (1827-1890), were the entrepreneurs who made a successful business of the manufacture and sale of aerostats from the 1850s onwards, to the extent that balloons became popularly known for a while as "Godards."

During

The great cup has overflowed.

The swell is camped where Tortoni was. All the balloons, torn apart by the atmospheric convulsions, have burst unanimously. Vengeful waves have taken up residence where the innocent cascades of the Palais-Royal once reigned. Unlike Vatel, Paris is complaining that the fish have arrived too soon,[4] for myriads of them have spread out in the streets, along the boulevards and in the squares.

Two oysters (opening their shells as they pass the Institut): Say, what if we were to go inside?

First oyster: It would be original.

Second oyster: Not half!

First oyster: Ha ha, Messieurs les Parisiens, you made our name into a term of scorn. Our turn has come to take our revenge. Wouldn't you like to be oysters today!

Second oyster. Let's go back out—there's no lack of room.

A sole (strayed into the kitchen of a restaurant on the Boulevard du Crime,[5] and perceiving a colleague): Heavens! My daughter! My progeniture, that a sweep of the net stole away from me the other day! Child, do you recognize your mother? No response. Dead! Dead! They've killed my child!

A turbot (on hearing these exclamations): Hey you, outside, when you've quite finished your tirade! Take your exclamations to the vicinity of the ex-theaters!

---

[4] François Vatel (1631-1671) was Nicolas Fouquet's butler, who famously committed suicide when a delivery from the fishmonger was delayed before an important dinner to be held in honor of Louis XIV. The fish arrived mere moments after he had literally fallen on his sword.

[5] The familiar term for the Boulevard du Temple, so-called for a clutch of theatres specializing in lurid melodramas of the kind likely to contains speeches akin to the sole's.

A lobster (caught on the tip of a lightning-conductor): Help! Rescue me! Help!

A whale (having just entered the Panthéon): So these are the monuments of which humans were so proud. A nice carcass! To be able to turn around, I'd need to smash a window with my tail.

At that moment, a de-masted ship entered at great speed what had formerly been the Place de l'Hôtel de Ville.

The last of the Prudhommes (having taken refuge on the summit of the Tour Saint-Jacques) A ship! Paris seaport! All my wishes are granted, and I can die![6]

The increasing tumult drowns out his voice; the waves are still rising.

After

Three thousand years have gone by. The waters have quit the place once occupied by Paris, having deposited a calcareous stratum there several meters thick. A new city has risen up, populated by new humans.

These new humans, endowed with new defects, have founded a new Académie des Science, where new deliberations often lead to nothing new.

Today, however, the day's schedule promises a curious report by a geologist on the debris of the antediluvian world that he has discovered.

The seats are occupied by an elegant crowd. The journalists are at their post.

At two o'clock in the afternoon, the famous geologist goes up to the podium in the midst of the most profound silence, unrolls a manuscript, and begins to read:

---

[6] The dream of making the Seine navigable to ships, popularly known as "Paris seaport" was almost as popular throughout the 19th century as the idea of building a channel tunnel, and schemes were continually produced, all of which languished on the drawing-board.

"Messieurs,

"Science, the indefatigable searcher, endows humankind with a new benefit every day, even in her infancy.

"Because, Messieurs, only three thousand years have gone by since a deluge destroyed a creation anterior and inferior to ours.

"It is precisely that deluge and that creation about which I want to talk to you." (*Attentive shuffling.*)

"Was the Earth before the deluge inhabited by human beings or not? Such is the grave question that immediately presents itself to the scientist.

Some of my colleagues say yes; others say no. Personally, I do not say either yes or no." (*Violent marks of approval.*)

"But from my excavations, Messieurs, I have extracted one certainty. That is that the Earth, prior to us, was covered by a gigantic creation, and I shall prove it.

"By digging in the ground in all directions, I have discovered for items of fossil debris of the greatest importance. The difficulty, however, was not finding them; it is necessary to recognize their nature, and, if you will forgive the expression, stealing from destruction the secrets of the past. I have done that!" (Unanimous bravos.)

"The first item of debris discovered by me is a perfectly conserved skeleton. Its form represents a truncated sphere; the bones are disposed in squares, and, bizarrely enough, the action of time has metalized them. The skeleton must be that of an animal having some analogy with the toys known to our children as bobo dolls. That animal, extinct today, must have been acephalous, moved by crawling and lived a vegetable existence.

"The second item of debris is a skull, which, given its restricted form, must evidently have belonged to a species of colossal bird of the family of our domestic canaries.

"The third item of debris, one of the most curious, is about a hundred feet long and is completely petrified. That debris, I have become convinced, is the dorsal spine of a gigantic fish run aground in these parts during the deluge. To judge by the extent of the backbone in question—it is still broken at its extremity—the monster that it ornamented was the monarch of the antediluvian seas and belonged to the species of which today's whales are the diminutives.

"As for the fourth item of debris, we have found specimens in fairly large quantities. It affects the same form, the same flatness and the same hardness everywhere. That hardness is such that it has resisted all efforts to break it down into fragments with blows of a hammer. It will be the subject of a special report.

"From now on, however, three capital facts have been acquired by science, to wit: the existence of enormous reptiles, birds and fish prior to the last deluge.

"Glad to have been able to play my small part in that retrospective progress, I leave to the Académie the honor of being the godmother of my discoveries and giving a name to each of the races that I have, by dint of patience, been able to resuscitate."

That reading was followed by a salvo of frantic applause. All the newspapers were filled with details of and praise for the marvelous discoveries for a month.

A pension for life of two thousand francs a year was granted by the Académie to the author s a sign of gratitude.

Moral

In all deluges and all cataclysms, only one thing will always rise to the surface without the help of any Noah's Ark, and that is the ridiculous.

Translator's note:
This story is an early inclusion in what was eventually to become a long series of tales, by various hands, in which future archeologists dig in the ruins of long-dead Paris discover artifacts mysterious to them, which they routinely misinterpret in an ironic fashion. The convention that eventually developed

in the series was to leave the discovered items unidentified, while planting sufficiently clues to allow an alert reader to work out what they really are, but Véron, working within an unusually tight word-limit, did not have the space to elaborate his descriptions to that extent. Instead, he inserted four curt footnotes identifying the four items discovered by the unenlightened scientist as a frame for displaying skirts, the head of a dandy, the Obelisk and a "32-sou beefsteak."

THE JOURNAL OF THE LAST CRUSOE

A Fantasy of the Future

Brest, January 1960

I'm embarking today aboard the *Mandragora*, a French vessel departing to go around the world and carry out a voyage of exploration in the most unknown regions.

Since childhood, the glory of celebrated navigators has kept me awake at night.

I too shall attach my name to some desert island; I too shall have adventures; I too shall tread lands still virgin of human footprints.

I have had enough, and too much, of civilization. I'm weary of strolling along the nine hundred and seventy-five boulevards that make up Paris. What I want to see is primitive nature—savage, even.

The fate of Robinson Crusoe seems to me, as an old song of the last century puts it, "the most beautiful, the most worthy of envy." Oh, if only I had been born in the times of Sir John Franklin!

Anyway, I shall find a corner of the globe to discover, to baptize, to colonize. What am I saying, colonize? No, I shall leave it religiously to its sublime solitude. I shall install myself there in the intimacy of the heavens, and I shall write for my descendants *The Journal of the Last Crusoe*.

We're raising anchor. To the grace of God!

Coast of Africa, February 1960

Since the commencement of our voyage, the heavens have seemed determined to harass us.

The weather has been admirable. Add to that that this frightful vessel is so ingeniously constructed according to the

20

rules and with all the modern improvements that one scarcely feels its movement.

It seems to me that I haven't left the Rue de Rivoli[7] and my third-floor front apartment.

However, the horizon is darkening, the captain is consulting his binoculars. There's no doubt about it—a tempest is in preparation!

My role is commencing, then!

Senegal, February 1960

I'm still seething with anger. The tempest was unleashed with insensate violence; the waves were sixty feet high; the thunder and lightning succeeded one another without interruption.

Sinister creaking sounds shook the vessel. I went to see the captain; he was impassive, smoking his cigar while commanding the maneuvers.

That impassivity irritated me. "We're in danger, aren't we?" I asked him.

"In danger of what?"

"Of being shipwrecked, of course. Don't hide it from me. I'm courageous, and..."

"Word of honor, I think you're very amusing, with your shipwreck. Do you think we're living in the nineteenth century? Pay attention at the helm! Today's ships are, thank God, sufficiently improved no longer to be subject to the caprices...pay attention there, at the helm!"

"But we're near the coast, and some reef..."

"Reefs! Where have you come from? Do you think we don't know the reefs? Look, there's one over there, thirty-three meters, twenty-two centimeters. It's a kilometer broad

---

[7] Véron lived in a third-floor apartment in the Rue de Rivoli. The weekly salons that he hosted there, in accordance with custom, became famous in the 1870s as a meeting-place for all the comic writers and artists in the capital.

and as long...reefs! I can list all of them for you, one after another. Would you like to take a closer look?"

"Then, any shipwreck in impossible with you?"

"I'd like to think so."

"But that's a treason!"

"You're mad, I assume."

A lively altercation followed that conversation. No more shipwrecks! No, I shan't remain for another minute in this impermeable hull, and will take advantage of the *Mandragora*'s stopover in Senegal to disembark.

I'll go explore the desert on foot; there, at least, danger and the unexpected are realities.

In the desert, March 1960.

They call this a desert! Don't trust people!

I've been walking for ten days, and for ten days I've found nothing but railway stations.

I'm writing these lines on an iron bench from the Tronchon factory, just like those one sees in the Champs-Élysées, near a little artesian well that reminds me of Grenelle, in the shade of fir-trees that one could take for a sub-branch of an English park.

On the horizon stand the houses of a town, and yesterday evening, experiments with electric lighting were visible on the roof of one of those houses.

A vehicle is going by. God forgive me, it's a fiacre!

The negro coachman is waving to me; another negro in a uniform is going over, and I understand by his pantomime that he's writing him a ticket for touting for trade.

This evening I'm going to retrace my steps, because a market-gardener I encountered taking his vegetables to the town assured me—in perfectly intelligible French, believe me—that the desert is all similar to this specimen.

I'm going to re-embark for the North Pole.

I'll probably be luckier in those icy regions.

North Pole, July 1960.

All my illusions have vanished successively.

I've traveled the Eskimo lands. Populated! Overpopulated! European colonies everywhere.

In a street in the last village I passed through, I read with my own eyes a notice advertising false teeth for five francs; another informed the inhabitants of a traveling salesman from the Belle Jardinière.

I should have anticipated the costume of the indigenes. Eskimos in overcoats with gaiters!

And all the women play the piano!

Let's flee! It's to be hoped that the virgin forests of America and the Rocky Mountains will be more inhospitable!

Virgin forests of America, September 1960.

Oh, Crusoe, Crusoe! Object of my admiration and my desire, is it necessary to renounce imitating you?

Virgin forests, says geography. With signposts at every crossroads and roads prohibited to vehicles without suspension.

To my right, a mechanical sawmill selling parquet floors at a fifty per cent discount; to my left a factory for the manufacture of gas.

This morning, however, I had some excitement. On emerging from a hamlet, after half an hour of walking through the country, I found myself face to face with an enormous snake suspended in a tree.

I approached stealthily; it didn't budge.

The monster's asleep, I thought.

I drew closer, and closer, and still it didn't budge.

When I was very close, I saw—I'm ashamed of my emotion—that the tree was a pear-tree and that the snake had been impaled there by a farmer to scare away the birds.

10 November 1960

If I don't inscribe any location at the top of this page, it's because I don't know where I am. Blessed is destiny!

But let's resume my journal at an earlier point. From America I went to New Caledonia—a France in miniature. Let's not talk about it; it hurts me too much.

Disgusted and harassed, I was about to return to Europe, when an idea popped into my head. One last desperate attempt, I said to myself, and then it will be finished forever.

Upon which I set off, without a compass, at the whim of the waves, in a small boat fitted with a sail, like those in which I often made the journey from Asnières to Saint-Cloud.

On the evening of my sixth day of navigation, a squall suddenly blew up; my boat sank, loyally, and an enormous wave threw me and my lifebelt on to a sandy beach.

Fatigue and joy are preventing me from writing any more today. Tomorrow, I'll resume the story.

I have the time now!

11 November 1960.

There's no more doubt about it, it really is a desert island! I've explored it in all directions. No one, so far!

I've started building myself a cabin.

One thing worries me, though. The vegetation of my island is admirable: grassy areas and verdant trees, which one might believe had been cared for by human hands. Save for a few birds, however, there's no trace of game.

What does it matter? The horrors of hunger will add to the poetry of my situation. I've eaten three roasted birds.

12 November 1960.

I'm on a desert island!

No matter how often I repeat it, I can't believe my luck. And yet, three days have gone by, and not a single human being...

In truth, I haven't yet discovered the other shore of my island. That nature also has an unnatural appearance.

Get away! Isn't nature the foremost of landscape gardeners?

I only lack a Friday, and I confess that it's a considerable lack. Game even more so.

I've eaten three roasted birds. Let's go finish my cabin. I'm happy!

13 November 1960.

I've just found a cigar-butt.

14 November 1960.

Abomination! Desolation! Malediction!

Yesterday's cigar-butt was only the prelude to my misfortunes.

Excited by the discovery, I undertook a longer excursion in my island, and came across a town—at least a hundred houses!

The place where I'm living is, therefore, the local Bois de Boulogne! One can see that land isn't dear here.

But those houses are all inhabited. I'm lost in conjectures, burning with impatience.

There still no game, and the doors of the houses are all firmly locked!

15 November 1960.

I have the key to the enigma. I'm mystified.

The inhabitants have just returned. They had all gone on a pleasure trip, to a play at the Gaîté.

I'm leaving in an hour for Paris. I have a plan.

Paris, 1 April 1961.

No more hope. My plan is unrealizable!

The only deserted place in the entire world, the last theater in which tragedy was being played, has closed in my absence.

Since everything is lacking at once, I shan't survive so much ridicule.

This evening, I shall no longer be. Pray for the last Crusoe!

THE MERCHANTS OF HEALTH

Preface

If I had to choose a name for our century I would call it the century of turnabouts.

Indeed!

What triumphant reactions! What comebacks by parties once lost!

I am not, of course, speaking politically, but only with regard to the social hierarchy. Look around. Victims have almost always ended up making a pedestal of their misfortunes—unless they preferred to make income out of them.

Ridicule, instead of killing them, has fattened them.

Take, for instance, the husband. There were not enough epithets in the dictionary with which to abuse him. Novels and plays, prose and verse, pen and pencil all conspired against him, all bombarded him, all took aim at his head.

Then, suddenly, the wind changed. The vanquished has become the victor, an aureole crowns the conjugal head, so long accustomed to another coiffure—to the extent that today, novels and plays, prose and verse, pen and pencil all set out to exalt the right of conjugal property.

The husband has killed the lover, and what is more, has inherited his sentimental wardrobe. Monsieur One-Too-Many is god, and the litterateurs have instituted themselves as his prophets.

And then there is the grocer.

O Homeric memories! O helmet of immortal luster! O epic of the grotesque! O treacle! O Gavarni![8]

"To be born a man and become a grocer!" people sniggered once, thinking that they had surpassed the Pillars of Hercules of disdain.

"To be born a grocer and to become a millionaire!" replied the man with the paper bags.

And he has done what he said. He has gained in seriousness as he has accumulated cash, has got used to frowning majestically and buying villas, and has been promoted to officer in the National Guard, alderman, perhaps mayor of the commune in which his estates lie.

Bow down to the counter that people once wanted to make into a pillory, and which had the talent to metamorphose into a throne.

Thirdly and finally—for I shall have to cut the list short here—consider the physician. What ironic nicknames were attached to that proud title! Monsieur Desfonandres here,[9] Uncle Murderer there, Purgon to the right, Diafoirus to the left,[10] and before the satires, the parodies, the pointed hats, the syringes.

---

[8] The reference is to the illustrator and caricaturist Paul Gavarni (1804-1866), once a leading contributor to *Le Charivari*, although he became more closely associated in the final years of his career with *L'Illustration*, when he also became intensely interested in science and aerial navigation.

[9] Monsieur Desfonandres [approximately, "Sinkpeople"] is a physician in Molière's *L'Amour Médecin* (1665) who favors enemas as a treatment; the name is rendered Des Fonanadres in most modern versions, but the spelling Véron employs is more frequent in older printings.

[10] Purgon and Diafoirus are two physicians features in Molière's last play, *Le Malade imaginaire* (1673). Molière collapsed during his fourth performance in the leading role, that of hypochondriac Argan and died shortly thereafter—

Our ancestors almost went from mocking their doctors to wanting to get rid of them.

There too the reaction has set in. Bow your head, proud Sicambre, adore the hero of the leech and the purgative that you once mocked.[11]

What was necessary for that reversal of fortune? A lot of science? Yes, if you life, but even more white cravats. What a subject of philosophical study: the influence of starch on human dignity!

What has happened to the augurs of medicine is the reverse of what became of the augurs of paganism. The latter began in respect to end in sarcasm; we are witnessing the inverse process.

That probably comes from the fact that the augurs of medicine, wilier than their predecessors, have learned to look at themselves without laughing.

Still, the turnabout is striking—too striking, in truth, and the idea of this book is inspired by that very excess. Not that I am weary of hearing Aristides called the Just, but there are contraband Aristides everywhere—fake good men and fake good doctors.

With their intention, I have written *The Merchants of Health*. If you sell chicory as coffee, you can be hauled up in court; you who sell adulterated health can at least be held up to caricature. True merit cannot be attained by this triage; to suppress weeds is to strengthen the good grain.

And now, may the shade of Molière protect me!

---

something that might be borne in mind while reading Véron's novella, which is a sequel of sorts to *Le Malade imaginaire*.

[11] This sentence adapts the famous phrase allegedly employed by the Bishop of Reims, Saint Remy, when baptizing the Merovingian king Clovis: "Courbe-toi, fier Sicambre, adore ce que tu as brûlé" [Bow your head, proud Sicambrian, adore what you have burned.] The Sicambrians were a Germanic tribe, although the term is applied very loosely in the remark.

I. I Have the Honor of Introducing to You...

Do you remember Argan?

Argan, the eccentric of the insinuative decoctions, preparations and remollients for softening, moistening and refreshing Monsieur's entrails?

Argan, the consumer of fine purgative and corroborative medicines for expelling and evacuating Monsieur's bile?

Argan the *Malade Imaginaire*, since it's necessary to spell it out. And perhaps you've often wondered what became of that eccentric after the famous session in which he was judged *dignus intrare in docto corpore...*[12]

The poor fellow, it appears, died of joy, but did not die entirely, and Mademoiselle Angelique, his daughter, took charge of continuing his posterity.

That posterity lived in Paris a few years ago, in the person of a male descendant whom I knew well, and whom you will permit me to introduce to you.

Monsieur Argan, by virtue of the frequent effect of skipping generations, was the exact image of his overly celebrated ancestor. In his cradle, his nurse had surprised him several times in the instinctive attitude of an invalid taking his pulse.

As a toddler, he stuck out his tongue at ever fragment of mirror he encountered.

At school, he professed a worship of the infirmary that earned him several hundred penances.

As a young man he replaced the beer and absinthe dear to his companions with mallow-flower and hot lemonade.

---

[12] The doctors in *La Malade imaginaire* deliver their judgments in Latin, in one key scene singing in chorus, as if parodying the Latin mass: "*Bene, bene, bene, respondere/Dignus, dignus est intrare/In notro docto corpore.*" [Very, very, very well answered/worthy, worthy is it to enter into our learned corporation.]

With the result that at thirty-five, you would have thought that he was sixty, if hazard had led you to encounter him walking slowly along the streets in his triple envelope of muffler, overcoat and flannel vest.

Fortunately for him, Monsieur Argan was rich, which furnished him with the means to devote himself to his fatal monomania. He was even rich enough, thanks to his father, prosperous in commerce, to be able to reject the latter's name—which he did not fail to do.

The law regarding noble titles had not yet been invented and he was permitted, in all security, to elevate himself with a *particule*.

There again his irresistible and hereditary predestination revealed itself in spite of him. At first he improvised Argan Du Tilleul, then simply Du Tilleul. Du Tilleul—so reminiscent of tisanes![13]

But wealth and nobility were not sufficient to secure the unfortunate's happiness. His life was populated by anxieties.

Sometimes it was the liver, sometimes the spleen, sometimes the heart, sometimes the lungs, sometimes... As a matter of sanitary precaution, he had not even dared to get married.

That is not all.

Argan, his ancestor, at least professed a boundless veneration for the men of the art: a blind credulity, a fetishism that admitted no verification—and although that faith did not save him, it always sustained him in his ordeals.

His offspring, on the contrary, added to all the diseases he thought he had one that he really had: the disease of doubt.

He wanted and did not want; he was avid for prescriptions, but when the prescriptions were drawn up, he set about querying them, interpreting them and discussing them, forgetting that medicine is a dogma that affirms but does not prove.

---

[13] Tilleul was (and still is) the name given to a very popular herbal tea made from an infusion of the flowers of the linden or lime tree, strongly recommended by its admirers as a cure for headaches.

In such a situation, imagine what mortal misery Monsieur Argan Du Tilleul must have found in every day of his existence.

II. A Supernatural Friend

One of those days—which was actually a night—Onésime Du Tilleul (his name was Onésime) was lying down, plunged in a profound depression.

A sedative potion had had no effect.

The hours went by, populated with insomnias that he attributed successively to the most redoubtable causes; his lassitude was extreme. Leaning his somnolent head in the hollow of one of his hands, and mechanically rotating a spoon with the other in a cup placed beside the tremulous night-light, the saddened bachelor was pensive.

A noise suddenly attracted his attention.

It was the door of his bedroom opening—and an individual of vaguely fantastic aspect appeared in the doorway.

The individual was totally unknown to Onésime, whose mouth was already open to ask him a perfectly natural question when the stranger got in ahead of the enquiry.

"Please excuse me, Monsieur Argan..."

"Du Tilleul," objected Onésime, shocked,

"Argan Du Tilleul, so be it, if you insist. You're nonetheless the descendant of the late Argan who married for a second time to Dame Béline. From that union was born..."

"I have no need for this genealogical instruction," said Onésime, interrupting again.

"That's true—I only wanted to prove to you that, although I'm unknown to you, I at least have the honor of being perfectly familiar with you and yours."

"What does that matter to me?"

"It will probably matter soon. You're ill, my dear Monsieur Arg...I mean, Du Tilleul."

"Who told you that?"

"No one; I know it. You're ill, or you believe that you are."

"I am."

"Granted—it's a family conviction on your part. And at the precise moment when I came in, you were occupied in racking your brains to figure out what unexplored genre of medicine you might appeal to your aid."

"Who are you, to be able to read my thoughts in that fashion?"

"A friend...whom you have never seen, but who is interested in you, and has resolved to come to your aid."

"Do you belong to the Faculty?"

The unknown smiled in a slightly ironic fashion, and then continued, in his penetrating voice: "My name is Master Helleborus,[14] but the sciences of the Earth are too petty for me to devote my precious time to them; it is to supernatural knowledge that I devote myself exclusively, and it is by supernatural methods that I shall bring about your cure."

"But..."

"No need! I've read your response in your brain. You take me for a lunatic."

The descendant of the *Malade Imaginaire* blushed slightly on seeing his thought so well-divined.

---

[14] The plant *Helleborus niger* [black hellebore] had been widely employed since Classical times as a treatment for various diseases, especially mental illness, although the preparation most commonly used from the Middle Ages onwards, probably polluted with material from more dangerous related species, was notoriously toxic, inducing such symptoms as vertigo, raging thirst, bradycardia, a feeling of suffocation and, ultimately, cardiac arrest. In Christian folklore, it routinely featured in recipes for summoning demons, but it is also featured in a sentimental legend in which the plant sprouted from the tears of a young girl who had no gift to offer to the child Christ, for which reason it is sometimes known as the Christmas rose.

"That ought to prove to you," the stranger went on, "that you will seek in vain to hide anything from me, and you'd do better to trust my word. So, I was telling you that I devote myself particularly to supernatural studies. I believe I can affirm to you that you have before you the foremost spiritualist in the universe. What, again! Now you're thinking secretly that I'm charlatan?"

This time, a superstitious terror took possession of Onésime, who sensed all his thoughts escaping him in spite of himself. He remained silent while his bizarre interlocutor went on: "Pay close attention! The foremost spiritualist in the universe, not on Earth. The Earth, I repeat, is unworthy of the focus of my preoccupations. But the immensity of worlds! All the planets! Your astronomers make me laugh, when they allow themselves to be heaped with decorations and stuffed with rewards for some petty celestial body they've perceived by chance. I, who am speaking to you, know thirty-nine thousand seven hundred and seventy-one planets."

That figure gave poor Du Tilleul goose-bumps.

"Thirty-nine thousand seven hundred and seventy-one with which I'm in regular communication. By the Inferno, that's travel that forms the mind and the heart! And I've resolved to take you on just such a trip with me, my dear friend."

"A voyage to the planets?"

"Horns of Beelzebub, how you go on! A thousand existences like yours wouldn't be sufficient for that, and you'd be quite content, I imagine, to visit one alone: the one that bears the registration number 29,388, is forty-nine million leagues distant from this globe,[15] and figures in the Atlas of Worlds under the name of Planet Fantasia."

"My God, Monsieur," stammered Onésime, "that would give me infinite pleasure, but nevertheless..."

---

[15] i.e. 196,000,000 kilometers—which would place "Planet Fantasia" somewhere in the "asteroid belt" among the minor planets of the solar system.

"Don't tell lies! Far from experiencing the slightest pleasure, you're feeling the most violent terror, and dying to call for help. Argan Du Tilleul, old chap, you're an ingrate, and you almost deserve to be abandoned to your paltry destiny..."

"I swear to you..."

"That you're half-dead of fear. Well, damn it, it's to prevent you from dying entirely that I've come. The example of our ancestor has done you no good, and you're preparing, like him, to die, not of disease but of medicine. For once, as it happens, I'll make an exception. The faculty of thought-reading of which I gave you proof a little while ago, you shall also possess during the voyage that we're about to undertake. Try to show yourself worthy of it and able to profit from it.

"Planet Fantasia will offer you, especially with regard to the subject that interests you, material for the most curious observations. Don't let them go to waste. Furthermore, I'll be there to keep watch, and underline the moral of the fable for you when your sight is too feeble to discover it. Are you ready?"

"What! To depart just like that, without making preparations of any sort?"

"Not even a will to write. We're not taking a railway train. No, I have a faster and less perilous means of locomotion."

"At least let me bring a few boxes of pills without which..."

"You'll find pills there, and more people to sugar-coat them for you than you could ever wish. Planet Fantasia has a medical and pharmaceutical reputation that isn't stolen, I can assure you. Let's go, my dear, let's go...still a residue of mistrust? Let's go—it will pass on the way.

"One, two, three...!"

So saying, Master Helleborus touched Onésime lightly with his fingertip.

III. Direct Transit

As soon as the contact occurred, it seemed to Onésime that his body became lighter than a feather, and that, like a balloon inflated with gas, he began to leave the ground and rise toward the ceiling.

But it was another matter when he felt the stranger's hand push him through the window that he had just opened.

At first, expecting to be precipitated on to the cobblestones of his courtyard, he wanted to shout "Help!"

"Don't shout," commanded his mysterious guide, with a snigger. "You won't fall. Far from it!"

And, indeed, once through the window, Onésime perceived that his body was continuing its ascensional movement.

Without being supported by anything, he rose up, and up, and up.

They passed the second story.

"A woman charming the leisure left to her by her husband's absence," said Du Tilleul's fantastic companion, showing him two shadows projected on the curtains of the casement by the light of a candle.

They passed the third, where a man was sitting up late in front of a strong-box.

"A usurer doing his accounts," said the cicerone.

They passed the fourth: "A poet searching for a rhyme!"

They passed the fifth: "Domestics busy drinking their masters' wine!"

"Sapristi!" Onésime exclaimed. "I recognize my groom!"

"Ha ha! Your peregrination is teaching you something from the very beginning, you see. Pay attention! We're off now!"

The rapidity with which the two travelers were rising had become vertiginous. It was a movement without jolts, but irresistible. The ground had already disappeared, and they were above the region of the clouds. On the other hand, the moon, with which the descendant of the *Malade Imaginaire* had only ever made the acquaintance through the intermediary of the telescope on the Pont-Neuf, appeared to him in monstrous proportions.

"I feel sick," murmured the unfortunate Du Tilleul.

"We'll take care of that later."

"The moonlight is blinding me."

"You'll get used to it—you'll see many others."

"I have a headache and I'm short of breath."

"When I tell you that I'm taking you to a place where you can consult at your ease regarding every ailment...come on! We're not making progress! Go faster!"

"We're not making progress! What a joke!"

At the moment when his companion addressed that reproach to him, Onésime estimated that he was rising at a velocity of about a thousand meters a minute. As the latter placed a finger on his breast, however, he suddenly experienced a complete relief, and ceased to feel the slightest suffocation, although the speed increased even more considerably.

"Confess that this is an excursion you didn't expect," his guide continued, chatting as casually as if they were sitting by the fireside in a peaceful drawing room. "It's said that a change of air is excellent for valetudinarians. You are, I think, served admirably! Do you see that star over there to the right? That's Sirius. Over there is Venus...further away, Jupiter... Change course slightly in order not to pass through Saturn's rings... That body which is moving to your left with such strange impetuosity is a great comet, which will soon be in the vicinity of the Earth...

"What? You're objecting that the Observatory hasn't said anything about it yet. When have you ever known the Observatory announce anything until six months afterwards?

"I won't make you a list of the fixed stars, much less those planets—between now and when they've all been baptized, as you can imagine, our scholars will have time to use up all the names in their vocabularies...

"Look out! You nearly bumped into one of those vagabonds, traveling with a velocity equal to that of a cannonball

36

multiplied by a hundred thousand…you could have sustained a bruise…

"Are you going to start trembling again? What I'm telling you is a matter of alleviating the tedium of the journey with a few innocent jokes…damn it! It's a matter of not chatting so much that we overshoot our station. 'Passengers for Planet Fantasia!' as the employees of our railways might shout! Stop there, Monsieur Argan!"

"Du Tilleul!" whispered the unfortunate, very quietly, having not dared to unclench his teeth throughout that monologue.

"Du Tilleul, so be it! That's no reason to overshoot the target. Stop, then!"

At the same time, Helleborus' hand fell upon Onésime's shoulder.

The shock was so violent that it seemed to the latter than he had been pulverized into a thousand smithereens. Closing his eyes and extending his arms, he sighed: "I'm dead!"

"Not at all! You've simply arrived, and I'm gallantly offering you my hand to help you down from the carriage!"

IV. Planet Fantasia

That last joke was not even perceived by Du Tilleul. He had lost consciousness.

When he came round, his cicerone was gravely administering a few little flicks to his nose and whistling a dance tune.

"Where am I?" he stammered.

"At the destination, damn it!"

The terrestrial voyager felt himself, to assure himself that he was intact.

"Did you think that you were going to be killed? Don't worry. None of your limbs has missed roll call. Our troll is over; you're resting on one of the benches of one of the pathways of one of the promenades of one of the quarters of the capital of Planet Fantasia. Oof!"

"We're really on the Planet Fantasia?"

"As really as you could wish. To convince you, deign to take the trouble of accompanying me to the summit of that nearby eminence. From there one can see in its entirety the immense city into which we're about to go."

One would think we were on the Buttes Montmartre, thought Onésime.

"That analogy isn't the only one you'll have occasion to remark. Planet Fantasia is, in effect, nothing but a kind of second Earth, seen through a magnifying glass. All the faults, all the vices, and all the vicissitudes of the world in which you're accustomed to living are found here, increased and exaggerated."

"Really?"

"Really; and that's what will comprise the principal utility of your voyage. Look!"

The two excursionists had reached the plateau that overlooked the capital of the planet.

A gigantic city extended at their feet, raising up into the air its thousands of steeples, roofs, domes, lightning-conductors, columns, triumphal arches, obelisks and factory chimneys.

"One might think that it was Paris," Du Tilleul murmured.

"The resemblance continues, as I warned you. Permit me to give you a few summary indications that will help you to orientate yourself in future.

"Do you see that area bristling with enormous chimneys, which are vomiting clouds of black smoke? That's the Workers' Quarter. There are a thousand laborers of every sort there, who use up their strength and their lives in the most crushing toil, and sometimes the most murderous. Most of them hardly earn enough to feed themselves. Their employers are sometimes millionaires.

"The fronton on the horizon is the center of the Speculator's Quarter. It's there that people gamble on the sale of bonds and shares. In general, one counts, in a good year or a bad one, three thousand honest men who ruin themselves in that recreation. On the other hand, the number of pickpockets who get rich there is less than half that.

"Do you see that dome? That's the center of the Literate Quarter. Forty individuals of the male sex have the mission of representing the literary intelligence of Planet Fantasia there, so those forty individuals are uniformly chosen from among men of the world, churchmen, advocates, military men, aristocrats, mathematicians and statesmen. There's talk of introducing at the next elections a manufacturer of woolen shawls who has made colossal profits in that game and who hosts superb balls. What one never sees there, of course, is a simple man of letters. One member who risked putting forward the name of talented writer two years ago was nearly lynched by his colleagues.

"Further away, that block of new buildings is the Quarter of Occasional Amours. It has become customary no longer to obtain provisions anywhere else, unless one addresses oneself, a kilometer further away, to the Quarter of Marriages Made to Measure. In the Quarter of Occasional Amours one does not love and one pays. In the Quarter of Marriages Made to Measure one does not love, and one is paid. That's the difference. Men ordinarily come to spend in the former, with Mesdemoiselles of the left hand, the dowries that they demand in the latter from Mesdames of the right hand."

"But that's just like Paris," said Onésime.

"In the capital of Planet Fantasia, everything is sacrificed to appearances: splendid houses make one believe that the residents are rentiers by right of birth, but there are no tenants in the houses, or tenants who eat pieces of cheese in their gilded dining-rooms; formidable rents, which aren't paid when the settlement is due; trinkets, but no comfort.

"Finally, as statistics details worthy of your interest, I will add:

"That in the capital of Planet Fantasia thirty thousand graduates are manufactured every year who have no employment, but who all replace that desideratum with the pretention of becoming, while still in their prime, Ministers or Great Men;

"That there are thirty-nine thousand sewers infinitely cleaner than the hovels of a host of poor people;

"That forty-one leagues of boulevards have been pierced since the last triennial census, even though thirty-five leagues of old boulevards are absolutely devoid of any construction;

"That playwrights number twenty-eight thousand three hundred there, only thirty-four of whom have succeeded in having plays staged during the last ten years, thirty-two of whom only figure in the list for a single act, the other two having furnished various theaters by themselves with eight hundred and eleven plays;

"And that, finally, of all the individuals arrested for vagrancy and questioned regarding their profession, there was not one who did not reply, imperturbably: 'I'm a photographer.'"

"Still just like Paris!" exclaimed Onésime, for the fourth time

Master Helleborus did not seem to pay any heed to the exclamation. "Now that you possess the most indispensable indications," he concluded, "adjust your clothing slightly, for everyone here is judged by external appearances. Keep your hands prudently in your pockets, because purses, like young daughters, cannot be too well-guarded. Finally, adopt a slightly insolent expression, because that will prevent other people from adopting one with you.

"As for the local language…just a second…" He passed his hand over Onésime's forehead. "Now you know it as if you had never spoken any other. We can now go into Capital Fantasia."

V. The Undersides of the Cards

The streets were filled with densely-packed moving crowds.

It was a holiday, and the crowds that were pressing everywhere differed so little from Parisian crowds, in terms of tumult and ugliness, that the two new arrivals might have thought that they had landed in the Faubourg Saint-Martin.

Onésime did not take long to perceive, however, that something extraordinary really was occurring in his life. There was a public market in front of him, and the vendors were striving to out-compete one another in their sales pitch.

"Believe me, Madame, if I wasn't sure of the quality I wouldn't give it to you; you can imagine that it isn't a practical person like you that I'd try to deceive."

"That merchant is an abominable thief," said Du Tilleul, turning to his guide. While he's heaping that worthy woman with protestations, he's thinking: *Yes, turn it this way and that, you won't see anything different, you miserly old crone! As if anyone will give you fresh poultry for that price! If you think I think you're practical, when you haggle for an hour over a miserable liard...*"

Further away, two friends were chatting.

"You can count on me."

"For sure?"

"I've already pleaded your cause warmly to the father. He already has less against you, and the marriage will be..."

"You're an abominable rogue!" stormed Du Tilleul, addressing his protests to the friend. "Don't believe a word of what he's just told you, Monsieur. He's thinking at this moment of means to have you driven out of your fiancée's house definitively, where he wants to take your place."

"You're a liar!" said the Monsieur who was making promises.

"It's you who are the liar!"

"No, damn it! It's you who's a busybody, getting mixed up in things that don't concern you," said the friend he had tried to enlighten.

"What—you too!" stammered Onésime in a reproachful tone.

"Yes, me too! Know, bumpkin, that hereabouts, one doesn't make a mock of friendship!"

"I can see that, damn it!"

"Is that an insult? Be careful!"

If Master Helleborus had not intervened, the dispute might have degenerated into a brawl.

"So," he said to Argan's descendant, when he was out of voice rage, "why did you interfere?"

"Could I allow him to be unworthily abused?"

"Not only could you have done so, but you should. It's to yourself that it's appropriate to apply the information you obtain by means of the second sight I've given you—and I can guarantee that you'll have enough to do with that."

The remonstration probably had its effect, for when, a few paces away, they passed two ladies exchanging the most affectionate courtesies, Onésime contented himself with muttering: "If they knew, reciprocally, that the husband of each of them is paying court to the other...but I don't understand what I'm experiencing...a sudden weakness...it's definitely some malign fever..."

"Rather say that it's hunger. Since the time that..."

The sentence was cut short by an exceedingly strange incident.

VI. Health for Sale

"A malign fever!" an individual dressed entirely in black had cried, approaching swiftly.

"A malign fever," repeated a second, no less black in his attire.

"A malign fever..."

"A malign fever..."

The phrase reverberated like a series of echoes, and within the blink of an eye, twenty individuals gathered around the voyagers, all speaking at the same time.

"Come with me, Monsieur!"

"Address yourself to me!"

"I alone have the veritable and infallible treatment!"

"I guarantee immutable health on payment of the invoice!"

"Monsieur...!"

"Monsieur...!"

"Monsieur...!"

And scrimmaging, tugging Onésime by the sleeves, the tails or the collar of his coat, they all tried to drag him away from the seductive attempts of their competitors.

"May Satan take you! Are you going to let us go?" the companion of the bewildered Du Tilleul said, in a menacing voice. "When we have need of you, we'll call you, and we certainly won't have any difficulty finding you, but in the meantime, try not to persecute us any longer."

The invective had its effect, and the obsessive individuals dispersed, but not without cursing and launching a few consolatory epithets. They were soon seen recommencing the same performance and the same solicitations around an indigenous passer-by who had stumbled while stepping down from a sidewalk.

"Who are those people?" asked Argan's grandson.

"Don't speak evil of them. Old friends of your family—and you."

"What?"

"They're the Merchants of Health. On Earth you call them physicians. We've arrived in the quarter reserved for them."

"What! This immense street..."

"There are forty-seven of similar length, exclusively inhabited by doctors of the most various Faculties, and the number increases every year with a rapidity that's frightful for them—and for their patients. You've just witnessed a scene that gives you a foretaste of the singularities that await you. The ones you've just seen are the professional hacks, the living-scrapers, the ones who, in France, advertise on the back pages of newspapers. Here, advertising is far from being disdained, but as it's considered insufficient, the merchants of health chase after clients in person. The magic word 'fever,' which you pronounced, rang in their ears like a clarion call. Now they're recommencing their attempts at forcible care elsewhere."

From all directions, in fact, nothing could be heard but offers of medical service. On the walls of every house in the quarter occupied by the disciples of Aesculapius, there were placards twelve feet high, and illuminated signs advertising the prices of consultations and the number of cures obtained during the year. Some had even taken the step of plastering their walls with portraits of patients before and after curative treatments.

That system, supported by the efforts of masterly writers was insufficient; the merchants of health were grabbing pedestrians by the arm, and striving to persuade them that the state of their health threatened the most terrible catastrophes.

"Once again," said Helleborus, "it's the common people who fall for it—but if the proletariat has its faults, the aristocracy has its own. We'll study both at our leisure, for our voyage here has only one objective. You'll need it! There are sixty-six thousand of them, not counting pharmacists, druggists, bone-setters, somnambulists, empiricists..."

"Sixty-six thousand!" murmured Argan's grandson, with joyful admiration. "Oh, thank you for having brought me. One needn't die here!" In a lower voice, he added: "It's singular, however, that since we arrived here, I've already counted twenty-two funeral processions..."

VII. Centralization

Quietly as he made the observation, it did not escape the subtle senses of the mysterious friend who was accompanying Onésime.

"My dear Monsieur Du Tilleul," he said, after a pause, "what you've just said proves that you're an observer, and augurs well for you."

44

"One doesn't need to be much of an observer! That funeral procession gives the city a lugubrious aspect that can't fail to make a deep impression."

"Permit me—let's not exaggerate. There are proportions in all things, which it's appropriate to respect, and which constitute the foremost of the sciences: the science of relativity."

"I don't really know what relativity there can be in the observation of a number."

"What about centralization, my dear Monsieur Du Tilleul?"

"I don't know."

"Can it be that you haven't read profound studies in the newspapers and magazines of the world we've just left of centralization and its importance?"

"I have a vague memory of it. Nevertheless, I confess frankly that my preferred reading is treatises of medicine."

"That's true—I should have remembered that. Centralization, my excellent Monsieur Du Tilleul, is, it appears, a perfect institution—except, as with everything else, when taken to excess.

"On Earth, when a peasant desires to dig a ditch in one of his fields, he has a word with the rural policeman, who tells the gendarme, who refers it to the alderman in order that the latter can inform the mayor. The mayor writes to the sub-prefect, who sends the petition to the offices of the Prefecture. After a rather prolonged interval in the offices of the Prefecture, the petition comes before the eyes of the Prefect, who sends it to the Ministry. At the Ministry, after a lapse of time that I can't estimate, the expeditionary is charged with drafting an account of the case. The account is reviewed by the editorial employee, who transmits it to the under-secretary, who passes it on to the section head, transmits it to the division head, who hands it on to the secretary general, who submits it to the minister.

"Then, when the minister had finally taken cognizance of the documents, he indicates the sense of the response to the secretary general, and the scale—descending this time—

recommences, passing via the division head, the section head, the under-secretary, the editor, the expeditionary, the prefect, the mayor, the alderman, the gendarme and the rural police-man to end up with the peasant, often with the two letters spelling the word NO.

"That, my dear friend, is one of a thousand examples of centralization.

"But here, of course, it's far worse.

"I've told you that all terrestrial ridiculousness is repro-duced on Planet Fantasia with uncommon magnification. Cen-tralization figures in the forefront of that ridiculousness.

"Everything is so effectively centralized that the entire planet is composed exclusively of one city, the capital in which we're standing. At certain distances there are traces of what might be called provinces, semblance of towns, villages and hamlets, but there's a distinct lack inhabitants there who resemble those of the towns, villages and hamlets with which you're familiar.

"My God, yes—and there's a rigorous logic to that.

"One day, the provincials perceived that they were ali-menting the budget, without being sufficiently alimented by it, and they said to themselves: 'In truth, we're being very stupid. Why, since the sun doesn't come to us, don't we go to the sun?' Men of letters thought: *there are only people of intelli-gence in the capital—let's go there!* Masons thought: *building only goes on in the capital—let's go there!* Pianists thought: *people only take piano lessons in the capital—let's go there!* Lovers thought: *there are only pretty girls in the capital—let's go there!* Bureaucrats thought: *there are only positions in the capital—let's go there!* Pickpockets thought: *there are only handkerchiefs to be easily filched in the capital—let's go there!* Speculators thought: *Monsieur Gullible is only to be found in the capital—let's go there!* Domestics thought: *the waste-bin dance has only been perfected in the capital—let's go there!* And they all went—all of them! And they arrived.

46

"Capital Fantasia is two hundred and eleven leagues around, and there's talk of pushing the customs-barriers further out next year."

"You're joking!" said Onésime, with profound stupefaction.

"Not at all. It's a little awkward for travel between districts, but with the steam omnibus, that inconvenience becomes secondary. Unfortunately, there's a more serious one, for which a remedy has thus far been sought in vain. Far from it—it seems to be getting worse every day.

"Not content with having centralized the planet in the city, each profession has been centralized in a different quarter, as I was explaining to you a little while ago. Imagine the pitch to which that agglomeration has brought competition! Imagine the poverty that the competition in question engenders in its turn! Imagine, finally, how that poverty must multiply the causes of death, and you'll no longer be astonished at the number of processions that frightened you so much..."

"Indeed...in spite of the affluence of physicians..."

"Because of it, my dear Monsieur Du Tilleul," Master Helleborus corrected him, with a sarcastic snigger.

VIII. An Illustration of Mores

That irony seemed a trifle irreverent to Argan's grandson, who adopted a disapproving expression not calculated to compensate for his natural disadvantages.

"Are you annoyed with me?" his guide asked him. "Is that because I've permitted myself to touch on the objects of your worship?"

"I'm tired," replied Onésime, dryly.

"In that case, would it please you to have some refreshment before going on? It's one of the singular charms of Capital Fantasia. Wherever one is, one only has to go into the ground floor of the first building one comes to, and one is in a café. Only cafés escape the law of universal centralization—they're everywhere."

"What, all these shops…?"

"Cafés, nothing but cafés. The other industrial and commercial enterprises have been obliged to take refuge on the upper floors. There are establishments selling lemonade that occupy a surface area of three square leagues—which obliges the waiters to serve the customers in little wagons driven by compressed air. Come in, then!"

"It's just that I'm forbidden to take anything between meals."

"The last one you had has had plenty of time to digest. Come on!"

Before they were even installed at a table, a noisy sound of wheels caused Onésime to jump. It was a waiter who fell upon the two customers in his wagon, at high speed.

"Absinthe, bitters, vermouth, eau-de-vie, alcohol, thirty-six, vitriol…!"

"What's that he's saying about vitriol?" asked Onésime, quivering with fear.

"Juniper vitriol, a very popular item," the waiter replied.

"A beverage imagined for palates jaded by the pertness of absinthe," explained Du Tilleul's guide.

"But that must cause frightful ravages to the internal organs."

"That's the attraction. You don't want to try it?"

"Great God! Me? My doctor forbids me so much as a simple sugar-cube dipped in brandy. If I could have an infusion of chamomile…"

"Get away! You're joking…drink a little coffee with me."

"It's very hot."

"Beer?"

"It's very cold."

"But since you have sixty thousand vigilant physicians around you… You keep forgetting that…beer, waiter."

"A keg or a half-keg?"

"What does he mean?" cried Du Tilleul.

"It's the usual measure. There are people who end up drinking six kegs a night, having started out with bottles, as in Paris."

"Merciful Heavens!"

The waiter had returned, as quick as lightning. "There you are, Messieurs! That's thirty-six francs, please."

"Damn!"

"And five francs for the tip."

"Are you mad? This waiter's insane..."

"Do hurry up, or I'll call a policeman."

"To force me to give you a five francs tip?"

"And for slowing me down."

"Well, I refuse. The tip is voluntary."

"You think so? Guard, arrest these Messieurs for me. What have I done to deserve such boors?"

Onésime's guide took the precaution of intervening momentarily. "Here are your forty-two francs, my friend. Accept Monsieur's very humble apologies—he's a stranger and not used to the local customs."

"Indeed!" muttered the waiter, drawing away. "Otherwise...and if he talks to me another time with his hat on his head..."

"Explain that to me," Du Tilleul demanded of his cicerone, quivering with contained emotion.

"Nothing simpler. The waiters of your homeland have only got as far as dishonesty, while these have acquired domination. It's the way that things are going in France, though. The tip to which you submit foolishly has become legal tax here; the insolence that you tolerate has metamorphosed here into subaltern autocracy. Let them get a foot in the door, etc. Have sip of this beer. To your health!"

"To my health! I certainly need it," replied the poor voyager, passing his hand over his face, on which those shocks had visibly had a deleterious effect.

IX. Provincial Medicine

Master Hellebore looked at Onésime intently. "So you're still the same? I'll wager that a good beefsteak will put you right."

"Me! But I'm on a diet!"

"You'd prefer a potion? You shall have one! You shall have one! The city is good."

"I swear to you that I'm seriously queasy," stammered Du Tilleul.

"So much the better, by the Devil's horns! So much the better! Messieurs the physicians have to live. Poor fellows! I was talking to you about centralization; they too have made the disastrous experiment. Well, provincial medicine is such a sad thing—there was good reason to renounce it.

"Picture a satanic locality where everyone knows everyone else. 'Hey,' says someone, 'they're sounding a death-knell.'

"'Yes, it's Père X.'

"'Bah! Who was looking after him?'

"'The tall dark-haired physician who's just settled here.'

"'Well, there's one who doesn't inspire confidence in me!'

"'Me neither!'

"'If that one ever catches on in the neighborhood, it'll be singularly astonishing.'

"'It's an abomination to let such blockheads practice.'

"'We ought to give him a charivari.'

"'For myself, I'm going to tell everyone that it's him who killed Père X.'

"'And you'll be right.'

"'Mother of God! People have been condemned to death who deserved it less!'

"Go practice medicine agreeably under the surveillance of the hundred eyes of Argus, with the responsibility for your slightest prescriptions!

"On the other hand, live in the great capital, where one can't count the invalids. One more or less on the heap…!"

"How you go on!" exclaimed Onésime, shivering. "I'm part of it myself, that heap!"

"It's hardly worth the trouble of interrupting me for that meager detail. I'll go on.

"The monitoring of the patients isn't the only one to which the provincial physician is subject. The pharmacist is there to keep an eye on him. The pharmacist of the capital has—as you'll see—mostly become the collaborator of the merchant of health, when he isn't an improvised merchant of health himself.

"In small localities it's different. Precipitated from more or less legitimate heights of ambition to the underworld of drug-supply, the pharmacist sees the physician as a favorite of fate, who has unjustly taken his place in the sun. That doesn't prevent him, when he encounters him, from lavishing his most obsequious reverences upon him, but if he embraces him it's only to be better able to stifle him.

"One centigram more in a potion, one milligram less in a prescription—and that's enough to stir up the entire town. And in the evening, while playing a hand of piquet with a neighbor, the jealous pharmacist insinuates: 'It's a good thing, though, that I never go away; even today…'

"'What?' the neighbor asks, quite naturally.

"'Oh, nothing…there are things which, for the honor of the corps, it's better to hide…but all the same, when one thinks of the carelessness with which they hand out diploma these days…three queens…and a point of fifty…'

"'Fifty's good. Do you mean that our physician has made another blunder?'

"'I haven't named anyone, as far as I know. I'll play clubs.'

"'Enough! One can take a hint. I'll take it…nine, ten. Eleven…anyway, you oughtn't to keep secrets from me, because, you know…mute as the tomb…'

"'There's no secret involved. Fourteen in diamonds, fifteen in clubs...only, I don't want to seem to be running him down. Fifteen. Word of honor...would you believe it?...he must have lost his head...to administer *nux vomica* to a child in such doses...'

"'Oh, it was the *nux vomica* for Madame ***'s kid!'

"'I haven't named anyone.'

"'My God, no...of course not! How odd you are to be suspicious of me. Your turn.'

"'I'm not suspicious.'

"'Which doesn't alter the fact that without you...'

"'The poor kid's number would have been up. You see, Monsieur Binet, it breaks one's heart, all the same, when one thinks that such disgraces to the profession have diplomas, and put on airs, while one vegetates in one's little shop, where it's still necessary to repair the blunders of these fine Messieurs... Ten o'clock. It's going to be fine tomorrow. I'll call it a day. Above all, not a word of this to anyone.'

"'Of course not!'

"And, the next day, Monsieur Binet has spread the word of the physician's error everywhere, which, but for the pharmacist, would have sent Madame ***'s little one *ad patres*."

Onésime had listened to that with an expression of incredulity. "It's a supposition you're making, isn't it?" he said to Master Helleborus. "No doctor ever commits such errors."

"The late Argan, your ancestor, would give you his blessing for such a question. Fine young man! You really are his direct and candid descendant. But on that chapter, I promised myself to let the facts speak for themselves, and they'll talk sufficiently, when the time comes.

"Permit me, in the meantime, to finish the portrait that I was in the process of painting for you, and complete the resemblance with a few final strokes.

"I've already shown you two redoubtable enemies of the provincial physician. There's also the authority! What suppleness of spine is requires by the man who wants to obtain its patronage! And the clergy! How many genuflections, if one requires its recommendation! And when the authority and the clergy are at odds, which can sometimes happen...how many detours and deviations to avoid the Charybdis of the mayor without running into the Scylla of the curé!

"And the immense distances to cover going from one patient to another. And the mutilating trot of the local horse or the mortal jolts of the cabriolet bogged down in the ruts! And the cold, and the heat, and the rain, and the wind and the insomnia to withstand. And the heart-rending paltriness of the salary that recompenses so many difficulties! And the arguments with the crafty peasant who doesn't understand that one has to be paid even though one hasn't sold him anything but words! And all the martyrology of which I'll spare you the rest!

"No, damn it, it's not astonishing that medical centralization has made such rapid progress, and that the sixty thousand physicians of Planet Fantasia are all in the capital. For from the moment that..."

While Master Helleborus was finishing his tirade, the waiter had approached.

"Now you've finished drinking," he said, without further ado, "do me the favor of surrendering the table."

X. A Carriage, Bourgeois!

Onésime was revolted once again by the uncivil procedure, but his guide closed his mouth with a sign and stood up in order to set an example.

When they had taken a few steps, Helleborus said: "My dear Onésime, I saw just now that you were about to get carried away again. I have, however, explained to you..."

"As you wish—but the insolence of that boor surpassed all limits."

"It doesn't differ as much as you seem to think from the insolence of terrestrial subordinates. In any case, it's only the logical progression of it. You've submitted back there to ridiculous demands; be punished here for the sins that you and your earthly brethren have committed."

"Furthermore," said Onésime, "I'm very glad to have quit the smoky atmosphere of that café."

"One of the certified caterers of Messieurs the Merchants of Health!"

"One couldn't see two paces in there, and that reek of tobacco combined with...I assure you that you shouldn't have made me drink that beer. It doesn't agree with me."

"Du Tilleul, my friend, your pusillanimity is the principal cause of your imaginary sufferings."

"Imaginary! There speaks one of those people who aren't afflicted by any illness! Imaginary! A poor man whose lungs and liver..."

"Spleen, heart, brain, kidneys, spinal cord, bronchi...," listed Helleborus, with ironic emphasis.

"It's easy for you to laugh. I don't know of anything that makes people crueler than being in good health."

"On that score, you can live here at the pleasure of your ideal, surrounded by compassionate and sympathetic hearts."

"What hearts do you mean?"

"Haven't I told you repeatedly that everything is centralized here? Just as there's a quarter of easy amours here, a workers' quarter and a literate quarter, there's an invalids' quarter, and that's the one that you'd choose for preference, isn't it?"

"I'd be obliged to, alas."

"That's what I thought. Taxi! Taxi!"

Master Helleborus addressed that appeal to the coachman of a vehicle that was passing along the street.

The Automedon turned his head with a movement of charming indolence, looked the two voyagers up and down in an adorably insolent manner, and then, making a gesture of scornful refusal, resumed his triumphant progress.

"But it's empty!" exclaimed Onésime.

"Certainly."

"Well?"

"Well, your face or mine didn't have the honor of pleasing him, and he disdained us."

"If I'd known, I'd have shown the scoundrel..."

"Violence? In order to be sentenced to a fine?"

"You're right. But there must be regulations..."

"There are, composed of several hundred articles, all conceived to correct abuses. Unfortunately, the regulations have been given to coachmen in order to procure them the pleasure of violating them."

"It's a little like that on Earth."

"Don't be astonished, then, that it's much more like that on Planet Fantasia. Always the magnification of the abuses that you've advertised... Taxi! Taxi!"

Master Helleborus hailed a second cab.

"You're too tall," said the coachman. "You'll tire out my animals."

"Taxi! Taxi!"

There was a third vehicle.

"Thanks, but it's necessary here not to have fat in your pockets," said the coachman, passing on.

"Taxi! Taxi! Taxi!"

They called a dozen in succession, all of which were empty, while the official stands remained deprived on any vehicle. Each of the twelve coachmen gave a different excuse for his refusal: one because the journey was too long; another because he didn't like Onésime's face; another because Helleborus' attire was insufficiently elegant; a fourth because he had promised himself never to carry any but decorated individuals...etc.

Finally, after multiple attempts, the voyagers ended up discovering a thirteenth coachman, who consented to take them, not without having laid down draconian conditions, such as:

Firstly, to go slowly, because his horse was hot.

Secondly, to stop at every tenth tavern, because the coachman and his horse were thirsty.

Thirdly, to set the passengers down on the way, if he found others who would give him a higher price...

And so on.

Onésime was furious.

"But my dear Du Tilleul, you'll overheat your blood," insinuated Master Helleborus.

Onésime immediately ceased to be furious.

XI. Strike Behind!

As he climbed into the carriage, Master Helleborus was necessarily obliged to give the address to which he wanted to be taken.

"To the Invalids' Quarter!" he had shouted. "Such and-such street! Number such-and-such!"

That was an imprudence—which he might perhaps have committed deliberately, and for the good of the cause that he had undertaken to win.

The numbered vehicle did, in fact, make progress for several minutes, and—faithful to the instruction given—did so at a measured pace.

Onésime, settled down in a corner and furtively applied his hand to his temple in order to assure himself that the beating of the artery had not suffered any serious perturbation.

Suddenly, a cry resounded, with significant determination, which had been proffered once or twice as soon as they were in the carriage.

It was the favorite exclamation of the Parisian gamin desirous of doing one of his comrades a bad turn: the "Look out, Sentinel!" of locomotion. "Strike behind! Strike behind! Strike behind!" sang a chorus of young ragamuffins.

Upon which the coachman sent a hail of whiplashes to the rear of his vehicle.

But the cries of "Strike behind!" continued to ring out with an increased ardor, which indicated that the objective had not been attained.

"Undoubtedly some young rascal must have climbed on to the springs," said Onésime.

His companion smiled silently.

"Why are you smiling?"

Master Helleborus made no reply. He contented himself with lifting up the little curtain that hid the small window set in the rear of the vehicle, with a gesture that signified: "Look."

Onésime looked, open-mouthed.

Sitting, clinging on, perched, and fighting to drive one another away from their positions, he perceived half a dozen merchants of health—the same ones who had assailed him on his arrival.

"Well, yes," said Master Helleborus, anticipating the reflections that Du Tilleul was about to formulate, "when one isn't used to it, and to the contrast between the severe costume and grave expressions of individuals with the bizarrerie of their attitude, it lends itself to astonishment—but what do you expect? It's competition!"

"What about professional dignity?" objected Onésime. "Never, in Paris..."

"Never...thus far. Don't make any promises for the future. Besides which, I can't see such an enormous difference as you're willing to admit. Chasing clients in writing or in person...it's a subtle difference. These worthy individuals have the sincerity of their role! They've heard that you're going to the invalids' quarter, and, having scented prey, they're following the trail..."

While Master Helleborus was explaining, the shouts of the street-urchins had increased—"Strike behind! Strike behind!"—to such an extent that the coachman was driven to the extreme of standing on his seat and turning his back on his horse, and striving to stretch out his arm in order to reach the intruders.

But another tumult suddenly burst out.

XII. The Vultures of Publicity

While the coachman applied himself to the repression of the crime of usurpation and had, as we have said, turned his back on his horse, the not-very-philanthropically inclined quadruped had thought it appropriate to use its head to give a familiar dig in the ribs to a deaf gentleman who was walking along the sidewalk with a security that might have passed for conceit on his part.

The deaf man stumbled and fell.

The horse—definitely no philanthropist—was utterly unmoved by that accident, and neither hastened nor slowed its pace—with the consequence that the deaf gentleman was about to make the intimate acquaintance of the wheels.

Fortunately, one of the street-urchins whose eyes were fixed on the carriage noticed a strange body on the ground.

"Man overboard!" he cried.

That was the signal adopted since a passer-by had perished by drowning in the improved macadam of Planet Fantasia.

Immediately, two policemen launched themselves intrepidly to the rescue, while two others extended poles at sidewalk-height. One of the policemen stopped the horse, the other dived, in order to reach the drowning man.

The deaf man was saved—but it was far from over. On the contrary, the comedy of accidents was just beginning.

The policemen rebuked the coachman harshly and took his number. The gathering idlers made speeches and formulated theses on the subject of surveillance of the public highway. Onésime tried to get down.

"What's the point?" said his companion.

"Perhaps the poor fellow needs attention. What a state he's in!"

"From the point of view of coquetry, his attire leaves much to be desired, but in a sanitary context, he can't have sustained any injury. Besides which, he's sure of being cared for to a greater extent than he would like."

In fact, as if driven by a spring, the six merchants of health who had climbed up on to the rear of the carriage had hurtled forward at the first hint of the accident. They surrounded the victim as if they were intent on fighting over the scraps.

One of them took his arm, another pulled his feet; one tried to feel his ribs, another to massage his spinal column.

"It's necessary to undress him!"

"He must have at least one fracture."

"A wound."

"A sprain."

"A graze."

"It's not possible that someone could have such a fall without any morbid symptom resulting."

"That would be indecent."

"It would be necessary to renounce the profession."

"Where does it hurt, Monsieur?"

"You must have dislocated something, Monsieur?"

"Unhinged?"

"Disconnected?"

"Bruised?"

"Have no fear; I'll have you back on your feet in a fortnight."

"I can do it within a week."

"Six days."

"Four."

"Isn't it me that you've chosen as your doctor, Monsieur?"

"Isn't it me?"

The deaf man did not reply, for the excellent reason that he did not hear a single word of all those questions.

"Monsieur!" persisted one of the merchants of health. "Hey, Monsieur!"

"Monsieur!" repeated all the others.

The deaf man, surprised by that unexpected *tutti*, risked a slight movement.

"He gave me a sign!"

"It was to me!"

"I saw him first!"

"So did I!"

"I must I care for him quickly, at all costs."

"I'm going to apply a sedative water compress."

"Just a minute—it's me that he's chosen."

The policemen, seeing that the battle was threatening to become prolonged, thought it necessary to intervene.

"Monsieur will be taken back to his domicile, and he'll send for you there if he wants to."

"In that case, please at least take my name," replied one of the merchants of health, handing his card to the policeman. "You'll be good enough to have the fact recorded in large print in the stop press of the newspapers that it was Dr. Ricochet who lavished first aid upon the wounded man."

"What! Don't listen to him, and accept this card, in order to have it recorded that it was Dr. Maniveau, with a devotion beyond all praise..."

"It's necessary to see that no one is mistaken about that matter! It's me, Dr. de Grandpré, 1233 Rue de Mule... do you hear?" Turning to the circle of onlookers that had formed, he repeated: "1233 Rue de Mule." In an insinuating tone, he added: "If there are other persons in the honorable society surrounding me who desire my address I can give it to them..."

"That's all right! That's fine!" the policemen intervened. "They know that."

"Permit me," another merchant of health insisted. "The interests of equity, I demand that this question be clarified. Isn't it me, Monsieur, who cared for you?"

"Isn't it me?" his colleague immediately repeated.

"Isn't it...?"

"Move along," interrupted the policemen, irritated.

Master Helleborus, who had wanted to ensure that Onésime witnessed that scene, saw that it was reaching its conclusion.

"Quickly," he said, "let's get away before they have time to attach themselves to our pursuit again. Let's go, coachman!"

"I'm going."

Meanwhile, the deaf gentleman had risen to his feet.

It doesn't matter, each of the merchants of health thought. *A man afflicted with deafness might become a client—let's stick to him.*

And they fell into step behind him, while the voices of the policemen could be heard grumbling, feebly: "Move along…move along…"

As for the coachman, when he judged that the performance was well and truly over, he decided to set off again, while muttering: "What a fuss! For one deaf man more or less! I've run over better men who didn't scream so loudly."

XIII. The Invalids' Quarter[16]

They arrived at their destination.

The Invalids' Quarter was offered to the gaze of the two voyagers. A blind man would have recognized it by its odor alone. Every street was redolent with the vaguely acrid odor that is the incestuous product of pharmacy and malady.

The carriage rolled dully over the straw that was scattered everywhere.

Onésime had put his head out of the door.

In front of him filed an interminable series of houses, punctuated at intervals by vaster edifices of—if you will pardon the neologism—barrackesque appearance.

---

[16] The "Quartier des Invalides" in Paris owes its name to the Hotel des Invalides, a complex of buildings in the 7th arrondissement that used to be a hospital and a retirement home for war veterans, hence its name; the joke here is that the name is taken literally and the entire neighborhood is a giant hospital.

The smaller houses were all "sanitariums," as attested by the signs placed in from of each of them, displaying names that were all more enticing than one another:

Bel Air

Pleasant Abode

Cosy Corner

Dolce Respiro

Therapeutic Paradise

Then came appetizing details regarding the salubrity, comfort and superiority of the different dwellings, which all claimed to be situated and organized in such a way as to render their guests centenarians.

As for the vaster edifices, they were hospitals. The nudity of their walls attested to their purpose. One sensed that the disdained to make advances to their gratuitous public. What is the point of making promises that one is not obliged to keep?

"Well?" asked Master Helleborus. "What do you think of your future domicile?"

"If once can believe the signs, the Invalids' Quarter is the nicest in the whole city. I can see faces at the windows, though, which reflect a different opinion."

"You're joking. Do you expect to see invalids dressed for a ball?"

"No, but the quarter seems to me to be a little sad."

"When you're cured, you'll have every opportunity to live in another."

"Alas, we're not at that stage yet," sighed Argan's descendant, sucking a Vichy pastille that he had discovered in the depths of one of his pockets.[17]

Master Helleborus did not respond to that remark. He leaned toward the coachman and pointed at a house of reasonable pleasant appearance. "Stop there," he said.

---

[17] Vichy pastilles are nowadays sugared and flavored (unsurprisingly, as the brand now belongs to Cadbury), but in 1862 they were pure bicarbonate of soda, taken to settle excess stomach acid.

On seeing the carriage pull up, a ground of invalids hastened to assist in the disembarkation. That novel escort was not exactly amusing, and the comments that emerged from it added to the unpleasantness of the situation.

The comments in question could be divided into two categories: those of discouraged invalids, and those of deluded invalids.

"They don't need to be here," complained some, looking Onésime and his guide up and down. "It's probably to insult our suffering. Are they going to be taken in looking like that?"

"Have you seen the short one?" whispered the others—"the short one" was Onésime. "That jaundiced complexion, those rings around the eyes...there's one spinning a weak thread. Thank God we're not in such a state, and will be long gone while he's still awaiting his cure! That's some consolation."

The unfortunate Du Tilleul, whom those reflections had not escaped, felt beads of sweat forming on his brow.

Master Helleborus probably noticed that, and deemed that it would be cruel to prolong the scene.

"Open the door and go in while I pay the coachman," he said. "I'll catch you up."

The porter of the house had advanced to meet Onésime. "What can we do for you?"

"I'd like...I've come..." He did not know how to translate a desire that was not exactly his own.

The porter, moreover, anticipated a more ample explanation. "It's for accommodation. You're not our affair. We don't take fatal maladies."

"What? What are you saying?" the unfortunate stammered.

"You heard. I'm telling you that the house is very well inhabited, and we only receive slightly indisposed people here, because the others, you understand...burials are so depressing."

"You're not...serious?"

"Do I look as if I'm laughing? Bonsoir. Go somewhere else."

Bewildered, Onésime went back to the door.

"No room available?" asked Master Helleborus. "Why what's the matter? You seem upset..."

"Oh, I knew that I was doomed!" And he recounted his misadventure to his companion.

"Is that all?" the other replied. "There's no need to be frightened by something so trivial. The porters of Planet Fantasia are like those elsewhere. Follow me."

"I can't."

"Good! You want to be ill now! Move, I tell you, and you'll soon see the counterpart of the scene that's affected you so much."

Indeed, they went into another house, the porter of which, with the good grace of his profession, greeted them with a: "Why have you come here?"

"To obtain accommodation," replied Master Helleborus.

"Never."

"And why not?"

"You're not sick enough, either of you."

Onésime felt better.

"What does it matter to you?" asked Helleborus,

"It matters a great deal to me, and to Monsieur the Proprietor. Monsieur the Proprietor and I let rooms by the year, but we take care to choose tenants who won't last longer than three months, because, you see, one then has the advantage of letting the same apartment four times."

"My companion is very ill, though," said Helleborus, with a snigger.

"Ha ha! Very ill! His appearance doesn't inspire me with confidence. I have an idea that he'll last a lot longer than you think..."

Onésime breathed out noisily.

"Do you know, bumpkin, that you're a scoundrel, with your system of letting to the dead!" exclaimed Helleborus, pretending to get angry.

"Don't we have the right any more to dispose of our property as we like?"

"It's crooked."

"Crooks, us? Us! A property-owner. Oh, that's it! Aménaïde, the broom! Help me!"

Aménaïde was otherwise occupied, and Helleborus, who was writhing with laughter, drew the comforted Onésime away.

In a third house, it was a woman—perhaps that title is a trifle pretentious for a portress—who came to meet the two strangers.

"The Messieurs desire…?"

"Accommodation for my friend.

"Ah! Monsieur is a bachelor?" she said, indicating Onésime.

"Certainly."

"Oh, then we have everything that Monsieur needs. Monsieur has no immediate relatives?"

"No."

"A superb room on the second floor. No collaterals?"

"No."

"What am I saying, the second? It's on the first floor that I'll accommodate Monsieur, and I'll care for him like my own son."

"Thanks, but I don't want to lodge here," Onésime interjected, abruptly. "Come on!" When they were outside, she added: "That abominable harpy. She didn't suspect that I could read her thoughts and that I deciphered her avaricious instincts through her kindly assurances."

"Oh well," said Helleborus, philosophically, "the gift I've made you has its petty disappointments. The underside of other people's thoughts isn't always rosy—but bitterness is often salutary. Ha ha! You ought to know that, being a drinker of tisanes."

After a few other fruitless attempts, Onésime was finally able to install himself in a domicile chosen by his friend.

"This will suit you marvelously," the latter told him. "It's late; you'd better go to bed. Adieu."

"You're leaving me?"

"I'll come back in the morning. I have to pay a visit to a fixed star a million leagues away."

XIV. The Safety Matches

When Onésime was alone he started examining the new domicile where he had run aground.

The walls of his room seemed to be decorated from top to bottom with paper crammed full of characters whose nature he could not quite make out because of the darkness that had fallen. The same characters were encrusted in the floor; they were also painted on the ceiling.

"That's curious," he murmured. "Let's verify the fact and complete our inventory."

So saying, he struck a match. It did not catch. He struck a second and a third. He went through the entire box: no trace of fire.

Impatient, he rang the bell. A domestic appeared.

"Monsieur rang?"

"I certainly did. I've been trying for an hour to strike your accursed matches, and not one caught fire."

"Thank God."

"What do you mean, thank God?"

"Our scientists had a great deal of difficulty making that discovery."

"What discovery?"

"Monsieur is not from these parts, then? He doesn't know?"

"No, I'm not from these parts."

"I thought so. Once, Monsieur, we had chemical match-es, as they were called. Those satanic matches caught fire as soon as one had the misfortune to strike them."

"It seems to me that that's an advantage for matches, not a defect."

"An advantage! Oh, one can certainly see that Monsieur isn't from these parts."

"What are you trying to insinuate?"

"Nothing, Monsieur...except that, if Monsieur were from these parts, he'd know that chemical matches are only good for setting fire..."

"Obviously."

"Setting fire to houses."

"When one commits imprudences."

"Perhaps so. In any case, we had fires every year, you see. So the scientists I mentioned got together, and they decided that if someone could find something better, it would be a good thing."

"Really? The scientists got together to make a decision of that importance?"

"Indeed, Monsieur. That's how things are done here. One can see that Monsieur isn't..."

"Enough."

"Apologies; I didn't mean it malevolently. So, after having decided what I told you, they waited for an amateur to present himself with an invention."

"And did one present himself?"

"Several, of course. One doesn't find such subtle things at the first attempt."

"What things?"

"For a start, one came along who'd imagined matches that would only catch alight if one struck them on special paper. The paper was stuck to the side of the box."

"That's ingenious."

"Ingenious, Monsieur, but imprudent. Because, you see, one had the match and the box at the same time. Paff! Once struck, it caught fire."

"It seems to me that the combination was convenient."

"And what about the fires? Once can see...no, forget it. After that inventor, another came along who proposed matches that it was necessary to dip in water before lighting them."

"Bah!"

"Yes, Monsieur, that was successful for a while, because children, who didn't know the means, were no longer at risk of roasting their father and mother."

"That's true."

"Unfortunately, at the first small fire that took hold in a house, people sprinkled water on all the floors. Bang! Immediately, all the provisions of matches went up, and an entire quarter burned down."

"And now?"

"Now, it's another pair of pistols altogether. There's the true recipe: safety matches."

"Of what do they consist?"

"Oh, Monsieur, it's both simple and improved. You have matches like the ones you tried…"

"Which didn't light."

"Of course! There's nothing but the wood."

"There's nothing but the wood?"

"Certainly, Monsieur. When you want to light a fire, you take one of those wooden matches, you dip it into a tin containing a liquid, then into a second, which contains a powder, and then into a third, which contains a paste, and crack! Your match catches!"

"But that must take a horribly long time?"

"Pooh! One gets used to it. And then, the security! One has every right to call them safety matches. Not to mention that a regulation has been made specifying that, for more tranquility, in each house, the tin of liquid should be in the cellar, the tin of powder on the third floor, in a cupboard lined with sheet metal, the tin of paste in the attic, and the matches in the individual rooms. With that method, you see, one can sleep easy."

"And go up and down a dozen flights of steps in order to have light."

"Oh, well…the security! One can see that Monsieur isn't…"

"We must hope that someone will invent matches that don't light at all. The security will be even greater."

"Monsieur is right; we must hope. You see, Monsieur, I take this little piece of wood; I go to the cellar; I go back up to the third floor; from there I go..."

"And I have to wait for a quarter of an hour?"

"Perhaps...always provided that the proprietor hasn't gone out, taking the key to the third floor cupboard with her. She's so scared of disasters!"

"Then I'd be obliged..."

"That's a supposition! Besides which, she'll be back later this evening. I'll hurry, Monsieur. But you'll see when you get to know this country that there's nothing like it for security..."

The domestic's voice faded away on the staircase.

XV. Onésime's Room

Finally, the safety match had decided to take effect. Onésime Du Tilleul was able to acquire a more ample acquaintance with the room in which he was residing.

He had not been mistaken.

First of all, on the shade of the lamp he was holding in his hand, he read:

Diseases of the Eyes
DR. PICHENETTE'S TREATMENT
Infallible Cure
From 4-6 p.m. every day at his consulting rooms
941 Rue des Éléphants

He examined at close range the characters he had remarked on the carpet;

Diseases of the Feet
(Corns, Bunions, etc.)
DR. BARDIZET'S TREATMENT
Infallible Cure
1102 Rue de la Bienfaisance

He looked at the paintings on the walls.

One represented "Autumn Leaves," and underneath it was:

Diseases of the Chest
DR. PISTOLOIS' TREATMENT
Infallible cure
9 Rue des Enfants-Verts

The second picture represented a lunatic asylum, and underneath:

Diseases of the Brain
DR. PALAVOINE'S TREATMENT
Infallible Cure
47 Rue de la Sauterelle

He looked at himself in the mirror. A poster was stuck to it, on which one read:

Diseases of the Liver
Infallible Cure
If you have a jaundiced complexion
Address yourself to DR. LANCINANT
1913 Rue des Chardons

He sat down on an armchair; a spring-mounted notice leapt out of the back:

Diseases of the Kidneys
DR. ADALBERT'S TREATMENT
Infallible Cure
22 Rue de la Rhubarbe

He drank a cup of tea. On the bottom of the cup, printed on the porcelain, was outlined:

Diseases of the Throat
DR. VALATIER'S TREATMENT
Infallible Cure
111 Rue des Comètes

He lay down on the bed. Woven into the sheets were the words:

Diseases of the Blood
(Insomnia)
DR. GANIMARD'S TREATMENT
Infallible Cure
123 Rue de la Syncope

Someone other than Onésime would probably have made different reflections on the appearance of this deployment of bait. But he—O Argan, from the height of Heaven, your final dwelling!—as he slid into those sheets full of damasked promises, contented himself with murmuring blissfully:

"Infallible cure! Always and everywhere! My new friend Helleborus has a slightly suspect and fantastic appearance, but I bless him nevertheless for having brought me here."

XVI. The Hygiopathic Sawmill

Rosy-fingered dawn had not yet done any more than open a crack in the gates of the Orient when Argan's descendant awoke with a start.

Close at hand—one might have thought that it was in the room—a concert of a novel species was making itself heard.

To the shrill grating of several dozens saws was added the sound of heavy pieces of wood being shifted noisily, and the echoes of exclamations, lamentations and injunctions, which formed the strangest of amalgams.

"Sapristi!" cried Onésime, propping himself up on his elbow.

Then he rubbed his eyes in order in order to gather his memories, troubled by the accumulation of so many unexpected events.

"Sapristi!" he repeated. "Where am I, then?"

As he addressed that question to himself, he felt his surroundings, for the half-light only illuminated the room imperfectly.

Suddenly, his memory was reconstructed. He had just perceived the paintings, the mirror, and the furniture with the singular recommendations.

"I remember now...Master Helleborus...the Planet Fantasia...the Invalids' Quarter..."

At that moment, the discordant concert somewhere in the vicinity redoubled its intensity.

Great God! he thought. *Have I landed in a lunatic asylum?*

Although he was not very familiar with the theater, Onésime went on occasion, and like everyone else, he had seen one of the sixty revivals of *Les Pilules du diable*, a play whose title must have had a particular attraction for him.[18]

It was a reminiscence of the famous fantasy in question that went through his head. He thought of the scene in the "rest home," and its dissonant racket.

"Is the fiction becoming a reality for me? It's abominable. I promised myself a lie-in! I'm exhausted after so much..." *Brring! Brring!* "Bellboy... Someone!" *Brring! Brring!*

---

[18] *Les Pilules du diable* [The Devil's Pills] was a pioneering "féerie" [fantasy play] in three acts and twenty tableaux with a libretto by Ferdinand Laloue and August Anicet-Bourgeois, with music by "Laurent" (Laurent Franconi) first produced in 1839, which became enormous popular and helped provoke a vogue for "fairy plays" featuring elaborate tableaux displaying lightly-costumed children (which became a focal point of child prostitution in both Paris and London).

The bell-pull to which he was clinging had caused a new placard to emerge from the wall, which bore this advice:

For the sake of the other invalids
please ring quietly.
If no one answers, wait, and
complain to the administration

"They're charming, with their *ring quietly!* And do they imagine that the other invalids can be sleeping, any more than me, with that serenade going on outside?" *Brring!* "Wait to complain, and die..." *Brring!* "while waiting..." *Brring! Brring! Brring!*

The bell-cord came away in the hand of the ringer, but his efforts did not seem capable of producing any other result.

Finally, however—a good half hour had gone by—the domestic of the previous evening appeared, half-dressed, with a fearful expression, rubbing his eyes.

"Did Monsieur ring?"

"Yes, I rang!"

"Well, Monsieur, in the first slumber..."

"The first slumber at five o'clock in the morning..."

"It's still my first, since I haven't woken up since yesterday evening."

"One would have had time to die..."

"Monsieur is right, since that has happened before."

"And you dare to admit it!"

"Well, Monsieur, it's the fault of the invalids; it's necessary to pay the night supplement, and then someone will come straight away."

"There's a night supplement?"

"It's quite simple. Fair's fair. On our part, this isn't philanthropy; it's commerce; we're trading our care for your money."

"I've never heard such brazen language…"

"That's because where you come from, people do the same but without telling you."

73

"Animal."

"If that's why Monsieur disturbed me, it wasn't worth the trouble. Only I'll make the observation to Monsieur that I'm not warm in this light costume, and I might catch a cold."

"That's all the same to me."

"And me too. Except, if I sneeze, that will be added to Monsieur's bill."

"That's a bit much."

"I can't catch a cold for nothing, though…it's not in my terms of service. Would Monsieur prefer it if I went away?"

"Not before telling me what that frightful racket is that's been pursuing me since daybreak."

"What racket is that?"

"Can't you hear it?"

As if to underline Onésime's question, the din caused the air to vibrate with a new fury.

"I can't hear anything extraordinary."

"What! That grinding, that whistling, that..."

"Oh, I get it! Monsieur is probably talking about the Hygiopathic Sawmill, which is next door. Another thing that proves that Monsieur is not from these parts—otherwise he'd be used to it."

"I could never get used to such a din."

"Monsieur isn't any different from anyone else. Anyway, the Hygiopathic Sawmill is an institution declared a public utility by a report of the Academy of Infallibles.

"But tell me, finally, what is this sawmill?"

"I'd like nothing better, except that I'm getting sensibly cold. Monsieur has been warned."

"Get on with it!"

"The Medical Sawmill, Monsieur, is a recent invention of Dr. Baltimer, an innovator, as we call them here. Dr. Baltimer has discovered that prior to him, medicine lacked common sense. That's generally how all innovators get started. Upon which, he tried to give it the sense that it lacked, and demonstrated in a large volume of 991 pages that violent and prolonged exercise is the sole and unique remedy against afflictions of all the organs.

"To prove what he said, Dr. Baltimer opened an establishment next door in which he's testing his theory, to which he's given the name of the Hygiopathic Sawmill. All the invalids there are required to saw from dawn to dusk a certain number of logs, in accordance with their strength and the more or less advanced stage of the treatment."

"What about those who don't want to?"

"They're forced to!"

"I don't see how."

"With strokes of the lash!"

"You're joking!"

"Not at all, Monsieur. The lash, according to Dr. Baltimer, is an indispensable complement, for whipping up the blood and restoring equilibrium to the humors. There, can you hear them? They're invalids rebellious against science."

One could, indeed, make out voices uttering plaints, and others proffering reproaches.

"That's necessary. If one listened to the invalids, you see, they'd never be cured. I once worked in the Hygopathic Mill myself, and I can guarantee that I didn't spare them. When one knows that it's for their own good...because, you see, when they've sweated a lot and sawed a lot, either they recover, or they die. If they recover, it's the treatment; if they die, it's the malady..."

"I doubt that many recover."

"Of course they do, Monsieur. I've seen one, with my own eyes."

"One out of how many?"

"The number is irrelevant. Anyway, the Academy of Infallibles is there to safeguard everything."

"And what is that Academy?"

"Our scientific elite. The luminaries of medical science."

"They must be mad to have approved such an absurd system."

"They've approved many others. You'll see, when you read the newspapers. After every advertised remedy, you'll invariably find the phrase: *Approved by the Academy of Infallibles.*"

"If I'm not mistaken," Onésime said, cocking an ear, "the noise has stopped."

"It's brushing time, Monsieur."

"For what?"

"For the invalids, of course. In order to refresh them, their bodies are raked with electro-chemico-houndstooth brushes—another invention of Dr. Baltimer's. After that operation, they'll resume sawing."

"I won't be able to go back to sleep, then?"

"Perhaps not today, but you'll get used to it, Monsieur, you'll get used to it."

"Thanks very much!"

"It's only a matter...I'll go back to my...my...damn it! Too late! Monsieur is my witness that I sneezed...*atchoo!* That will cost Monsieur a hundred sous."

XVII. The Indiscreet Square

What can one do in a bed when one can't sleep?

Onésime, away from home, anxious and isolated, waited for the daylight to arrive completely, while indulging in monologues that voiced a series of impressions unfavorable to Planet Fantasia.

So, in order to react against his preoccupations, as he saw that his guide had not yet returned, he got dressed briskly, went downstairs and went out into the street, thinking: *A morning stroll is eminently healthy, according to all the physicians I've seen, so let's take a walk, without any prejudice to the opinions of the physicians I've yet to see.*

At the end of the street, he perceived a space twenty meters square, covered with artificial grass and planted with half a dozen trees enveloped in flannel vests.

He asked a passer-by what the space was.

"Monsieur," replied the passer-by, "that's what we call a *square*."[19]

"Ah! Very good—I know."

"We know too—we know only too well. In the beginning, when these playthings were put in the middle of our public places, we thought the idea agreeably frivolous, but we didn't take long to change our opinion."

"Once, in fact, we had magnificent public gardens in Capital Fantasia, very shady and very leafy. But while, one the one hand, we were given these toy fields, on the other, the beautiful gardens were gradually eroded and mutilated—to such an extent that one morning, we perceived that we had released the prey for the shadow.

"At present, the sacrifice is consummate. The 'squares' are the only greenery to be found in our great city. If you want to take a stroll, I advise you to hurry before it's too late, for the 'square' will be full up and you'll be obliged to take a number while you wait for someone else to come out. I have the honor of saluting you, Monsieur."

"Monsieur..."

Onésime resumed walking, bewildered once again.

His astonishment soon had a very different motive however. He had forgotten the faculty of second sight with which his friend Helleborus had enriched him, and was strangely

---

[19] The word *square* is here given in English, to emphasize that it has a different meaning from *place*, which would normally translate into English as "square." The French had observed, although many Londoners had not, that there is a marked difference between large open spaces like Trafalgar Square and smaller ones like the nearby St. James's Square, which typically have a small railed garden in the middle—although the establishment of such narrow urban plots did not, in the long run, lead to the annihilation of St. James's Park or any of its analogues, any more than Paris was eventually deprived of the Jardins du Luxembourg and its annexes.

surprised to find that he could read the thoughts of all those he encountered as clearly as if he were deciphering an open book.

On several occasions, the result of that reading was so startling that Onésime passed his hand over his eyes, as if to escape a painful vision.

"No, it's impossible! It's impossible!" he murmured.

Meanwhile, he had arrived at the principal "square" of the Invalids' Quarter.

Various groups of strollers were circulating—or rather, following in single file a circular course, which, by virtue of the tightness of the circle resembled the evolutions of Franconi's horses.[20]

Onésime joined the file, on the instruction given to him by a warden.

In front of him, an old gentleman was walking, who was leaning on the shoulder of a young man. Because of the short distance separating them, Onésime did not miss a word of their conversation.

"Dear boy," said the old gentleman, "thank you for having got up so early in the morning in order to assist me in my habitual walk!"

"Of course, my dear uncle; am I not only too happy to oblige you?"

"You're a charming fellow; I shall remember you in my will."

"Oh, uncle, why speak of such things?"

"It's necessary! I'm under no illusions about my age or my situation."

"Uncle, my dear uncle, if I thought you supposed that interest was guiding me..."

"Far from it! But you can't prevent me from showing my affection by means of a small legacy."

---

[20] Antonio Franconi (1738-1836) founded the equestrian theater known as the Cirque Olympique, whose tradition was carried on after his death by his descendants.

"So be it, uncle, as I'm sure that with a chest like yours you'll bury twenty young men like me..."

"You're joking!"

While they expressed themselves thus, Onésime read in their thoughts:

I know full well, fool, why you're going out of your way this morning; you've sniffed the odor of an inheritance, the uncle said to himself. *It's not my chest, it's my strong-box that you're thinking about.*

If you imagine, the nephew said to himself, *that without your money, I'd be stupid enough to serve as your cane...*

But he who laughs last laughs longest.

I'll have my revenge; patience!

For a start, I'm not leaving you a sou.

How vexed the other heirs will be when they find that I've copped the lot!

I'm certainly hoping not to die so soon...

Except that if he doesn't hurry up and die...

Revolted by these duplicities, Onésime turned his attention away from that pair of hypocrites.

Behind him, a husband was advancing, lending his arm to a wife emaciated by suffering.

"How are you feeling today?" the husband asked.

"Better, much better," replied the wife.

"I came a little later than usual because I was obliged to be in my officer at eight...because of extra work."

"I'm very grateful to you."

"Isn't it a pleasure for me? And what kind of night did you have?"

"Very bad."

"You didn't sleep?"

"Hardy at all."

"What does the doctor say?"

"Oh, the doctor..."

"Well? You're not going to despair? I've never seen you looking better."

"I'm in a great deal of pain, though."

"What kind of pain?"

"A kind that…that…"

"It's necessary not to tire yourself out, then. I'll take you home—all the more so as it's getting late, and that accursed office…I don't know what I'd give to be able to spend all day every day with you."

"Poor love!"

And while the pair continued aloud on that sentimental note, Onésime deciphered, in a much lower register:

Oh my office, how I bless you! thought the husband.

Oh, no, I won't tell him that, the cause of my illness, thought his wife.

Without the bureaucratic pretext, I could see myself obliged to spend all day in the company of a woman in pain, who's jaundiced, getting old…

A month and a half without a letter from him…

Fortunately, one is able to create compensations. She's charming, little Eudoxie.

Albert, Albert! I love you so much!

Damn! Let's hurry, or I'll miss the rendezvous she's given me to go to lunch in the country—and she hates waiting.

If Albert doesn't come back, I think I'll die.

What a difference there is, all the same, between a mistress and a wife!

When I think of him, and then look at my husband!

She's become shrewish, my wife, since falling ill.

He's aging horribly, my husband.

While she…

While he…

Let's hurry so that I can meet her.

If he's betrayed me, I won't survive it…

Meanwhile, the two spouses and stopped, and, while exchanging mutual kisses on the cheek, repeated:

"Adieu, my dear, until this evening."

"Adieu, my love."

"Look after yourself."

"Take care of yourself—don't work too hard."

"Think about me."

"You too..."

They went their separate ways, murmuring as a secret conclusion:

"If I were a widower, though..."

"If I were a widow..."

Before the elegiac couple had time to complete their double hypothesis, Onésime, ceding to an abrupt surge of indignation, had quit the "square."

And, as he turned the corner of the street, he perceived the sarcastic face of Master Helleborus at the window of his room.

XVIII. An Exception

Master Helleborus smiled on observing his protégé's stride from a distance, and called out to him in an ironic tone as soon as he reached the foot of his staircase: "Well, have we run away already? How goes your health, this morning? Personally, I'm very well, thank you. The eight million kilometers I traveled last night have given me the heartiest appetite...

"Oh, have we, by chance already been to consult a doctor? We're perfectly capable of it. No? So much the better. So we've been taking our little morning stroll, then? Tell me what nice things you've seen. Damn it, what a face! Are we discontented, then?"

"One will be, at least, and I advise you not to joke about it!" exclaimed Onésime. "I'd like to quit this horrible planet as quickly as possible and get away from its infamous inhabitants."

"Damn! How you slander people!"

"I repeat to you that I want to leave."

"You'll permit me to have my humble determination too?"

"But it's an abomination! I can still hear them heaping one another with tender words, caresses, assurances of devotion, while I, for my part, know what ambitions, what hypocrisies, what..."

"There you go!" said Helleborus, sardonically. "One should never confide anything to children. Because I had the misfortune to lift a little corner of the curtain for Monsieur, he gets carried away, shows his fist to his fellows..."

"To my fellows! Know that there is nothing in common between the rogues of the Planet Fantasia and me!"

"I admire that pride from an artistic point of view, but from the viewpoint of reason, I'd like to speak in order to make a correction. Truly, my good Monsieur Onésime, there's nothing in common between you and the new world that you see here? Impossible!"

"No, certainly not."

"Then take the trouble to convince yourself."

And with the tip of his index finger, Helleborus traced a cabalistic sign in the air.

Immediately, it seemed to Onésime that he could see his domicile in the Rue Odéon again, and in that domicile...

"Enough! Enough!" he exclaimed, choking. "It's only two days since I disappeared, and already my friends, relatives and servants, back there, are robbing me, vilifying me, mocking me...

"That blackguard of a domestic who swore he was so attached to me, won't leave me a single bottle of wine if I don't get back to Earth soon.

"That cousin in whom I had a blind confidence..."

"Blind is the word. So don't calumniate Planet Fantasia so cruelly. Its faults leap to your eyes, but those of the sublunary globe escape you. It's a simple question of wearing spectacles.

"In addition, no matter how general a rule is, it always has exceptions. The exception exists here, as it does elsewhere, and if that's all that's necessary to reconcile you to your new abode, be satisfied."

As he concluded, Master Helleborus had drawn closer to the window, and he showed Onésime the top floor of the house situated facing theirs. In a somber, stifling and lugubrious mansard, a seated woman was leaning over a child that she was holding in her arms.

The unfortunate woman was not saying anything, or uttering a single sob, but her haggard features and her avidly immobile eyes spoke eloquently on her behalf.

"Read her heart at your ease, Onésime," said Helleborus. "She's poor, but you won't find any concern regarding the misery that's lying in wait for her; she's exhausted, but you won't discover any thought in her regarding her own fatigue; her dolor is immense, but you won't hear her utter any plaint."

"Indeed," stammered Onésime.

"Am I not right? Isn't it true that you can't catch her red-handed in any duplicity?"

"I admit it."

"Good. And when you're revolted by the iniquities of Planet Fantasia, have a little indulgence, and remember that woman at her child's bedside."

XIX. The First Day

A pause of a few minutes followed that argument *ad hominem*. Helleborus wanted to allow Onésime's thoughts time to evolve fully. Onésime wanted to give Helleborus' mockery time to lay down its arms.

It was the latter who broke the silence first. "With all that, my dear Du Tilleul, we're not occupying ourselves with the principal motive that brought us here. You must have some new malady since I last had the pleasure of seeing you."

"You're wrong to make a joke out of everything, Monsieur Helleborus. I feel a great need for medical care."

"Of course! I was sure of it, and I'd be desolate if it were otherwise. I even want you to commence, without delay, to experiment with the indigenous medications. Let's go."

"It's just that...I haven't had anything to eat today..."

"Appetite—not the most redoubtable of symptoms. Let's go all the more quickly; we'll have breakfast on the way."

"It's just that…," Onésime reiterated.

"Go on."

"It's just that I'm a trifle embarrassed. I left the Earth so abruptly that I didn't bring any…"

"Money! You're mistaken. I brought the contents of your strong-box for you. Your capital is in that writing-desk."

"By what means…?"

"Did it get there? That's my secret—a rather curious secret, I might add. There are too many people studying methods of getting cash out of their neighbor's strong-box without them finding that one. Personally, I find it more original to put it in *incognito*."

"I'll be with you," said Onésime, "as soon as I've filled my wallet."

"Are you ready?"

"Yes."

"Now, above all, beware of thieves."

"Are the police so inefficient, then?"

"On the contrary—and that's the danger. The police here are so efficient that all the thieves are obliged to maintain the appearance of honest men."

XX. Nothing in the Hands, everything in the Pockets[21]

Master Helleborus' recommendation did not take long to bear fruit.

Onésime, who was very suspicious by nature, remained on the alert. Already, several times, he had seen individuals whose appearance seemed suspect prowling around him, approaching him and then drawing away rapidly. He even thought that he noticed signs of intelligence changed between them, but in his uncertainty he had not dared to share his concerns with his traveling companion.

---

[21] A play on words on something stage magicians used to say before performing a trick: "Nothing in the hands, nothing in the pockets."

Suddenly, he spun around, seized a hand that had slipped into his coat pocket, and shouted with all the force of his lungs: "Finally, I've got one! Thief! Thief!"

The poor fellow thus caught *in flagrante delicto* was trembling like a leaf.

"Monsieur, I beg you..."

"Thief!"

"I'm an unfortunate father of a family..."

"Good excuse. Thief!"

"Don't turn me in—the law is so severe.

"Perhaps you need laws that would assure you impunity to rob passers-by in broad daylight."

"Rob, me!"

"You dare to deny it?"

"But certainly."

"You didn't try to take my handkerchief?"

"On the contrary!"

"Presumably, it was to slide a hand into my pocket..."

"Yes, Monsieur...which is to say, no. Not a handkerchief, but...reach into it. Monsieur!"

Mechanically, Onésime carried out the requested gesture, and felt that, since his departure, his pockets had swelled prodigiously.

At the same time, he pulled out wads of paper

"Monsieur, I swear to you that it wasn't me who put all of it in." He pointed to two pieces of paper, one white and one pink: "Those are mine," he added.

Onésime understood less and less. As for Master Helleborus, he was sporting his mocking smile.

"Yes, Monsieur, believe me; I'm an honest father of a family; it wasn't me who put the others in. I know that two is too many, but work is so hard to come by that one earns what one can. Don't have me arrested, Monsieur, I beg you. I confess that they're charlatans, that their drugs aren't worth two sous, but a father of a family...if you like, I'll tell you how they manufacture their syrup of pulverized platinum for lymphatic temperaments. It's a sucker-trap. You can see that I'm not hiding anything, Monsieur. Don't have me arrested..."

Onésime, half out of compassion and half out of astonishment, let go of his prisoner, who made off as fast as his legs could carry him, without further ado.

Argan's descendant was still looking at his two fistfuls of paper.

"If you contemplate them for two hours," Heleborus put in, "they'll still be pharmacy prospectuses."

"All of them?"

"Yes, all of them."

"But how were they able to get them into my coat pockets?"

"I'll wager that you have many more. Here! Here! Here!"

The prospectuses extracted by Helleborus emerged in a flood from Onésime's trousers, waistcoat and collar.

"Confess that they're dexterous rogues."

"Then all those individuals that were prowling around us...?"

"That's right! Since the police started pursuing them, the distributers of printed documents have been obliged to become veritable experts. They use the same ruses and go to the same trouble to inundate you with their wares, as cut-purses do to relieve you of your cash. And in fact, there's only a difference of procedure—the result remains the same. Read, then!"

Onésime had cast his eyes over the pink prospectus, which was thus conceived:

A MARVEL OF MODERN TIMES!!!
SYRUP OF PULVERIZED PLATINUM
Regenerator of Populations
Providence of Families

NOTICE

The mysteries of the Lord are impenetrable, and one wonders why he wanted our epoch alone to have the joy of discovering Syrup of Pulverized Platinum!

The true sage, when asked such a question, bows his head, murmuring: *Fiat voluntas!* Then he gets up again in order to exalt himself in actions of grace. For, as our illustrious Ducastor[22] has said, *Syrup of Pulverized Platinum is a blessed remedy.*

A modest instrument of celestial decrees, Monsieur Brigandeau-de-Saint-Français, pharmacist, chemist and hygienist, has no desire other than to propagate a discovery that he is pleased to attribute to the initiative of the Supreme Inspiration of all great thoughts.

Syrup of Pulverized Platinum is the fruit of twenty years of indefatigable research. Twenty more years of experiments have been consecrated to it and sanctioned its success.

Away, then, with all the ferruginous compounds of routine! Make way for platinum, which, as well as being the most precious of metals, has become the most useful.

Syrup of Platinum sells for 150 francs per half-bottle; the bottles are returnable for 20 centimes.

CURES SPECIALLY AND UNIQUELY:

Dyspepsia, apepsia, catarrh, rabies, phthisis, rheumatism, overheated temperaments, ringworm, scurvy, gout, toothache, cuts, sprains and burns, cancer, smallpox, angina, typhoid, mucous, malign and bilious fevers, goiters, lupus, apoplexies, styes, dysentery, warts of the nose, hepatitis, red eyes, bone cavities, calluses, etc., etc., etc.

---

[22] An oblique reference to the famous medical treatise by Jean Marius, *Traité du Castor* (1746), which extravagantly sang the praises of castor oil and established it as one of the most popular medicaments of the 19th century. It still features as an ingredient in many branded medicines, although its therapeutic benefits remain unproven.

9,875,734 certificates, all signed by the most high-status names, attest the prodigies operated by our sublime invention.

We cite a few selected randomly:

No. 7,361,424

Monsieur Brigandeau,

I believe I would be failing in the most imperious of my duties if I did not send you durable testimony of my eternal gratitude.

For thirty-nine years nine months and eleven days I suffered from a cancer, which all the merchants of health had declared incurable.

I drank sixteen coffee-spoonfuls of your divine Syrup of Platinum, and today, at the age of ninety-three, I eat a two-pound loaf of bread and six courses at every meal.

Such facts cannot be too widely spread in the interests of suffering humanity.

Du Godin
Nephew of the aunt of a former ministerial officer.

No. 4,111,111

Monsieur,

Three days ago, I fell from a second-floor window while watering my flowers.

By a fortunate chance that saved my life I fell, Monsieur, on to the head of one of the most fervent admirers of our inimitable Syrup of Platinum, Monsieur Durupot, whose son entered the École Polytechnique in seventeenth place this year.

Monsieur Durupot injured his head and I injured my stomach, for the impact was terrible. Impassively taking out of his pocket a bottle of Syrup of Platinum, however, Monsieur Durupot drank two gulps, and made me drink three, and in the evening we played a game of billiards lasting thirty-five frames. In attesting the veracity of these supernatural facts I am, Monsieur,

Cornivet,
Rentier

No. 8,234,517

Monsieur,

I believe it to be my duty to hasten to inform you of a case of instantaneous cure that happened before my very eyes.

My daughter was complaining of frightful headaches. On the recommendation of an old friend of the family. I bought her a bottle of your magical Syrup of Pulverized Platinum.

Scarcely had the bottle been given to her than my daughter declared that she felt a sudden relief.

At the moment when I have the honor of writing to you, we have not yet uncorked the bottle, but the improvement is continuing,

I owe you the life of my dear child, Monsieur, and I intend to proclaim it loudly, saluting you as one of the benefactors of society.

Adelaide Borylas
Living in the same house as General de Pardinel.

"Do you know," said Onésime, after having finished. "This Syrup of Pulverized Platinum could well be an excellent thing."

"What! What about the other remedies, which you're forgetting. They have singularly attractive entitlements, though."

So saying, he riffled through the collection:

CONCENTRATED OIL OF CROCODILE BONES
Replacing,
with a marked superiority, cod liver oil.

PILLS
of South American Scarab Thoraces

POWDERED CHARCOAL IN GOAT'S MILK
for delicate chests.

"My God!" Onésime interjected. "I can't see what you think extraordinary about these discoveries. Besides which, as I've just remarked, they furnish the proof of what they claim."

"Proofs, even—for there are two sorts: the written proofs, in the genre of the certificates that have just had the good fortune to influence you, if only for a moment; and the living proofs, which you will probably never see."

"Can't you inform me?"

"Messieurs the pharmacists do not leave me the leisure; they have foreseen everything, anticipated everything. Judge by this note, which I've just encountered at the bottom of all the prospectuses:

"N.B. In order to put the public on guard against the tricks of which so many unworthy companies have rendered themselves guilty, we have adopted the best means of confounding incredulity and defeating fraud.

"Every day, between noon and four o'clock, people who desire to do so may converse in our store with the patients who have been cured by our preparation and who have been kind enough to put themselves graciously at our disposal."

"Well, that's decisive," said Onésime. "Which remedy does it concern?"

"From the first to the last, as I said, they all carry the same note."

"Patients attesting themselves to their own cure! Such a system wouldn't be possible on Earth, with all the deceptions of exploiters of bad faith."

"It seems to me, however, that something analogous has been imagined..."

"What's that?"

"The child of a carp and a rabbit, the father and mother of which are never displayed..."

"The example might be witty, but I confess that I don't see the analogy..."

"Well, here's an application that's arriving in a timely fashion."

XXI. The Certificate Man

A man was, in fact, just coming toward Onésime and his companion.

When he reached them he took off his hat respectfully, the brim of which bent under the pressure of his hands, and he said, in an obsequious tone: "Please excuse me, Messieurs. I've been out of work for a month, and if one of you could employ me..."

"Employ you to do what?" Master Helleborus asked.

"As to that, Messieurs, I do anything that concerns my estate, and I can say that I'm quite well-known. I spent a year working for Dr. Jubilard, three months for Dr. Buchon, nine months for Dr. Lacouture, eight months for..."

"Pardon me, but you haven't told us what kind of work you do.

"Once again, Messieurs, I do everything that concerns my estate; first of all, I was a certificate..."

"What, a certificate?"

"Yes, Messieurs. I show myself to sick people as an attestation of the remedies that someone wants to give them."

"What did I tell you!" said Helleborus, turning to Onésime.

"Without vanity, Monsieur, I can say that I'm one of the best at that game, especially for the variety of physiognomies. With Dr. Jubilard I worked in the liver, with Dr. Buchon in the lungs, with Dr. Lacouture in the spinal cord—and you'll realize that the true merit is there. There aren't two like me for taking on the face of a consumptive."

"What do you mean by that?" asked Onésime.

"Well, Monsieur knows as well as I do—unless Monsieur is very new to the game. When a new invalid arrives, he's brought to me—or, rather, I'm taken to him—in order to show him that his case isn't as desperate as mine. That's my triumph. You'd have given me two hours to live. So, when the same invalid sees me appear a week later, fresh, cheerful and smiling, he's vanquished and convinced; my doctor could get anything out of him he wanted."

"And how is it that you've renounced that métier, which must have been lucrative and restful?" asked Helleborus.

"I haven't renounced it, Monsieur, but competition depresses everything it touches. It ended up with good-for-nothings coming along who'll play cerebral congestion or typhoid fever for you for twenty sous a day."

"The rogues!" exclaimed Helleborus, with a solemn expression.

"Aren't they, Monsieur? So, I branched out and I went into antechambering."

Onésime opened his eyes wide at everything he heard. The word "antechambering," in particular, sounded so bizarre in his ears that he could not help interrogating once again.

"What is antechambering?"

"Decidedly," the man went on, "these Messieurs are new to the game. "Antechamberers are employees that the doctors pay for sitting in their antechambers—because, you see, the clients aren't half a funny lot."

Onésime pulled a face, but Master Helleborus put in: "Oh, yes, you're right—a funny lot!"

"When they arrive in the home of a merchant of health, and they're not made to wait for a good hour, they go out convinced that he's a donkey. A doctor who doesn't have a single patient in his antechamber!

"Hence the creation of antechamberers. One takes up one's station at consultation time in the waiting room, ornamented with a sonorous name, elegantly dressed; one engages the new arrivals in conversation, cleverly singing the praises of the merchant of health to whom one's attached.

"That's my forte, especially with the ladies. That's down to my education…former honor student, at your service."

"How is it, Monsieur Honor Student, that you also abandoned the noble career of antechambering?"

"Same reason—the spoilsports. Would you believe that you can now get antechamberers to work for food? So they make grammatical errors while chatting with the clients—and what howlers! When a profession has degenerated to that point, a self-respecting person has no alternative but to abandon it."

"Naturally," agree Helleborus.

XIII. The Deceased

"And then," the man went on, "I had an idea."

"Aha!"

"Yes, I tried to found a newspaper: *The Deceased.*"

"Nice title, isn't it, my dear Du Tilleul?"

"I don't think so," Onésime muttered.

"Bah! Fear apart..."

"Besides, Messieurs, my intention wasn't to make it a literary affair, but a commercial one."

"I suspected as much," said Helleborus.

"My idea was excellent, Monsieur—and practical! And simple in its conception. *The Deceased* appeared twice a week, with a list of all the slightly notable people who had died on Planet Fantasia, except that, to the routine necrology—this is the important point—I added the names of the doctors who had cared for the deceased individual."

"Just think!" laughed Helleborus. "Free advertisements!"

"Advertisements! You think so? My God, you must be new to the game. On the contrary; I could envelop the mention with such euphemisms as 'In spite of the devotion of which Dr. So-and-so gave proof...,' 'In spite of his efforts, the science of Dr. So-and-so failed...' or 'Dr. So-and-so did everything he could without succeeding in avoiding...' but the effect was produced nevertheless. Those were terrible registers that I was keeping—terrible for the reputation of those I mentioned in connection with the deaths."

"Well, well, well! Do you know, Onésime, that Monsieur is first rate?"

"Monsieur is very kind...but I don't merit his eulogies, for *The Deceased* was only a partial success."

"What a pity!"

"In the beginning, people came to offer me considerable compensations for me not to print their names in my paper."

"That's understandable."

"Nevertheless, after a rather short interval, an embarrassing complication emerged. A merchant of health gave me, for instance, fifty écus not to be named. I pocketed it and I scratched him out—but then another merchant of health arrived, a rival of the first, who had learned that the other had lost some patient or other, and he offered me a hundred écus to name him.

"How could I refuse the hundred écus, I ask you, Messieurs? One isn't made of bronze, damn it."

"Otherwise one could melt oneself down to make money," Helleborus observed.

"So, it turned out that the doctor who had paid the fifty écus was featured in the lists in *The Deceased* even so, because of his competitor's trickery. It was as confusing as double-entry book-keeping!

"In brief, by dint of seeing those little accidents repeated, the merchants of health ended up avoiding me, and I fell from the heights of my realized dream in no time at all."

"You must have done yourself considerable harm."

"A lot of harm, Messieurs. I've been out of work for a month."

"You told us that."

"And if you'd care to utilize my knowledge...I'll do anything. Do you need a certificate man? An antechamberer? Any price...when it's a matter of life or death..."

"My dear fellow, we only had need of your information. Thank you."

"What! So you aren't...?"

"Merchants of health? No. Purchasers, yes."

"Invalids! And me, who's let the cat out of the bag!" exclaimed the man, making a gesture of disappointment.

"The cat! It was an entire litter!" said Helleborus, laughing. "My friend is particularly obliged to you, aren't you, my dear Du Tilleul?"

"Let's get away from this adventurer," replied Argan's descendant, hotly. "His revelations will make me hate medicine, and I need it too much to lose my taste for it."

As for the man, he had drawn away rapidly, muttering: "Invalids! They hide it well. The big one, in particular, didn't look like a client at all!"

XXIII. A Prince of the Science

Master Helleborus said to Du Tilleul: "My dear friend, you're ill, or think you are."

"I am."

"You are. It's important to you, in consequence, to have the advice of a competent man as soon as possible. If I were you, I'd begin right away with what is known on Planet Fantasia as a prince of the science."

"I'd like nothing better."

"In that case, without bating around the bush, I'll take you to the illustrious Dr. Gorniain, the chief merchant of health of Mercy Hospital, decorated by the three hundred and ten different orders instituted on the planet, Professor of Pathology in the Faculty, and member of all the scientific societies past, present and future."

"Take me," said Onésime.

And they headed for Dr. Gorniain's dwelling—but the Road to Corinth was no more difficult than the one leading to that exceedingly famous abode. As soon as they were within a quarter of a league of it they discovered an enormous queue of invalids snaking through the streets in two ranks, people in carriages to the left, pedestrians to the right.

Onésime remarked, moreover, that the pedestrians were obliged, before going in, to wait until the people in carriages had been expedited.

It's no better than Earth, he thought, silently.

It was, at any rate, a curious spectacle, that of the crowd laying siege to a single door, while the discontented faces of other doctors appeared in the windows of all the surrounding houses, devouring those coveted patients with their eyes.

"All on one side, nothing on the other," said Helleborus. "That's how divisions generally work out. Where one sheep jumps, the others jump. One sheep is perhaps all that's needed for those starving merchants of health whose profiles you can see to become celebrated. Poor fellows! How this torture of Tantalus must make them suffer!"

"This extraordinary urgency," Onésime retorted, "appears to me to prove one thing above all—which is that Dr. Gorniain has an incontestable superiority over all his colleagues."

"That's one way of looking at it..."

After an hour and half of waiting, Onésime reached the doctor's house.

At the door two domestics, seconded by four guardsmen, were preventing the crowd from forcing a way in. The domestics, doubtless penetrated by their master's importance, were very insolent—so much so that one of them, looking Onésime and his guide up and down, said: "You're number 1,223.

"What's that, please?" asked Onésime.

"I repeat that you're number 1,223."

"To do what?"

"You're annoying me! If it were necessary to give similar explanations to every invalid, we'd never finish."

"But it's still necessary that..."

"1,223 is your order number. There are 1,222 people ahead of you. Now, if you're not content, don't take it. There's no lack of others who will."

"Give it to us," said Hellebore, putting out his hand. "Can you just tell us what time our turn will arrive?"

"I don't know. Probably about half past midnight."

"Merciful Heaven!" Onésime exclaimed. "Twelve and a half hours to wait!"

"I believe you're mistaken, my friend," replied Helleborus, placidly. "It isn't half past midnight that you meant to say..." At the same time he seemed to slip something into the lackey's hand that had the glint of gold.

"Indeed, Monsieur. I beg you to excuse me. I don't know where my head is. It's number 223 that I've given you...."

"123, isn't it?" said Helleborus, slipping him another coin.

"Yes, Monsieur, 123," replied the valet, brazenly.

"And we'll get through in about half an hour?"

"About that."

"Then, my dear Onésime, we just have time to have a quick lunch."

"What!" said Du Tilleul. "He'll see 122 invalids in half an hour?"

"My friend, it's easy to see that you don't know anything about the commercial value of the title 'Prince of the Science.'"

XXIV. The Sanitary Table d'Hôte

The choice of a restaurant is always a thorny matter for a man who respects his stomach; imagine what it must be like for man who fears his!

Onésime was that man, and furthermore, he was in a country of whose gastronomic customs he was absolutely ignorant.

There was, however, no lack of lures.

In the Restaurant Quarter—confining, perhaps by way of precaution, that of the merchants of health—one read nothing but pompous announcements and enticing excitations, from the restaurant at fifty francs a dish to the one that offered, for seven sous, a choice of six dishes, soup, bread at indiscretion, dessert, coffee and a digestive clarinet solo, executed at liqueur time by a virtuoso attached to the establishment.

There were establishments that pinned up their menus outside. There were some that, in order better to fascinate the clientele, exposed in the display window a small-scale facsimile of a table laden with all the dishes announced on the menu, before which a spring-loaded diner was sitting, passing his hand back and forth over his epigastrum with a voluptuous expression calculated to penetrate the utmost depths of the hearts of famished passers-by.

Onésime's embarrassment increased before that deployment of culinary riches.

Fortunately, Master Helleborus came to his aid spontaneously.

"My dear Du Tilleul," he said to him, "if you were in better health, there would be matter here for a complete course of comparative eateries, but let's not stray from our program. You're ill, so it's to the Sanitary Table d'Hôte that we must go. Luckily, lunch is served at noon there. Go on ahead, I beg you."

The Sanitary Table d'Hôte was on the eleventh floor—some houses in Capital Fantasia have as many as twenty. Onésime arrived there out of breath, and could not help exclaiming, as he pressed the bell-button: "Sapristi! That's a long way up!"

"Salutary and aperitif exercise," replied an individual seated in the first room in front of a sort of office counter. "We're hoping to go up another two floors soon, in the interest of our customers. That's five francs, Messieurs. Here's the menu."

After having plaid for two seats, Onésime passed into the dining room, holding in his hand the sheet of paper on which was printed a truly regal menu, as the reader may judge from the following literal transcription:

SANITARY TABLE D'HÔTE
Directed and Founded by a Doctor of the Faculty

The majority of maladies originate from the carelessness that gives rise to the fundamental axiom: *You must to eat to live, not live to eat.*

Hence the idea of the Sanitary Table d'Hôte.

Placed under the surveillance of a physician, who will previously have observed his state of health, each guest will be sure of escaping the dangers of an alimentation left to hazard and directed without the verification of the art.

TODAY'S MENU
(Lunch)

Chicken vol-au-vents
Peppered fillets of roe-deer venison
Truffled grouse
Fresh *petits pois*
Asparagus tips
Lobster remoulade
Iced parfait
Assorted Desserts
Coffee
Liqueurs

"You know," said Onésime to Helleborus, "for five francs, that's not dear. Except that the large quantity of succulent dishes frightens me slightly."

"Don't worry! You'll see."

The individual dressed in black who had previously been seated by the door came to place himself in the middle of the table.

He's going to carve, Onésime thought. *Why has nothing been served yet?*

Instead of carving, the man in black addressed his guests.

"Forgive me, Messieurs, but before beginning the meal, would you be kind enough to stick out your tongues?"

The other customers having obeyed the injunction, Onésime did likewise.

"Damn…! Damn…! It's doubtless due to the temperature—those tongues are extremely furry this morning! Science, to my great regret, makes it my duty to forbid you the chicken vol-au-vent, very heavy by nature... I shall now make a circuit of the table, in order to take each individual's pulse."

He carried out the announced maneuver, pausing to whisper in the ear of each person.

When Onésime's turn came he leaned toward him, and said: "Temperament slightly exhausted, temporary gastric embarrassment, irregular pulse. The pepper sauce would irritate you, the *petits pois* are flatulent and the asparagus too harsh for the blood. I don't insist on the lobster, known for its indigestible character, nor the iced parfait, dangerous for stomachs as cold as yours. Two boiled eggs and water with a little red wine in it are all that you can tolerate this morning.

He had probably said the same to everyone, for the meal continued in the same fashion for all of them.

When they left, Onésime was delighted. "That really is an excellent invention!"

"You think so?"

"Certainly. Without the sage advice of that excellent doctor, I might have given myself a terrible indigestion!"

"Incorrigible!" sniggered Helleborus, in a low voice. More loudly, he said: "You didn't read his thoughts, then?"

"In truth, I forgot—but I promise you that I'll redeem myself henceforth."

XXV. Medicine at the Double

Have you ever seen a military review?

If you have, you must remember the part known as the march-past. The general is motionless in a corner, and the compact battalions and tightly-packed squadrons file past him at the double.

That memory was exactly what was evoked in Onésime's mind at the sight of the great reception room inhabited by the prince of the science.

The room, oblong in form, was furnished with a luxury that embodied a premeditated austerity.

In the center, on a platform—one might have thought it a throne—was the illustrious Dr. Gorniain.

Dr. Gorniain was a man of about fifty, wearing a rosette in his buttonhole striped with all the colors of the rainbow. His gaze was harsh, his gesture abrupt. As for his speech, it was impossible to pass judgment, because Dr. Gorniain did not speak.

The invalids were arranged in a file in order to pass, one by one, in front of the platform. As they crossed the threshold of the reception room, an usher with a steel chain round his neck called out: "Have your money in your hand! Have your money in your hand!"

Then each one went with the flow, which was rapid, and soon arrived in the presence of the doctor.

Onésime, for whom Helleborus was waiting outside, conformed with that general itinerary.

The fashion in which the patients were lined up and the cry of "Have your money in your hand" had already made a disagreeable impression on him; nevertheless, the important thing, so far as he was concerned, was to have the advice of such a prominent person, and that consideration overrode all others.

Suddenly, he shivered. Dr. Gorniain's gaze was fixed upon him.

"Monsieur," he stammered. "I...?"

"Your thousand francs?" interjected a second usher, placed to his right.

"I've come to consult you..."

"Your thousand francs!" repeated the usher.

"...To consult you on the matter of..."

"Your thousand..."

Realizing that it was necessary to pay for the consultation in advance, but not without a constriction of the heart, Onésime handed the banknote he was holding to the usher.

"Foreign currency," grumbled the later. "We can't give you change. No matter, Move on! Move on!"

"Monsieur," Onésime resumed, addressing the doctor. "I believe I'm afflicted..."

"Come on! Will you move on, now!" said the usher, pulling him by the arm.

"What about my consultation?"

"It was finished long ago. If it were necessary for Monsieur the Doctor to amuse himself writing consultations for everyone...! Take the prescription that Monsieur the Doctor is holding out to you."

The illustrious Gorniain was, indeed, holding out a printed piece of paper, which he had taken from one of the pigeon-holes placed in front of him.

"But I haven't explained to the doctor what I'm feeling..."

"A Prince of the Science has no need of information; that's strictly for quacks. Move on!"

"What an abomination...a thousand francs for this scrap of paper!"

"Do you imagine that for that price you can spend an hour in private with a man whose every minute is worth fifty louis? Move on! Move on!"

Onésime tried to continue resisting, but the file had resumed its rapid pace, each invalid handing his thousand-franc bill to the right and receiving his printed prescription from the left. He was transported thus all the way to the street, where he found Master Helleborus again.

"My friend," said Onésime, tapping him on the shoulder.

"Aha! You, already! That didn't take long, did it?"

"Rather say that it's worthless. He didn't listen to me and I only saw him for the moment that I paused. To pay a thousand francs for a slip of paper like this! What does it say, though? *Lymphatic temperament. Decay in the leg bones.* But that's crazy! I've never had any trouble with my legs. It's inside my body that I'm suffering."

"My poor Du Tilleul, what's happened to you happens quite often. In his haste, the illustrious doctor mistook the pigeon-hole. Your thousand francs are lost. What do you expect? Dr. Gorniain was an excellent doctor when he was unknown; since he's become famous he's changed into a money-minting pendulum. Tick tock, tick tock! Too bad for those who get caught in the gears."

"Isn't it you who advised me to go to see him?"

"Because I know you. I was sure that if you hadn't visited him first, the prestige of his renown would always have dazzled you, to I began by bringing you right off the bat, to spare you from coming back."

"I'm nevertheless a thousand francs lighter, and at that rate..."

"Don't worry, not all the merchants of health have arrived at such extravagant tariffs. There are even a large number who give free consultations."

"Free! That suits me. I'll redeem on the one hand what I lost on the other..."

"Lost, ingrate? What about the lesson? That thousand francs might perhaps have saved you ten thousand."

XXVI. The Vadiuses and the Trissotins[23]

"Are we going far?" asked Argan's descendant, after having walked for some time.

"We're nearly there—but you understand that in a centralized society like this one, one can't allow the gratuitous merchants of health to live side by side with those for whom one pays so dear."

"You're right. But what's that crowd I can see in the distance?"

---

[23] Vadius and Trissotin are two characters in Molière's *Les Femmes Savantes* (1872); they are two supposedly-distinguished scholars, who begin one scene by paying one another extravagant compliments, but quarrel violently thereafter. The latter pretends to be in love with the heroine, but is only after her money.

"Well, I can guess, merely by the location where the scene is unfolding. That's the frontier of the allopathy sector and the homeopathy sector. Yet another quarrel between the disciples of the two doctrines!"

"The rivalry that divides them is, from what I can see, as keen as it is on the Earth."

"Even worse! In the twenty years since homeopathy has made its appearance on Planet Fantasia, there have already been eight pitched battles between those irreconcilable adversaries."

"Has the number of fatalities been considerable?"

"Not too bad; it was stipulated that each army would leave its remedies at home. On another occasion, it was resolved to put an end to the eternal question by means of a decisive trial. They selected eight homeopathic physicians and eight allopathic physicians, and forced them to treat one another."

"And?"

"Well, the chances were equal on both sides."

"Really?"

"Yes—eight out of eight."

"Cured?"

"Permanently. So they gave up trying to cut short a debate that is perpetuated in a host of individual lawsuits, and battles of the kind to which circumstances have conveyed us.

Master Helleborus and Onésime were now, in fact, no more than a few paces from the melee. They mingled with the crowd of curiosity-seekers who were standing on tiptoe, probably better to enjoy an interesting spectacle.

In the center of the circle, two merchants of health were hurling abuse and threats at one another.

"Get away! Get away!" cried the allopath. "Everyone knows what's in your globules.

"Get away yourself!" replied the homeopath. "Everyone knows what your bleedings and moxas are worth."

"I'm strong enough to swallow a whole box of homeopathic medicaments in one go dine thereafter with a perfect appetite."

"I certainly couldn't say as much. A single one of your drugs would be sufficient to take away my taste for bread."

"You can talk—you who sent a poor old woman to the other world only yesterday."

"You're the one who took her on."

"And you're the one who finished her off."

"Insolent."

"Ruffian."

"Do you even known what a cure is?"

"It isn't you, at any rate, who could teach me."

"Damn! Messieurs, I take you as judges..."

"Messieurs, decide for yourselves...

"These ignoramuses, these rogues, these impostors...

"These liars, these pedants, these hypocrites..."

"You give people clear water to swallow...

"You torment them with horrible instruments of torture..."

"Hold on—Messieurs, if one of you, who is ill, would care to approach..."

"If someone who is suffering will step forward..."

"I'll show this sycophant..."

"I'll prove to this calumniator..."

"Well! Messieurs..."

"Let's see…Messieurs..."

At that proposition the crowd had moved back in an abrupt impulse of panic.

"No one's responding—that's because you're all convinced already of the superiority of allopathy."

"No one's saying anything—that's because your minds are already made up as to the preeminent excellence of homeopathy."

"What! What! What are you claiming there?" said a third antagonist, cleaving through the crowd. "The true medicine is entirely in hydropathy."

"In electropathy," argued a fourth, who had also just parted the ranks in order to confront the other three.

"Water for all! The medicine of ducks!"

"Electricity! The medicine of fairground performers!"

"Messieurs, these charlatans are deceiving you!"

"Taking you for a ride."

"Leading you astray."

"Listen to what I say. I swear to you—do you hear?—I swear to you that they're plotting against your existence."

"I swear by Hippocrates that they'll put you to death!"

"By Hahnemann!"

"Oh, that's the way it is..."

"Don't you take that tone..."

"We'll see..."

"We'll teach you politeness..."

With that, the four champions began to grapple with one another, with a fury that the love of science was insufficient to alleviate.

The guard arrived, under the leadership of the traditional corporal.

"What's this?" demanded the corporal.

"It's these merchants of health quarreling with one another," cried the crowd.

"Merchants of health! Platoon—arrest those men!"

The soldiers did not budge.

"What! Brave men who've spent ten years on campaign, recoiling before four feeble citizens?"

"Well, Corporal, excuse me if I object," said one of the soldiers, "but with doctors, being brave isn't enough. They'd only have to recognize us one day in the hospital..."

"That's true. Well, anyone who arrests them anyway, I'll recommend for promotion."

The four soldiers immediately launched themselves forward, with a temerity that seemed greatly to impress the audience.

XXVII. Free Consultations

Master Helleborus was watching Onésime from the corner of his eye, but he carefully refrained from asking him for an account of his sensations.

It was, consequently, in silence that they arrived at the office of free consultations—or, rather, one of them.

The number was, in fact, considerable, and Capital Fantasia must have hidden many philanthropists in its bosom for them to devote themselves to the exercise of a medicine so disinterested.

Such, at least, was the reflection that comforted the descendant of Argan, who was visibly demoralized by the previous scene.

It was noticeable that the queue for the free consultation was much shorter than the one for the thousand-franc consultation. Onésime had not yet been able to account for that detail when he found himself in the presence of Dr. Tatonnet.

Dr. Tatonnet's lodgings affected a simplicity bordering on nudity; there was not a single picture on the walls, not a single mirror or tapestry—nothing but pine shelves laden with thick medical textbooks, a white-wood desk and two wicker chairs, one for the doctor and one for the patient.

Here, one consulted sitting down.

All these details made a favorable impression on Onésime.

This time, I think, I've put my hand on a model of probity and devotion...

Dr. Tatonnet was mild-mannered, paternal and charming.

"Monsieur," he said to Onésime, after having examined him, apparently very carefully, "it's the entrails that are the seat of your malady, but the affliction of the entrails is propagating through your whole body. Frankness makes it a duty for me to tell you that; in any case, my language cannot be suspect to you. You know, in fact that I always give my care gratuitously.

"In exchange for that procedure, the delicacy of which I hope you appreciate, I only ask one thing of a patient: to conform scrupulously to the medication I prescribe. I will add, in particular, that it is of capital importance that the remedies be properly prepared. Everything depends on that, Monsieur, everything depends on that. Thus, I have associated myself with a local pharmacist of whom I am certain, and to whom I want my prescriptions to be taken exclusively.

"You understand, Monsieur, that it is your interests alone that guide me in that, since the benefits that might be realized cannot enter my pocket. Here is your prescription." He displayed a placard in six columns. "It's necessary not to neglect a single item, or modify it by one iota. Permit me—for the sake of greater security, and still in your interests—to place the necessary orders myself. My pharmacist is on the floor below; my familiar remedies are prepared there in advance…it will only take five minutes."

So saying, Dr. Tatonnet slipped is prescription into a kind of tube, which communicated with the floor below.

After a few minutes, two apprentice pharmacists appeared, each carrying a voluminous package.

"Put them on the table," said Dr. Tatonnet, simply. "You'll answer to me with your heads for the quality of the products..."

"Doctor…!"

"I'm not joking, you know. Thank you!"

Then, turning to Onésime, he said: "My dear Monsieur, I think you will be one of my best cures. Here's the pharmacist's receipt: 921 francs 50, which I'll take responsibility for passing on to him on your behalf."

"Nine hundred and twenty-one francs' worth of drugs!"

"It ill behooves you, Monsieur, to haggle. It seems to me that I, who devote my late nights and my strength to the suffering classes, am not haggling over my time..."

"Nine hundred and twenty-one francs," repeated Onésime, paying mechanically, and allowing Dr. Tatonnet to stuff one of the bulging packets of remedies under each of his arms.

XXVIII. I Make That Two Thousand

It was in that grotesque attitude that he offered himself to the gaze of Master Helleborus, who asked him, still in the same mocking tone: "Where the Devil are you taking those parcels? Not content with offering you a free consultation, have they also made you those gifts in there?"

"Shut up, I beg you. The impudent rogue! His disinterest! His philanthropy! To tell me such shameful lies when I could see him thinking to himself: *This fellow's a cretin; that's obvious at first glance. Let's not let go of such a prey. It's three months since I had such a windfall. He has the appearance of a fellow who can pay. Bah, let's bleed him of nine hundred and twenty-one francs at one go. The twenty-one francs will add plausibility to the nine hundred. Six francs for the raw materials, a third of the profit for my associate, leaves six hundred and ten francs...*"

"And you paid!" said Helleborus, laughing out loud.

"Of course I paid."

"You're very naïve."

"Nine hundred francs on the one hand, a thousand on the other..."

"Total nineteen hundred francs."

"Plus the additional expenses, about a hundred francs..."

"I make that two thousand."

"Two thousand francs in one day!"

"In fact, it's not bad."

"Two thousand francs lost...absolutely wasted..."

"My dear chap, you're not very grateful."

"Leave me alone."

"I repeat that you're not very grateful."

"For what?"

"You claim that your money is absolutely wasted."

"Undoubtedly."

"Well, not at all. Since those Messieurs have told you what's afflicting you, that's two maladies you're almost certain of not having, for the moment."

XXIX. *A Consolation* in extremis

Onésime was not cheerful.

Adding up his expenses on the one hand, and his disillusionment on the other, he was finding increasingly that it was impossible to establish an equilibrium between the active and the passive. Master Helleborus was sniggering, as usual, but he was sniggering internally.

Externally, there was complete silence.

That silence was suddenly troubled by the echo of heart-rending sobs.

"My baby! My dear child!" moaned a voice. "If it's not barbaric to mock the dolor of a mother so cruelly...my baby! My little darling!"

The two voyagers turned round instinctively. A woman was walking behind them—a woman whom Onésime recognized immediately as the neighbor whose sincere despair had moved him so forcefully that very morning.

As in the morning, she was holding in her arms a paltry and suffering creature whom she was hugging convulsively while repeating incessantly: "My baby! My dear child!"

Argan's descendant was sensitive; the cries touched him, and he spoke to the weeping woman as she went past him.

"I beg your pardon, Madame...I'm doubtless being indiscreet, but your dolor appears to be very profound. If we knew the reason, perhaps we could..."

"You can't do anything, my good sir! The blow has fallen. Would you believe it? But what I'm telling you can't be of any interest..."

"You're mistaken, and all our sympathies are acquired in advance."

"It's a matter of my son, my good sir, my only treasure...that I'm going to lose. My God! My God!"

"Why such ideas?"

"Oh, he said it, him! Can you imagine sir, that I took my darling to the physician at the Public Assistance…because, you see, one isn't rich…I knew full well that they don't always pay much attention, because it's a chore for them, but in the end, I never supposed…

"Anyway, my good sir, I arrive. I have to wait and wait…it had to be done. I hugged the little dear as tightly as I could, because in our room there was no fire. That's only in the room for the paying customers…finally, I go in. The merchant of health takes the little one in his arms…he turns him over, feels him, then, with an indifferent expression, shaking his head, he says: 'He's a child who needs fortifying. A season in the country, or a voyage. Red meat. Old wine. Nothing else. Otherwise…'

"'Otherwise?' I said, shivering.

"'Well, without that, goodbye!'

"Oh, I promise you, my good sir, that I didn't hear any more. It seemed to me that I had the executioner before me. For in the end, is it just? Is it good to talk to poor folk about voyages, succulent dishes, generous wines, when one knows that it's only twisting the knife…?

"They call that Assistance. But my God, assistance comes from the heart, before anything else. Did he need to cause me pain? To make me jealous of other mothers?

"In truth, my good sir, I'm not wicked; he could have given me a few soothing words instead of remedies, if nothing else…but instead of that…isn't it an abomination?

"My baby! My dear child!"

The unfortunate woman stopped, interrupted by sobs.

"Indeed, it is abominable," said Onésime. "Come on, Madame, come on! Console yourself a little."

"How can I console myself? When from now on, everywhere, I'll hear that voice repeating its anathema on poverty…"

Onésime could not find any reply to make.

"Isn't it true, Monsieur Du Tilleul," said Helleborus, "That for the moment, you're not thinking so much about regretting your two thousand francs?"

"The fact is that in the presence of such an affliction..."

"Yes indeed! I, for one, wouldn't have wanted the merchants of health to take that away from you."

"Thanks very much."

"You're welcome. Anyway, defrauding someone of money is a misdemeanor, but reproaching someone for not having any is a crime."

"How is it that such monstrosities can occur...?"

"At every moment, my excellent Monsieur Du Tilleul, at every moment. Well, what do you expect? The Medical School of Planet Fantasia has always neglected to offer a course in sensitivity."

XXX. The Neurobiologists' Banquet[24]

The day was decidedly concluding under the most somber auspices, and that final episode was by no means calculated to restore serenity to Onésime's ideas.

As if by mocking contrast, however, at the very moment when they parted from the mother who had been so cruelly tested, a joyful clinking of glasses and plates reached their ears, and odorant gusts of culinary perfumes reached their nostrils.

"Those who are enjoying themselves today are very lucky," murmured Argan's descendant, between his teeth.

"And do you know who they are?" asked Master Helleborus.

"Some wedding party?"

---

[24] The term "neurobiology" had not yet been coined in 1862 to refer to the science that now bears the name, so Véron doubtless felt fully entitled to attribute it to a fictitious school of therapy.

"You're wide of the mark, my friend. First, know that on Planet Fantasia, marriage is much too serious a business to be mingled with the futility of pleasure. On a wedding day here, the husband and wife shut themselves up alone, and spend the whole day adding up figures, to calculate how much they have stolen from one another reciprocally by the terms of their contract."

"A nice occupation, but that doesn't tell me..."

"The provenance of those sounds of merrymaking. Well, I confess that the juxtaposition seems piquant to me. You've heard what others say about the merchants of health; you're about to hear what the merchants of health say about themselves. The banquet of which those cheerful echoes are reaching us is a medical banquet."

"Again!"

"Still! It's the banquet that the Neurobiologists hold annually to celebrate the anniversary of the birth of Divagmann,[25] the famous founder of the neurobiological doctrine. The windows of the banqueting hall overlook the street, and, as a ground floor is very convenient to permit passers-by to overhear the enthusiastic eulogies that those gentlemen are lavishing upon to one another, I can promise you that they'll carefully refrain from closing the casements. Let's take advantage of it to get closer. The spectacle is interesting, especially when the time comes for the toasts.

"Oh, we're in luck! There's one of the guests getting up now. The fire of the speeches is about to burst forth. Pay attention!"

The inhabitants of the Planet Fantasia were probably used to solemnities of that sort and were blasé with regard to the post-prandial eloquence of Messieurs the Neurobiologists, because no one else stopped to listen. Only a few street-urchins indulged in anti-academic comments on the wigs, noses and spectacles of the learned assembly.

---

[25] A joke name combining "divag" from *divaguer* [to ramble] with –Mann as in Heinemann.

"A veritable front-row seat," said Master Helleborus, showing Onésime a window completely devoid of spectators.

The first orator had blown his nose, passed his hand over his brow, picked up his glass in his right hand, and, raising it in a nobly impetuous gesture, said: "I have the honor, gentlemen, of drinking to the health of Divagmann, the medical prophet, Divagmann, our venerated master, Divagmann, the valiant founder, initiator, revelator and propagator of Neurobiology."

Frantic hurrahs responded to that proposition. All the guests had stood up and were clinking their glasses against one another. The orator was obliged to wait for calm to be restored, and he utilized that respite to place his hand on his heart several times, as if to suppress its beating.

After ten minutes, he was finally able to resume: "It is with pleasure, gentlemen, that I have seen the welcome that you gave to the illustrious name that serves us as a rallying cry. That unanimous surge of filial recognition is one more proof of the energy with which we have decided to march in the path so broadly frayed by the admirable Divagmann. Yes, gentlemen, let us persevere, for we are great, we are strong, we are knowledgeable and we are inspired." (*Yes, yes! Prolonged cheers.*) "To Divagmann! To his work! To Neurobiology!"

"Do you know," said Onésime, that if what they're saying is true..."

"Du Tilleul! My poor friend!"

"In any case, it's not precisely by virtue of modesty that the toast I've just heard shines."

"What are you going to think of the others? Modesty, in Capital Fantasia, is avoided like the plague. Does one get anywhere with modesty? So, no futile subterfuges. On Earth, in gatherings like this one, Mr. X raises a toast to the merits of Mr. Y, in order that Mr. Y will raise a toast to the merits of Mr. X. Here, the mechanism is simplified, doubtless because people are better served by themselves, than by the system of you-scratch-my-back-and-I'll-scratch-yours.

"As proof..."

A second orator had succeeded the first.

"Gentlemen," he said, "it is the custom when we come to these fraternal agapes..." ("*Very good! Very good! Take a bow Orator!*") "...to expose, one by one what we have accomplished for the triumph of the Neurobiological method. I can affirm, gentlemen, that my devotion has been demonstrated this year even more than during previous years. I am, for my patients, simultaneously a friend, a savior and a father. With an intuition above all praise, I have discovered the secret of more than eighty maladies against which the science of my colleagues of other sects had failed, as usual." (*Prolonged laughter. Cheers.*) "My trophies, gentlemen, are those of Neurobiology; sure of your sympathy, therefore, I can drink to my rare talent, and my marvelous cures!" (*Prolonged acclamations.*)

"This is dementia," Onésime thought aloud.

"No, it's simply the frankness of the *savoir-faire* of which you have only thus far known the hypocrisy on Earth. However, in order to be agreeable to you and cheer you up a little, I'd like to risk an intervention in the midst of that feast, which will probably not be to everyone's taste."

"You're going in?"

"Not at all—even better than that, thanks to a certain talent for ventriloquism. Anyway, you'll see..."

A third orator had just risen to his feet.

"Gentlemen," he began, "I can say with a just pride that this year has been fecund for me. Not one invalid has left my hands without being radically cured..."

Suddenly, it seemed that a voice escaping from the crowd drowned out the words of the merchant of health.

"Dr. A***, you're lying!"

The orator looked in all directions, as if to assure himself that he was not the victim of an illusion, and then, gathering his courage on perceiving nothing extraordinary, he continued: "Yes, my dear colleagues, I have vanquished the disease in every..."

"Dr. A***," said the voice, again, "you haven't invited me, but here I am. Do you remember the patient whom your ignorance killed in the Rue Neuve? It's the least you can do to invite me to dinner—would you like to, Dr. A***?"

Dr. A*** went horribly pale.

The other guests did not know what attitude to adopt. One of them, however, attempting a diversion, prepared to speak.

"Dr. B***," said another voice, "don't boast about your skill, for I'm here—the young woman from the Rue des Rosiers, whose life your stupidity cost."

Dr. B*** went pale in his turn.

The voice continued: "Dr. C***, what did you do to the old man you were treating for gout while he was dying of gall-stones? Dr. D***, are you also preparing your little speech? Stop there, my man—I'm here to provide the reply—me, your victim at the Carrefour des Incurables.

"Dr. E***, Dr. F***, Dr. G***...!"

The members of the audience were no longer able to contain themselves. Prey to a panic fear, the merchants of health were shoving one another, knocking one another over, trying to flee as if they were being pursued by vengeful shades...

"Well," said Master Helleborus, turning to Onésime, who could not help laughing, "how do you like the comedy? I promised to cheer you up and I've kept my word...it's only justice! If one could make them believe in ghosts, I can assure you that those gentlemen wouldn't dare to drink to anyone's health!"

XXXI. In Quest of the Genuine Article

The lessons had multiplied and accumulated sufficiently to correct the most obstinate—but Onésime was the heir of four generations of imaginary invalids: think of that!

The very next day, he resumed his lamentations. Three days later, he set out on campaign again.

116

O Homeric lists! Colossal enumerations, you would not be sufficient to evaluate the merchants of health that he saw, who attributed different afflictions to him, how many remedies he consumed, and how much anguish he endured!

The consultants were only in agreement in disagreeing with one another Furthermore, each one gave the lie to the previous diagnosis, only to be called a liar in is turn by the next.

One affected brutality, the next bonhomie, a third elegance and a forth untidiness. He consulted young ones, old ones, consolers, desolators, the earnest, the frivolous, the tall, the short, the fat, the thin, the fair-haired, the dark-haired, and the gray-haired. One heaped him with drugs, another absolutely forbade him everything that was not in the domain of pure and simple hygiene.

Onésime was going out of his mind.

Seeing that, Helleborus said to him: "My dear friend, I think the moment has come for you to enter a new phase of consultations."

"Is that more irony?"

"Of course not! Only, it's inexcusable for us to disdain an entire sector of the science—perhaps the most numerous."

"Which is?"

"That of the specialists. It appears that invalids have more confidence in men who only declare themselves capable of treating one malady than those who think that they can cure them all. Hence, the exploitation is considerable.

"First of all, every species of ailment has its specialty, then every division and every subdivision. We now have specialists for the left lung and specialists for the right lung; specialists for the upper body and specialists for the lower body; specialists for the ankle, the calf, the knee, the thigh, the hip, the forearm, the shoulder, etc., etc., etc. You can imagine that people who have localized their knowledge in such restricted areas must have arrived at a prodigious erudition!"

"You're right," Onésime replied, without perceiving that Master Hellebore was biting his lip in order not to burst out laughing.

Every single specialist declared him to be suffering from the malady that he had adopted as a specialty.

That circumstance became increasingly embarrassing.

XXXII. The Sucker, *a Weekly Periodical*

Onésime, however, in order to enlighten himself further, had subscribed to the leading medical journal of Planet Fantasia, *The Sucker*,[26] a periodical as weekly as it was influential.

It was overflowing with in-depth articles on the discovery of a new system of "mechanical leeching," generic articles on "the pathological functions of the periosteum," and feuilletons on...

Oh, the feuilleton, especially, was the triumph of *The Sucker*.

The periodical and much-maligned publication had understood that the aridity of the science put off a certain number of readers that it might be able to conquer in the absence of that nullifying vice. It had dreamed up a means of conquering it.

The Sucker was edited by a merchant of health who, incapable of succeeding on his own merits, had resolved to succeed on the merits of others—which is to say, by exalting or criticizing their endeavors, discoveries or innovations.

Hence the idea of the medico-romantic feuilleton. It was exquisite and ingenious.

Judge by the following sample:

---

[26] *Ventouse*, which I have translated literally as "sucker," was also the term used in medical circles at the time for a cupping-glass, which French physicians preferred to leeches as a means of bleeding their patients.

That day, Marguerite was as pale as a corpse.

Albert, who had followed the progress of the disease with anguish, fell prey himself to a discouragement that he could not hide from his fiancée.

"What's the matter, Albert?" she exclaimed, when she saw him come in.

"With me? Nothing."

"You're lying to me Albert."

"A slight amygdalitis."[27]

"What did I tell you!"

"It's nothing—don't worry. I took two spoonfuls of the excellent Dr. Dulaurier's syrup[28] yesterday evening. But you, my adored Marguerite, you, my angel, you, my life!"

"Me! Oh well…"

"Well, I want you to look after yourself."

"What's the point?"[29]

"Child, you're forgetting that we're engaged and that I have the right to demand that you conserve the treasure of my happiness for me."

"Albert, I swear to you that I'm no longer suffering. In any case. Haven't I tried all the remedies. I've taken Sympathetic Snail Paste."[30]

"An abominable drug."

"*Tamariva curativa* powder."[31]

---

[27] At this point, the author inserts the first of seven footnotes supposedly attached to *The Sucker*'s feuilleton: "See our *Dictionary of Medical Knowledge*, 2nd edition, published by Barbichon, price 20 francs."

[28] "15 francs a bottle, available from any pharmacy."

[29] "See our *Treatise on Indifference in Matters of Health*, Barbichon, 30 francs.

[30] "Dr. Picard's."

"Brazen charlatanism."

"The delicious health-flour known as Resuscitalescery."[32]

"Red bean flour sold as a panacea."

"But Albert, in what do you want me to place my trust, then?"

"In whom: Dr. Bibolin,[33] who has just discovered the lung-renovator. Listen to me carefully; I'll explain the theory of the lung-renovator, for it's what will ensure our happiness..."

(Followed by two columns of medical dissertations, after which the feuilleton concludes with the marriage of Marguerite, saved by the Bibolin lung-renovator, between 3 and 5 p.m.)

From the earliest days, these serials had captured Onésime's attention and emotion. He ended up perceiving, however, that the names of certain doctors always recurred with the same sarcasms, and certain others with the same eulogies. He pointed that out to Helleborus.

The latter's only response was to point to *The Sucker*'s advertising tariffs. The strip was torn out, and that rip was followed by a heroic resolution, which Du Tilleul signified to his companion one day in the following terms:

"Monsieur Hellebous," he said, "Would you care to let me return to the Earth?"

"What's the point, my dear Monsieur Du Tilleul? Don't you have here all the ridiculous things you had back there? Are you lacking a single one?"

"But my health is deteriorating."

"That's necessary for your cure."

"I'm spending crazy sums."

"No one's forcing you to."

"My confidence in medicine is weakening by the day."

---

[31] "Dr. Tratinois'"

[32] "Dr. Fuyotard's."

[33] "1410 Rue Bon-Apôtre, 3-5 p.m."

"Fortunately."

"Monsieur Helleborus?"

"Monsieur Du Tilleul?"

"In order to find out what's wrong with me, I want to become a merchant of health myself."

"I was about to suggest that to you," replied Master Helleborus, coldly.

XXXIII. The Model Mercy Hospital

Argan's descendant had fulfilled all the condition without which one cannot aspire to the honor of being a merchant of health on Planet Fantasia.

He had paid the subscription tax, the medical bag tax, the dissection tax, the professional tax, and others...there were a lot of taxes on Planet Fantasia.

Those formalities accomplished, he was permitted to enter into the exercise of his new studies, so, naturally, his first visit was to a hospital.

He chose the Mercy Hospital, the most renowned in the entire capital—so renowned, in fact, that it had been awarded the title of the Model Hospital.

Onésime, expecting violent emotions, had asked Master Helleborus to go with him, to which the latter had consented. He also expected to witness a spectacle full of gravity, dignity and melancholy. From the first moment, he was disillusioned.

A group of students was standing at the foot of the great staircase, awaiting the arrival of the merchant of health who was the chief of staff. Their conversation seemed to be in the ultra-cheerful mode.

They were laughing, talking about a new play, recounting tales of good fortune and making puns. Meanwhile, through an open window on the floor above, the groans of the inmates of the sad abode could be heard.

A matter of habitude—but Onésime was not an habitué, and that insouciance seemed to him to be bordering on profanation. He did not have time to express that personal impression, however. The chief merchant of health had just arrived.

At a glance, Onésime recognized him as the Prince of the Science who had passed him in review as such an accelerated pace.

Decidedly, the man was always in a hurry. He traversed the courtyard at a rapid pace, ran upstairs four at a time, took a white apron from the hands of an orderly, which he put on while waking, and went into ward no. 4, escorted by the group of pupils, who continued making puns—in a lower tone, to be fair.

The chief merchant of health went to a bed.

"Ah, my good sir!" sighed a voice.

"Pernicious angina!" pronounced the merchant of health.

He went to another bed. "Pulmonary congestion."

A third: "Typhoid fever."

And the race began again immediately.

Suddenly, however, he stopped.

That pause seemed miraculous to Onésime, whose gaze questioned Helleborus.

"You'll see," said the other, by means of a wink.

The patient was a young woman.

"Superb! Magnificent!" exclaimed the merchant of health, as he examined her.

The poor woman was trembling in every limb. The pupils had drawn nearer and were standing on tiptoe in order not to miss a single word or gesture.

"Magnificent! Superb!" the merchant of health was still repeating.

"Is it something dangerous?" hazarded the patient, timidly.

"Come closer, gentlemen," said the Prince of the Science, seemingly without paying any heed to the question. "It's one of the finest cases I've encountered since I've been practicing. How old are you?"

"Nineteen."

"Nineteen—in that case, it's a real find. I've never known a cancerous tumor develop in such a young patient. So inflamed! So voluminous! You, sir—yes, the blond one— palpate it. Hard as stone! But if I'm not mistaken, here's another, another two...three tumors. Which proves to you, gentleman, that plurality isn't always forbidden."[34]

As he made that remark, the merchant of health risked a smile, which was accompanied by the general hilarity of his audience.

"Three...*numero deus impare gaudet*,"[35] added the doctor of Mercy Hospital. "Are you quite sure you're only nineteen?"

"Yes, sir. How much time do I have left? You're hurting me! You're hurting me!"

"That's splendid, gentlemen! You'll see the progress that it will accomplish from day to day. A fine fellow, that disease! My God! A lovely case! A lovely case! No complication lacking! I'll make it the subject of a report to the Academy. Let's go! I haven't wasted my morning. Nine o'clock already! Damn!"

And while the sick woman, half dead with fear, fell back inert on her bed, the merchant of health resumed traversing the room at a rapid trot, scarcely darting a word to the right and the left.

There were no more lovely cases.

XXXIV. The School of Medical Commerce

On Earth we call the relevant institution the Faculty of Medicine, but on Planet Fantasia, as the physicians have adopted the name of merchants of health, it was both logical

---

[34] *Cumul* [plurality] is usually encountered in the context of a political rule forbidding the holding of a number of different of offices.

[35] "God delights in an odd number." The quotation is from Virgil's *Eclogues*.

and honest to follow the metaphor through—hence the title "The School of Medical Commerce"

Onésime, who was taking the elementary course, went into a lecture room.

A professor was gravely chalking up: *On the Art of Multiplying Visits*. He expressed himself in these terms:

"In my preceding lesson, I had the honor of explaining to you the general theory of the great art whose precious resources we are studying together. Today, we are entering into the details, and I am approaching one of the thorniest questions: that of multiplying visits to an invalid known for his avarice.

"The solution to that, problem long regarded as insoluble, is surely one of the most glorious conquests of modern science. It is to what one of our masters, the great Bassinard, owes his imperishable renown.

"In the past, the merchants of health sought, stupidly and without concern for themselves, to abridge maladies. One is tempted to laugh now at the thought of such naivety.

"The first precaution to take, gentlemen, in order to multiply visits to a patient is to insist on a diet. In fact, a man who does not eat loses his strength; a man who loses his strength loses his will-power."

Onésime hastened to pass on to the next room.

The lecture in progress there was on "Means of Recovering Medical Debts."

In the next, the topic was "Consultation Tax."

"But people here are only occupied with money!" exclaimed Onésime.

"With what did you expect them to be occupied in a school of commerce?" asked Master Helleborus.

"Medical Commerce!"

"Oh, yes—you'd like to hear them talking about medicine? Be satisfied."

So saying, he opened a door, and they both went into a kind of amphitheater, the center of which was occupied by a table, on which stood cages of all sizes.

From those cages escaped multiple mewls, clucks, barks, bleats, growls and croaks. One might have thought that they were in the Jardin des Plantes.

That unexpected symphony, combined with a strong menagerie odor, caused Onésime to take a step backwards—a movement that he repeated on perceiving two rows in front of the professorial chair, one of rabbit skins and the other of skinned rabbits, all alive.

"Don't be afraid," whispered Master Helleborus. "You have before you one of the celebrities of Planet Fantasia, the famous Lourens.[36] He's certainly the practitioner who has killed the most animals…not counting clients.

"What's the point of these executions?"

"What's the point? You don't know, then, that by means of that exercise, the famous Lourens has obtained fifteen decorations, six salaries, eight academic chairs, nine…"

"And what has medicine obtained?"

"You're always asking silly questions. Listen, instead, to the peerless scientist."

In fact, the famous Lourens had just started speaking.

"Gentlemen, you know that my previous experiments have led us to a precious certainty: the knowledge that the bones of a duck can receive all kinds of dyes. I dare say that I am the first person on Planet Fantasia to open up that new horizon.

---

[36] Most of the names attributed by Véron to his fictitious physicians are derived by wordplay, but this one is an obvious contraction of the name of Pierre Flourens (1794-1867), the most famous French pioneer of animal vivisection as a research tool, who was the Secretary of the Académie des Sciences and Professor of Natural History at the Collège de France.

"You have seen my chocolate, pistachio, crimson, *cuisse de nymphe*,[37] bottle green, pearl gray and buttercup duck bones. Well, gentlemen, all that is nothing. Today, with the aid of a method of nourishment combined with a method of acupuncture that permits me to act directly on the tissues, I shall color not only bones but flesh! I shall color not only in one shade but several. And that of all sorts of animals!

"Pass me a rabbit."

The laboratory assistant hastened to take a rabbit from one of the cages, which the professor seized by the ears.

"This rabbit, gentlemen, does not appear to have been prepared in any way, does it? Pass me a knife. In three strokes, I'll skin it for you. One! Two! Three!

"Now look, gentlemen. That is the fruit of twenty years of late nights! That is the result of twenty years of research! Twenty years that I do not regret, gentlemen, since it has finally enabled me to obtain my life's dream: the tricolor rabbit!"

Onésime took advantage of the enthusiasm caused by that speech to slip away, and go to recover in the fresh air from the legitimate nausea that the sight of the triply colored rabbit had caused him.

XXXV. The Academy of Infallibles

The first time that Onésime had heard mention of the Academy of Infallibles he had experienced the disagreeable sensation produced by a discordant note. "Infallibles" almost smacked of charlatanism. Fortunately, he remembered in time that Paris possesses "immortals," and, comparing the two instances of antiphrasis, he was obliged to recognize that one was no more grotesque than the other. Master Helleborus had even insisted on giving the prize for ridicule to the terrestrial vocable.

---

[37] *Cuisse de nymphe* [literally "nymph's thigh"] is a variety of pale pink rose, the name of which was often applied to pigments of a similar color.

That Master Helleborus was a terrible person. He had not lifted any corner of the veil of mystery that surrounded him, he had not departed by one iota from his habit of perpetual satire, and he had not given Onésime an inch.

He no longer gave the impression of weighing up any of the decisions of his invalid. He acquiesced to all his desires, and unless he had the power to inspire those desires at will, that was incomprehensible.

Thus, when Argan's descendant manifested the intention to attend a session of the Academy of Infallibles, it seemed the Master Helleborus had foreseen that the manifestation in question would occur.

"There's a meeting this very day," he replied, simply. "An important discussion will occupy the Infallibles. You can judge them in full knowledge of the case."

The Academy of Infallibles was installed in a location of funereal appearance. A dubious daylight filtered through the ceiling and had difficulty illuminating the depths of a vault devoid of architectural style.

The first part of the hall, divided into stalls, was reserved for the Academicians, the second for the public, which was generally conspicuous by its absence.

As for the Infallibles, gathered in groups, they were chatting about their petty affairs in the sharpest tones, while a gentleman standing at a kind of podium read out a document of which it as impossible to hear a single word.

"Who is that man?" asked Onésime.

"It's the secretary, reading the minutes of the previous meeting."

"But one can't hear a word of it."

"Of course not! He isn't speaking."

"How can he read without speaking?"

"Nothing simpler. As it has been the rule, since time immemorial, for the Infallibles not to pay any attention to this part of the program, the reader limits himself to a pantomime, as a matter of pure formality."

"Bah! And who is the other man now taking his place?"

"A foreign merchant of health who has a communication to make."

"On what? No one's listening to him."

"Because it will be in the minutes."

"But since no one listens to the minutes either..."

"You're asking too much of me. Anyway, you'll be able to divert yourself. The great debate I mentioned to you is about to open."

An Infallible unfurled a voluminous dossier with a superb gesture. Then, in a trenchant tone, he commenced: "*Brief Observations of the Curative Properties of Rat Poison.*"

"I demand to speak," another Infallible interrupted.

"A diehard enemy of the orator," Master Helleborus murmured rapidly to Onésime.

"I'm astonished that my colleague wants to contradict me before I've breathed a single word," objected the first Infallible.

"Pardon me! You said *Brief Observations* and your manuscript is at least two hundred pages."

While everyone laughed, the first Infallible recovered his aplomb.

"Rap poison, that toxic substance..."

"I demand to speak!" cried the second Infallible. "You said 'that substance'—but rat poison is a composite of several substances, not a simple substance."

"That toxic substance, of which the ancients..."

"I demand to speak! The ancients never employed that poison, of modern origin."

"...of which the ancients were unaware..."

"I demand to speak! The ancients did not employ it, it's true, but between that and being unaware of it there's an abyss."

"...has conquered its place..."

"I demand to speak! You want to make it a conqueror, but nothing gives you grounds for that."

"You're not giving me time to express myself."

"You're abusing the podium."

128

"It's envy that's driving you."

"And jealousy you."

The Infallibles appeared to be relishing the spectacle of that altercation.

"Courage, Dr. Carbonet!" cried some.

"Bravo, Dr. Danipeau!" cried others.

"Kiss! Kiss! Kiss!"

The Academy was evidently divided into two camps. Interpellations were already flying back and forth, fists were being waved; but the president, who had been asleep until then, thought the moment had come to wake up and shout over the tumult: "The session is closed! Until next week..."

"It won't be me who'll come back," said Onésime. "When it's reason that speaks they don't want to listen; when it's rancor, they don't want to listen to one another. I can see that here, it's better to be a buyer than a merchant of health."

"To suffer evil is to do it," said Master Helleborus, by way of commentary.

XXXVI. The Waters of Blaguen-Blaguen

A new access of prostration succeeded that further disappointment on Onésime's part. He was wilting, yellowing, and becoming thin.

In the meantime, the rumor suddenly ran around Capital Fantasia that a spring of mineral water had just been discovered whose marvelous properties left all those previously known far behind.

Everywhere, nobody was talking about anything but the waters of Blaguen-Blaguen,[38] so unexpectedly discovered by Dr. Balissan.

This is what had happened.

Dr. Balissan was vegetating—an unoccupied occupation that he had in common with many colleagues. He had tried to

---

[38] Another funny name, lampooning Baden-Baden, a *blague* being a joke.

latch on to all the branches of his art successively, but the branches had remained in his hand.

He was about to drown. In what does one drown? In water. What a flash of enlightenment! Dr. Balissan was saved.

"Imbecile!" he said to himself. "Triple imbecile, who hasn't thought of the specialty of waters. Planet Fantasia already counts, it's true, considerable quantities...damn, 9,976, according to my hydrological dictionary. There are sulfurous ones, ferruginous ones, arsenical, alkaline...but there isn't one that has all of them at the same time. I'll make one!"

Take note that Dr. Balissan had not said: "I'll find one."

And with a confident step, he had gone to see a close friend, a manufacturer of chemical products, whose workshops were situated in one of the suburbs of Capital Fantasia, forty-six and three-quarter leagues from the great central square of the city.

"My dear friend," he said, "would you like to make a fortune? Yes? Me too. You manufacture chemical products? Yes again. For the running water you use, you have a collection pipe conforming to police ordinance no, 33,654, modified by ordinance 41,365, modified by ordinance no. 111,313, modified by ordinance no, 534,322."

"I do indeed have a collection pipe conforming with ordinance no. etc., etc. etc."

"That's all we need. At what depth? Five meters. Very good. We'll block the pipe at one end. By night, we'll make an opening through which the water can gush. You'll prepare a mixture of which this is the formula, and then...pch pch pch pch!"

Dr. Balissan finished whispering the rest of his idea in his colleague's ear. The latter threw his arms around him and embraced him effusively.

The next day, all the newspapers announced the discovery of the waters of Blaguen-Blaguen, which had sprung forth during the night. All the chemists, on analyzing it, had found different ingredients. Lured by a commission that Balissan had generously sown in order to reap more abundantly, all the merchants of health recommended the waters of Blaguen-Blaguen, one because of the sulfur, another because of the iron, a third because of the arsenic...

Dr. Balissan was on the way to a fortune.

XXXVII. Thermal Amours

That true story told to Onésime by Master Helleborus did not convince him. Probably, that was the reason that Helleborus had told it to him, for when he saw his friend shake his head, he said to him: "I've divulged to you the art of fabricating a spring and creating an income of millions."

"That's all well and good, but once can't deceive an entire population like that."

"Deceive them how? The other natural mineral waters of Planet Fantasia have never done any good, and these don't do any harm, so it's quits."

"If those who go there weren't satisfied..."

"They'd be sure not to inform anyone else, in order to allow them to share their disappointment."

"You're disillusioning."

"And you're deluded. But I've foreseen the circumstance, so our bags have already been taken out to the steam-carriage that's waiting for us downstairs."

"To take us where?"

"To the waters of Blaguen-Blaguen, of course."

Voyages do not last long on Planet Fantasia, and in twenty minutes, the two tourists had covered the forty-six and three-quarter leagues.

In fact, they only had to cover forty, for the queue of steam-vehicles bringing drinkers to the waters of Blaguen-Blaguen extended to a distance of six and three-quarter leagues.

An employee approached.

"These gentlemen are coming for the waters?"

"Yes, of course, but we're not there yet."

"It's impossible to go any further, sirs. Everything is booked until the twenty-eighth of September."

"But it's the first of May."

"Yes, sir. On the twenty-eighth of September, at two thirty-five in the morning, sir will be admitted to drink a glass of the precious spring. Not before."

"That's prodigious," said Onésime, almost enthused.

"Do you want to wait?" asked Helleborus, sarcastically.

"If the gentlemen don't wish to remain in the carriage for all that time, they can stay at one of the nine thousand waiting hotels founded under the patronage of Dr, Balissan. One is well-accommodated there for three francs a day."

"Damn!" Onésime could not help exclaiming.

"Oh, that's food included, sir!" the employee objected.

"I should hope so. But how the Devil are we going to pass the time until two thirty-five in the morning of the twenty-eighth of September?"

Just as Onésime was asking himself that question, as he got down, he glimpsed the silhouette of a woman who appeared to be young and seductive.

What if I were to fall in love to kill time? he thought.

From which it followed that by the twentieth of September, Onésime had not yet drunk his glass of water, but he was on the point of marrying Mademoiselle Sylvandire de Hocheval.

XXXVIII. The Inspector of Expectations

Fully preoccupied with his future marriage, Argan's descendant was standing at the window of the hotel in which he was staying, opposite that of Sylvandire de Hocheval.

Two reasons militated in favor of that attitude. The first was that he was trying to catch a glimpse of his fiancée's profile; the second was that he was shaping his beard.

And while running the razor over his cheeks he reflected: *She's charming and she seems to adore me. I believe that marriage would restore my health. At least, that's the opinion of the doctor I went to see yesterday. It's true that I consulted another the day before yesterday who threatened me with the greatest misfortunes if I didn't remain a bachelor...but dear Sylvandire...it would be impossible for me to renounce her. She's charming, and then, she definitely adores me...*

The tinkle of the doorbell interrupted that mental monologue.

"Come in!" shouted Helleborus, who was smoking a cigar on the divan while following the expressions on his protégé's face with his gaze.

A stranger in official attire came in, making forced reverences, and addressed himself to Heleborus.

"Is it to Monsieur Du Tilleul that I have the honor of speaking?" As he spoke he extended his hand as if to grip Helleborus' arm.

The latter fixed him with a sarcastic stare. "You're confused, Monsieur. Over there, by the window."

The stranger resumed his advance with the same profusion of reverences and said, in the same tone: "Is it to Monsieur Du Tilleul that I have the honor...?" At the same time, he seized—really seized, this time—Onésime's arm, making as if to take his pulse.

"Pardon me, but what do you want?" asked Argan's descendant, not understanding that maneuver at all.

"Inspector of Expectations!" said the stranger, with one more bow.

"Oh! Very well," replied Onésime, "except that I don't know exactly..."

The unknown man was counting, placidly: "One, two, one, two, one, two..."

"I don't exactly grasp the motive that brings you..."

"One, two, one, two! The pulse answers fairly well to what I've been told," said the bizarre visitor. "Will you please take your clothes off?"

"Take my clothes off? Why?"

"Haven't I just said, Monsieur, that I'm the Inspector of Expectations?"

"I'm damned, Monsieur, if I know what you want from me, with your expectations, your inspection, your fashion of taking my pulse and wanting me to take off my clothes."

"Aren't you about to be married?"

"Yes, certainly, to Mademoiselle Sylvandire de Hocheval..."

"Well, then?"

"Well then, what connection is there...?"

"Pardon me," intervened Master Hellebore, "but Monsieur is a foreigner, and as such, ignorant of the customs of the land. Would you be good enough to explain your titles and qualities to him."

"It seems to me that when one lives somewhere," grumbled the Inspector, "one ought at least to learn to respect the public functionaries."

Onésime looked at the intruder with an expression that clearly demanded to know with what sort of function he was invested.

"Monsieur," the newcomer went on, "Mademoiselle de Hocheval has sent me here, in conformity with the law that authorizes fiancés of both sexes to have the expectations enunciated by each of them in the marriage contract verified officially and medically."

"The expectations...wait a minute...in France, one gives that charming name to calculations of interest based on funereal covetousness..."

"I don't know what happens on the planet that I heard named just now for the first time, but here, our legislators have prudently made provision so that fraud and deception do not insinuate themselves into amours. Once, before the institution of the corps of which I have the honor to belong, it was a veritable scandal. Every day, one saw young women, in their impatience to get married, representing uncles who had at least ten years to live as being on their death-bed, and old men deceiving unfortunate young women by simulating, at the moment of the marriage, infirmities that deceived them as to the imminence of the heritage to come. Thank God, we've regulated all that now. You're going to marry? That's good. Your future anticipates so much ready cash, and so much cash to come from various relatives. Immediately, I or one of my colleagues go to see the relatives, and we ascertain whether their faintness of complexion or decrepitude authorizes the presumptions of an imminent legacy. I or one of my colleagues then makes a report—and that, Monsieur, is what defines the useful and noble functions of the Inspector of Expectations."

Slightly pale, Onésime was making an obvious effort not to lose his temper.

"Pardon me, Monsieur," he said, "but I still don't see what you're doing here. I haven't mentioned legacies from any relatives to Mademoiselle Sylvandire..."

"No doubt—but as for yourself?" continued the Inspector, with a terrible smile.

"Myself! What does that mean?"

"You have a certain personal fortune, which is determining Mademoiselle de Hocheval to marry you."

"Ah! It's my fortune..."

"You can't be unaware that no marriage is contracted on any other basis. In the vicinity of the waters, above all, where young people difficult of placement seek a valetudinarian, it's quite natural that the poor things acquire a few guarantees. Permit me, therefore, to continue my examination..."

"Don't touch me! Don't touch me! You horrify me!"

"If it's the dread of some saddening revelation that animates you, have no anxiety. We're very discreet, and never tell a subject how we evaluate the remainder of his duration."

"I repeat to you that you horrify me, you and your abominable attributions."

"Insolent!"

"Because I want to be married for myself..."

"In your condition? I'd like to see that!"

"And you can go to the fifty thousand devils in the company of Mademoiselle de Hocheval, whose infamous calculations have cured me forever of a foolish amour."

135

"A fine lover! With that concave chest and that complexion!"

"Get out, scoundrel!" cried Onésime, overcome by wrath and fear.

"I'm going, I'm going, but he who goes last will go best!" grated the Inspector, with a wink redolent of the tomb.

Argan's descendant fell back into an armchair, exhausted.

"She! To have me inspected...to count on my sufferings...oh, this frightful country! That frightful girl! That frightful man!"

"You're not being fair, Du Tilleul," Master Helleborus objected, philosophically. "On Earth, people carry out that kind of verification on the sly. Here, it has been legalized. Fundamentally, matrimonial cupidity counts; don't always speak ill of frankness..."

XXXIX. Judiciary Medicine

For such a feeble mind, such an emotion was already a great deal—but it was not, alas, the end of the matter.

A week later, Onésime received a document ornamented with seventeen stamps, each one costing six francs, the treasury of Planet Fantasia having successively raised the required number from one to seventeen.

On that paper was written, in a rigorously formal style:

Monsieur Onésime Du Tilleul, of no known profession, is summoned to appear tomorrow before the CCXXXth chamber of the Civil Courts of Capital Fantasia, otherwise known as the Matrimonial Chamber, in order to be sentenced, by law, to the reparation of damages caused, by an unmotivated refusal of marriage, to the health of Mademoiselle Sylvandire de Hocheval; the aforesaid damages having resulted in an incapacity of engagement of more than twenty days, misdemeanor specified by articles 6, 875, 773 and 9,395,263 of the two hundred and sixtieth Code in vigor.

"I told you so, my dear Du Tilleul," Helleborus hastened to respond, when he heard the news.

"But it ought to be me who is seeking damages and compensation, for all these shocks have reduced me to a piteous state."

"It was necessary to get in first; everyone is a lawyer here, and you'd have found a thousand advocates ready and willing."

"I would have recoiled before the ridicule of such a suit."

"Mademoiselle de Hocheval doesn't recoil—she's brave, that one!"

"She's a monster of impudence, a perfidious individual whom I shall confound in no uncertain terms—for it's impossible that any judge...by the way, what does she mean by *incapacity of engagement*?"

"The incapacity in which her indisposition has put her of searching for another potential husband, of course. That's the amiable maiden's work."

"What a country!" murmured Onésime. "What a country!"

It was, however, necessary to comply with the legal injunction, and on the stated day, Onésime appeared before the CCXXXth Chamber, accompanied only by Master Helleborus. He had not obtained an advocate; the first he had seen had asked him for seventeen thousand francs merely for the preparatory expenses of his plea.

A hostile murmur greeted Du Tilleul's arrival, and everyone manifested a scornful antipathy toward the foreigner who had wanted to exempt himself from the sage prescriptions of Fantasian laws.

A second murmur, as flattering as the other had been hostile, saluted the entrance of an old man with a venerable air, whom the president invited to read his report on the facts of the case.

The old man was Dr. Patachu, an expert in judiciary medicine for the tribunals of the planet.

Dr. Patachu, a man of the world, a distinguished scientist and an exceptional toxicologist, had only one fault: he saw guilty parties everywhere. Instead of conserving an equitable neutrality, his reports were sharpened into speeches for the prosecution. Before examining a case, he had already drawn a mental conclusion. From then on, all his efforts tended to organize the facts and combine the arguments able to confirm that initial conviction. He could have discovered poison in a pair of spectacles.

Thus, Dr. Patachu was reputed to be a terrible opponent. In his lectures in judiciary medicine, he took pleasure in proclaiming his successes with a pride mingled with cheerfulness, and repeated to his pupils in a sweetly satisfied tone: "Yes, gentlemen, I had the pleasure this morning of having my three thousandth man condemned to death..."

Dr. Patachu advanced to the bar, darted a glance at Onésime that presaged sinister conclusions, took a pinch of snuff, and started to read a long report, which concluded thus:

"Such are, sires, the medical elements of the case. Gastric embarrassment, the obstruction of the liver and cerebral overexcitement are constant in Mademoiselle Sylvandire. Let no one object that the indigestion might be accidental, the overexcitement temporary. The guilty party is before your eyes; it is Monsieur Du Tilleul.

"As I have proved in my *Researches on the Influence of Mental Suffering*, chagrin reacts powerfully upon the organs. What happens, then, when chagrin turns to despair? That is the case here. When I visited her, Mademoiselle Sylvandire was prey to a most characteristic despair, and her dolor is only too explicable by the ruination of the hopes inspired in her by the sanitary state of the accused.

"To lose a valetudinarian fiancé with a private income is a blow that might have been mortal for Mademoiselle Sylvandire. Heaven has not permitted that, but the incapacity of engagement is established and that incapacity is terrible with regard to the age of the victim. Twenty days lost when one is nearing thirty are twenty centuries, and I do not think the tribunal will find excessive the request for six months in prison and a hundred thousand francs in damages and compensation."

Cheers from the audience punctuated that conclusion on the part of Dr. Patachu, to whom the president granted permission to withdraw, in view of the importance of precious work that demanded his attention.

As for Onésime, he wanted to reply, but suddenly felt dazed, remained incapable of uttering a word, and vaguely heard himself condemned to pay the hundred thousand francs in damages. The tribunal, admitting extenuating circumstances, set aside the prison term.

XL. Vir Bonus[39]

The crisis had been frightful.

So many vicissitudes, capped by complete ruination, had shaken poor Onésime physically and mentally, to the extent that he had really fallen ill.

Thus, one morning, he said to his companion, with tears in his eyes: "Listen, my dear Helleborus, I sense that I'm very poorly. I haven't made any reproaches to you until now, even though you are, in large measure, responsible for my misfortunes...but please, have pity on me. You know what I've endured, and you know what I've lost; you won't refuse to render me one last service.

"Master Helleborus, if I don't receive conscientious care, it's all over for me. Is there not, on the entire Planet Fantasia, a single doctor in whom one can have confidence?"

"My dear Du Tilleul, there is one. That is the doctor truly worthy of that name, and not an odious or banal merchant of health. He is as modest as true science always ought to be. He is disinterested, because his sweetest reward is the sentiment of the services he renders. He has never fatigued the renown of his name, because he understands the dignity of the duty

---

[39] Latin for "Good Man," frequently used as a standard epithet,

that he exercises. No poor person ever calls him in vain, because for him, all humans are equal before suffering. He has never given an erroneous diagnosis, because, when he is uncertain, he has the good sense to abstain from one. In brief, my dear Du Tilleul, he is the doctor that all of them ought to be."

"Oh, Master Helleborus, take me to him," begged Onésime.

"Gladly," replied the other, with a singular intonation.

When they had arrived, Helleborus rang at a door of poor appearance, saying: "Here it is."

An old woman peered out through a loophole. "Who do you want?"

"Doctor Loyal."

"He's no longer here."

"Oh! Has he moved?"

"Yes, the dear brave man, he certainly has moved."

"Where is he resident now?"

"In the cemetery."

"What, dead! Of what?"

"Of poverty, of course."

XLI. An Extra-Lucid Somnambulist

"Since that's how it is," Onésime said, after walking in silence for a few minutes, "since certified medicine can no longer do anything for me and has done me nothing but harm, I'll go ask its enemies for the cure it refuses me."

"That's all that was lacking!" said Master Helleborus.

"I've recently heard mention of a somnambulist..."

"Extra-lucid?"

"Yes, extra-lucid. Why shouldn't she be? Why shouldn't I believe in her power?"

"You have an absolute need for credulity, then?"

"A drowning man clutches at any rope that's thrown to him."

"But he doesn't put it around his neck."

"It's definitely the Rue des Aveugles," said Onésime, as if talking to himself. "But that's where we are! Indeed: *Mademoiselle Brigitte, fluid gold medal at the Universal Exhibition of the Supernatural Arts...*"

With a bound he launched himself toward Mademoiselle Brigitte's residence. Master Helleborus gravely climbed the staircase behind him.

Mademoiselle Brigitte had been destined by her family for the career of milliner. During her childhood she had taken courses; during her youth she had made hats. At twenty-five, finding the métier unprofitable, she had decided to make miracles.

For that, it had been sufficient for her to say to herself one day: "I ought to be a somnambulist. If I'm not, I'll become one."

With that aim, she had procured an associate in the person of a former salesman of insurance against conjugal misfortunes. There are insurance companies of every sort on Capital Fantasia. That one had, however, gone bankrupt because of the enormous quantity of disasters on which it had to pay out annually. The salesman had, therefore, gratefully accepted Mademoiselle Brigitte's project; he had already been in sympathetic communication with her for a long time.

The ex-salesman was occupied in consuming a ham with the modern sibyl when Onésime presented himself, with Helleborus. He got up hastily, and wiped his mouth with the corner of his napkin.

"The gentlemen desire an oracle?"

From the start, the term "consultation" had been judged too prosaic by the pythoness of the Rue des Aveugles.

"Only my friend," said Helleborus.

"Very good. If the gentlemen would care to go into the waiting room while Mademoiselle prepares herself..." As he spoke, the ex-salesman opened a door, and went in with them.

"Sir would like a consultation for...?" insinuated the magnetic accomplice.

Onésime was about to reply, but Helleborus got in ahead of him. "My friend desires to leave all the merit of the divination to the somnambulist."

"Perfect!" said the accomplice, with a smile that resembled a grimace. "Would you like to read a newspaper? There's an account of a very curious robbery. It's astonishing how many robberies there have been this year..."

"Ah!" said Helleborus, having signaled to his friend to remain silent. He said "Ah!" indifferently.

It's not for a theft, thought the knight of industry. "There's also a palpitating romance by the Vicomte Basson du Mérail—a feuilleton that's been running for thirty-seven years. The prologue has just concluded; it's full of emotion. In particular, there's a separation between two lovers...such separations are cruel..."

"Ah!" replied the impassive Helleborus, again.

He didn't flinch; it's not for an affair of sentiment. "Would you like me to open the window? It's so close today—such unhealthy weather. The mortality rate has tripled in a week."

"Heaven!" exclaimed Onésime, before Helleborus could stop him.

He said "Heaven!"—it's an illness, thought the ex-salesman. Then, having clarified the question, he added: "The séance is about to commence. Please follow me."

Mademoiselle Brigitte was standing next to an armchair. She looked at her accomplice, who gave her the conventional signal to indicate that it was a matter of a medical consultation. Immediately, at the mere contact of the ex-salesman's hand, she rolled her eyes, coughed three times, and let herself fall into the armchair.

"She's asleep," said the ex-salesman.

"Impossible!" Helleborus acquiesced, feigning surprise.

"She's asleep but she's lucid. Mademoiselle! The gentleman desires..."

"I know what he desires. He's ill...very ill."

Onésime became tremulous.

"I can read his body like a book. His heart is there," she said, pointing at the left side.

"That's true," said Onésime.

"His liver is there..." (to the right).

"How clearly she sees!"

"His stomach there..." (in the middle).

"What lucidity!"

"Oh, the stomach! It's the stomach...thousands of insects."

"I have thousands of insects in my stomach!"

"They're as large as a grain of sand."

"Oh, my God!"

"And there are...wait while I count...there are seven billion nine hundred and thirty-seven million, one hundred and twenty thousand and fourteen..."

"That's prodigious!"

"No...a hundred and twenty thousand and fifteen."

"One more or less doesn't matter."

"It matters a great deal," the ex-salesman put in, in an intense tone. "Our house wants the exact truth!"

"That's admirable."

"Continue, Mademoiselle."

"It's necessary to kill them or they'll kill you. Kill them or they'll kill you. And there's only one means. Write! Write! The invalid will collect, or have someone collect, on the third day of the full moon, three leaves from the second chestnut-tree on the left on entering the eighth row in the Square des Innocentes. It's necessary to boil those three leaves with a black radish, two ounces of gutta-percha, half an ounce of snuff, three rifle bullets, and a cake of soap. Let it marinate for eleven days, bring it to the boil again, and drink five liters of the mixture every day. He'll be cured in a month. Ah...!"

As she finished, Mademoiselle Brigitte agitated her head as if she were prey to an attack of nerves.

"The sibyl is exhausted," said the ex-salesman. "Here's the prescription. Above all, don't forget to follow the instructions."

"Oh, Monsieur, you can count on it," replied Onésime, breathlessly.

As they went down the stairs, Master Helleborus heard the pythoness say: "I was a bit hasty, but damn it, the ham doesn't like waiting!"

"And he had to fork out his thousand just the same," added the ex-salesman.

But when Master Helleborus told Onésime about this dialogue, the latter shrugged his shoulders.

XLII. A Nurse

A room, illuminated by the tremulous flame of a nightlight. In the room, a bed. In the med, a moribund man. Next to the bed, an old woman.

The moribund man was Onésime, to whom the somnambulist's potion had delivered the final blow. The old woman was a nurse.

"Madame," said the unfortunate.

"Rrron! Rrron! Rrron!"

"Madame!"

"Rrrron!"

"Madame!"

"What! Is it common sense to shout like that? What do you want now?"

"My friend Helleborus hasn't returned?"

"Since you've been told that he'd be gone for three days."

"Why?"

"Do you think he told me?"

"I'm very thirsty."

"You'll permit me, I suppose, to make my black coffee first. You know that I threw away the stuff I found. I only take coffee that I grind myself. Your wine doesn't do my stomach any good—it's too cold. I've ordered twenty-five bottles of vintage. By the way, don't you have a maid to polish my shoes in the morning and do my parting? Don't worry about it—I'll get one from the agency, because the housework isn't my concern. And one has to look after one's hair, doesn't one? That's what keeps one looking young..."

"I'm very thirsty."

"All right...when my coffee has boiled. He's very demanding, this one! And with all that, I don't know what I'm going to have for supper. As it happens, I have a chicken here, a leg of mutton, asparagus, a little fish...but I fear that the mutton might be a bit heavy for me..."

"I'm thirsty..."

"Still! It wouldn't even be content to give me poor advice for my stomach. It would rather weight heavily on my heart..."

"I'm thirsty..."

"Oh, but it's not necessary to burn my ears, you know. I'm a good person, it's true; I look after the sick, it's true; but that doesn't prevent me from having had a position. And then again, I can't tolerate obstinacy. Damn it...I've left the brandy in my coffee-pot. It's his fault, all that whining...yes, it's your fault..."

"I'm...I'm...I'm..."

"Well, what's got into him? He's rolling his eyes. Hey...you know that I don't like people dying without warning me...sir? He's a funny invalid. He's not moving any more...hey! No one in! No...no...I knew it! He won't have any more toothaches.

"Now, to work!"

XLIII. Every Man for Himself

In the blink of an eye, the nurse had opened the cupboards.

With a curt gesture and a rapidity that denoted long-ingrained habitude, she hurled into the middle of the room everything that appeared to her to be desirable. She accompanied that inventory with little reflections: "Cotton chemises...they always come in handy...damn! He certainly wears them out. What a miser! Couldn't even order new underwear before packing his trunks for the other world.

"A nut-brown overcoat. I can't abide that color. Decidedly, he was a man devoid of taste. Anyway, I can always sell it.

"A black suit. That's convenient. My husband and I have been invited to a wedding next week, and poor Aristide doesn't have a black suit. You shall have one, my man! It's as good as new. He'll look like a lord.

"Hmm—the shoes aren't in very good condition, Worn soles…worn soles…scuffed inside…

"He had legs in shirtsleeves, that's for sure...

"Jewels…don't be stupid…someone might notice the disappearance. One either has delicacy, or one hasn't…let's just take that little ring…a matter of keeping a souvenir of the deceased. I haven't watched over a single one without keeping some trinket to remind me of him.

"It's silly, if you like, but sentimental things…I call it my little museum..."

The list went on.

When the nurse judged that she had stripped the cupboards of everything suitable, she made three parcels of it, which she hid in the fireplace until nightfall.

Then she went back to sit down tranquilly beside her coffee-pot, giving it three little taps because nothing was getting through the filter.

XLIV. The Certifier of Death

Onésime was only in a state of catalepsy. He could see and hear, but could not move.

He had watched the packaging scene, but an incredible force of inertia had prevented him from crying out: "Stop, thief!"

The whole night passed like that.

Toward midday, the nurse, who had gone to put her loot in a safe place, came back and started dusting the furniture.

That precaution seemed extraordinary to Onésime, but it did not take long to obtain an explanation, because, while dusting, the old woman muttered: "No stupidity! Everything has to be clean and tidy, because, when the certifier of death comes..."

The certifier of death!

At that title, Onésime's hair stood on end.

They won't perceive that I'm alive! That will be horrible! I want to go home, return to Earth, get my own back on Helleborus. They're capable of murdering me. But no, the certifier of death—it's his mission to prevent such frightful errors. He'll see at first glance how things are. My God! Why is he taking so long to arrive?

A voice cut short Onésime's somber reflections: a voice asking; "It's here that there's a deceased person?"

"Yes, sir."

"Ah!"

The certifier of death seemed to be a man who lived well. In fact, people in the neighborhood told amusing anecdotes about that.

Among others one of his quips to a practicing doctor who seemed scornful of the funereal doctor's functions was the remark: "Ha ha! I don't see that much difference between you and me. You play the shots—I mark up the score."

In the practice of his métier, the certifier of death had acquired a professional insouciance. A decease was an excursion of variable duration; death was his living—so he did not waste time.

That day, the certifier of death was even busier than usual. He has two friends coming to dinner to help celebrate his wife's birthday, and on the way to Onésime's house he had said to himself: "The fellow really ought to have died on another day. It's as if he's done it on purpose, because it wouldn't have been so inconvenient then. My stuffed artichokes will be overcooked. Artichokes like to be eaten just right..."

The certifier of death stuck his head through the door, looked in the direction of the bed where Onésime lay, impotent to give any sign of life and tortured by anguish, and he pointed at him. "That's him over there? Good."

After which he went home for lunch.

After lunch he shut himself in his study in order to finish a chapter he wanted to add to a book that ought to earn him a gold medal from the Academy of Infallibles.

The book was entitled: *Precautions to be Taken to Recognize Cases of Apparent Death.*

XLV. The Pack

Onésime's anguish was becoming increasingly poignant.

That doctor didn't even look at me...but I'm doomed, then! Come on...it's impossible! Helleborus will come back. He'll save me. For he isn't malevolent, Helleborus...

Helleborus did not come back. All day long, however, there was an interminable procession. The pack of the parasites of death descended upon the house.

The nurse, who had found the money in the drawers and who intended that "her deceased" should be buried in a suitable fashion—it was a point of honor, in fact—arranged things on a large scale, taking care to retain a commission on all her orders.

"Don't forget my establishment," said one. "Artistic funerary monuments a specialty. We'll make the gentleman a beautiful Gothic chapel. The Gothic is very much in fashion at the moment. With stained-glass windows. That gives a tomb a more cheerful appearance. As for the inscription, we have *Eternal Regrets* gilded by a galvano-chemical process; it's indelible..."

"Madame," said another, "I have an honorable reputation, I dare say, in my specialty: epitapher, at your service. No one turns a mortuary quatrain and a posthumous elegy better than me. Besides which, I have antecedents. Here are my papers, attesting that I'm a laureate of the floral tournament at which I obtained, five years ago, the antimony ranunculus. Would you like the grand dolor quatrain or the demi-mourning sonnet? It's the same price—it's a matter of taste."

"Madame, said a third, would you care to cast our eyes over this prospectus? Rubber coffins, patented s.g.d.g.[40] The impermeable and soft rubber coffin has obtained the approval of the competent authorities. One is as comfortable within it as in one's own bed..."

And Onésime, alive but immobile, heard all of that...

XLVI. A Dialogue of Crows

He was to hear many more.

Time marched on, without any sign presaging an end to the torture.

The fatal moment arrived.

Two individuals in uniformly sober dress came into the room. They were the undertakers.

The excellent fellows, while proceeding with their task, chatted.

"So you're in love, then?"

"What do you think? It's not compulsory."

"Is she pretty?"

"A peach! Five foot three...not to mention a tempting wine business. Get hold of that plank."

"A wine business. I'll be a regular, because, as you know, that's my weakness."

"Joker. Pass me the screws."

"Will you be quitting the game, once you're married?"

"Not likely!"

"Good!"

"Once one's got used to it, it's impossible to change."

---

[40] *Sans garantie du gouvernment*: the standard precautionary formula attached to all French patents, signifying that the granting of a patent did not imply any official guarantee that the patented device actually worked.

"Same here."

"Too true! If I didn't have my little routine every day, I wouldn't know what to do with myself."

"That's true. Isn't it funny to get attached like that? Christ! The fellow isn't light."

"A man of substance."

"Ha ha!"

"There'll be speeches you know—so I've heard."

"That's lucky. Suits me—I like rhetoric. *Ladies and gentlemen, in the midst of the mourning that surrounds me, I feel that my feeble voice is insufficient*...or even, *Ladies and gentlemen, there are times when speech is impossible...*"

"All the same, he's jolly heavy, the fellow."

And Onésime could still hear!

XLVII. The Funeral Oration

The bier had just descended into the funerary crypt.

The few people who had accompanied Onésime to his final resting place were arranged in a circle.

The undertakers, fond of rhetoric, had drawn closer.

Someone did indeed, begin a speech.

"Ladies and gentlemen, on the edge of this still open grave..."

But that's Helleborus! Onésime thought, as the sounds reached him inside the coffin. *The traitor! To have abandoned me like that! It's about time he showed himself...and why? To pronounce a few words of banal regret...*

Meanwhile, the voice continued: "On the edge of this still open grave, I would like to enable those surrounding me to hear a few items of salutary advice, which will, I believe, replace advantageously the compliments of condolence usual in such cases.

"The man who has just left us forever cannot, in any case, have any right to our tears, since his death was, in a sense, the result of a long suicide."

What! What's that he's saying? thought Onésime, indignantly.

"Our friend had, in fact, everything that a creature can desire. He was young; he was independent in his means; he was able to render himself useful by his endeavors.

"Instead of that, he preferred to concentrate all his thoughts on himself; he sacrificed to egotism, and was sacrificed by himself. For he had the most dangerous egotism of all: the egotism of health. He was not afflicted by any malady, ladies and gentlemen, but by the end of his life he had succeeded in giving himself all of them.

"Let that example, both terrible and ridiculous, not be wasted on you."

It's an infamy! complained Onésime, mentally. *To insult me in my grave!*

"My friend was indebted," Helleborus continued, "to all the maladies of the merchants of health. Fear commenced the work, remedies continued it, and nature completed it—and nature, I proclaim, would have done better to revolt.

"May you all remember the example of Onésime Du Tilleul—and in order that the memory should be supported by evidence, I shall have engraved at my own expense on the marble tombstone that will cover my unfortunate friend's remains, the names of all the merchants of health that he consulted on Planet Fantasia.

"If that custom can be propagated, it will be the only service that Onésime Du Tilleul has rendered in the course of his existence. Adieu, Du Tilleul…you asked for it!"

XLVIII. Help!

The voice had died away...

Onésime, his hair standing on end, with sweat on his brow, listened hard.

Nothing more.

So it was all over.

Then, in a fit of immense despair, the unfortunate cataleptic started roaring: "Rogue! Scoundrel! Blackguard! He's no longer speaking...they're going away...oh, I couldn't cry out! Helleborus! My friend! Helleborus...frightful vagabond... Heaven! The first spadefuls of sand are falling...with that dull sound...

"Help me! I'm choking...my throat is tight...my breath is...

"Help me! I..."

...

...

...

Epilogue. Onésime's Vow

Suddenly, Onésime opened his eyes again.

O surprise!

He found himself in his bedroom in the Rue des Martyrs, with daylight flooding in through the window.

He looked at the clock.

Three o'clock!

So he had been asleep for twelve hours—dreaming for twelve hours!

Master Helleborus, his fantastic voyage, the Planet Fantasia, the merchants of health, his marriage, his trial, his catalepsy—everything—had all been the effect of a dream, doubtless occasioned by the potion that he had taken the previous evening, the bottle of which still remained in the night-table.

But dreams bring counsel, it appears, for Onésime, having felt himself in order to make sure that it really was him, leapt out of bed, got dressed and, while putting on his trousers, said: "Decidedly, it was a warning from Heaven. I've been as grotesque as my poor ancestor Argan. I don't want to be any longer. I've never felt so robust. I swear never to consult another physician as long as I live!"

"Bravo!" cried one of his friends, who had heard the end of the speech as he came in. "Bravo, Onésime. Is it true, what you just swore? No more physicians?"

"Never!"

"Well then; I've just inherited a hundred thousand francs—permit me to buy an annuity guaranteed by your life."

MONSIEUR NOBODY

I. The Mob

Geography, which is enthusiastic to form the mind at the same time as the heart, never fails to combine the names of the cities that it enumerates with one or more indications appropriate to furnish the memory of its readers comfortably. It tells you, for example, with an agreeable mixture of realism and sentimentality:

ROUEN. Population 84,000. Famous for its apple-favored barley sugar and the birthplace of the great Corneille.

MONTPELLIER. Equally renowned for its Faculté de Médecine and its brandy.

ORLÉANS. Has given its name to the immortal Jeanne d'Arc and excellent quince jam.

Thus with all our cities, each recommended in turn by what might be described as the advertising of the science: to each its mention.

Now, if ever a conscientious scientist—may heaven preserve him—were charged with spreading printed news to the five continents of the world, arrives at the article PARIS, he will not fail, in order to conform to the immutable habit of geography, to add: *Birthplace of Molière, idlers and mobs.*

The idler and mobs constitute, in fact, one of the most Parisian of the Parisian specialties that might serve as an identifying mark on the passport of the great capital. Idlers are required for mobs, and mobs are required for idlers. The live by courtesy of one another, and for one another; they cannot live without one another.

For the formation of a mob, any pretext will do: a political event or a charlatan's prospectus, a shooting star or a stopping carriage, a woman throwing herself out of a window or a taffeta merchant after horns.

What does it matter to the idler?

He contemplates with the same banal gaze the parade of men with walking-sticks and the body of an unfortunate who has just been run over by an omnibus. He has the same idiotic pleasure in contemplating a man staggering because he has drunk too much and one who has collapsed because he has not eaten enough. He is there, standing on his two feet, to watch a government at odds with a revolution, or an old lady at odds with her cat.

The mob is the miracle of the multiplication of imbeciles.

There is one of them; in ten seconds he has become a hundred—and perorates like a thousand.

The mob has axioms in all circumstances, remonstrations for all authorities, and remedies for all ills.

It occupies itself with affairs of State with the *Moniteur* stuck to walls; meteorology with the engineer Chevalier's thermometer;[41] dramatic literature with the queue that snakes around theaters in which croixdemaméries[42] are playing; mat-

[41] The Chevalier family were instrument-makers who had shops on the Quai d'Horloge and the Palais-Royal. They installed a thermometer outside the former establishment which became a kind of official monitor of the temperature in Paris, frequently mentioned in novels.

[42] This improvised portmanteau word refers to melodramatic plays routinely employing the narrative device baptized by such sarcastic critics as Paul Féval as "la croix de ma mère" [my mother's cross]; Véron also cited the cliché in *Les Marchands de santé*.

ters of public order involving a policeman escorting a delinquent to the station; astronomy, with the lunar telescope on the Pont-Neuf; fine arts, with Mangin's pencils;[43] and gymnastics with the skater of the Place de la Concorde.

The mob knows everything—except how not to let itself be taken in by any exploiter who come along—and sees everything, except for the pickpocket stealing its handkerchiefs. It has a great deal of advice for those who cannot act on it, and no spare change for those who have need of it.

The mob consists of the sheep—but sometimes also the wolves—of Panurge.

Which makes the mob an object of hatred, like the idler, and the idler like the mob; and one has all the more right to be impatient with their stupidity because one senses that it is eternal.

II. In the Year 1901

What has just been said in general about the malady of the mob can, with much greater reason, be applied in particular to the Paris in which this story asks for permission to transport the reader: the Paris of the year of grace 1901.

In that first year of the twentieth century, the movement of pedestrians and vehicles had acquired such an activity that is some places, notably at the intersections of several streets, one was obliged to apply the day before to *ad hoc* ticket offices for an order number, in order to be allowed to cross the streets or boulevards the following day.

The encumbrance of the sidewalks had naturally increased in the same proportion.

As the spirit of indiscipline typical of the national character had prevented passers-by from submitting to multiple ordinances intended to oblige each citizen to keep to the right

---

[43] The reference is to the popularizer of science Arthur Mangin (1824-1887), a prolific publisher of illustrated books.

while walking, there were continual collisions between comers and goers on either side of the asphalt.

Furthermore, the administration finding itself confronted by an immense increase of the Parisian population, unable to multiply surveillance too considerably, had ended up by establishing a policeman on sentry duty outside every fifth shop. These estimable and otherwise very useful functionaries had the inconvenience of forming on the bitumen, already obstructed, an embarrassment of zeal that added a further obstacle to circulation.

It is easy to conceive that, in such a state of affairs, the most trivial motive or the most insignificant event might suddenly become the focal point of frightful agglomerations.

It is easier still to understand that more than any other thoroughfare, the Rue des Petits-Champs, that uncomfortable corridor of the illustrious capital, was exposed to such congestions of citizens. Thus, you will not be surprised to learn that on the first of August in the year 1901, at about three o'clock in the afternoon, the said street was completely blocked by an assembly of at least six thousand people.

What was happening, then?

That was what everyone was trying to see, either by raising themselves up on their own feet or treading on other people's.

In spite of so many gymnastic efforts, however, all that those whom hazard had not placed in front-row seats could succeed in discovering was an agent of the authority at odds with an innocent griffon dog.

III. Cellular Dogs

This is what had happened.

In the year of grace 1901 the police, like everything else, had necessarily made as much progress as possible. To cite just one example, which directly concerns the commencement of this story, they had, for several years, rendered in honor of the canine race a series of a hundred and fourteen decrees.

The aim of the first hundred and ten had been to bring successive improvements to the construction of muzzles, which had been fitted with springs, safety-locks and other devices designed to reassure the public against the perils of hydrophobia.

Soon, muzzles, no matter how well-bolted, had no longer seemed sufficient—because, as one local bigwig said in a luminous report: *There is no guarantee that a dog with intelligence—and the race has it—cannot succeeded in forcing the lock of its collar.* The same report might well also have emphasized the hypothesis of the fabrication of false keys, but although that aspect of the argument had been wrongly left in the shadows, the urgency was decided nevertheless of depriving the redoubtable quadrupeds of the use of their forepaws.

In consequence, every dog-owner was instructed to shackle the said forepaws, with the aid of a chain riveted to an iron ball.

Then it was the turn of the rear paws, which were submitted to the same formality.

Then, finally, these external restraints were recognized once again to be insufficient, and the following decree was published:

Considering that in the matter of regulations, when there are enough of them, more are required; and considering that the dog is man's best friend, the latter ought to surround the former with all imaginable precautions; and considering that hydrophobia is an incontestably dangerous disease, since the most terrible dangers can result therefrom, the following articles are decreed:

Article One. From this day forward, dogs may no longer appear in the streets unless enclosed in small cages mounted on four wheels and equipped with iron bars, the length and diameter of which will be determined by a committee of engineers, civil servants and blacksmiths.

Article Two. Ever dog-owner must draw his dog's cage personally, and never let go of the rope to which it is attached.

Article Three. Any contravention will be punished by a fine of between a hundred and a million francs.

Article Four. In case of recidivism, that penalty may be supplemented by a term of imprisonment between a week and twenty years.

Article Five. Any dog encountered circulating on the public highway without its cage will be immediately taken to a Clinic, where the luminaries of medical science, to whom the destruction of their diseases offers insufficient recreation, will have the pleasure of vivisecting the delinquent.

Article Six. In order to spare dog-owners the trouble of constructing cages in conformity with the present decree, the administration has granted the exclusive right to manufacture and sell the article for more than its value to a subsidiary.

Article Seven. The latest ordinance always being the only rational one, all those preceding it are declared to be ridiculous, contrary to common sense, null and void.

The authoritarian crescendo had stopped for the moment at the above dispositions, and it was a contravention of this draconian law that had occasioned the gathering in the Rue des Petits-Champs.

An unfortunate griffon had strayed into the sunlight without a precautionary prison. A policeman had perceived it, seized it and restrained it.

The dog struggled.

The policeman pulled.

The dog choked.

The policeman pulled harder.

As for the crowd, its members were watching without any other sentiment than the pleasure of enjoying a free performance, when a man suddenly appeared, fraying a passage through the lovers of open-air spectacles, and fell like an aerolith into the middle of the circle surrounding the two combatants in the unequal struggle.

IV. The Man with Green Eyes

The newcomer was a strange individual.

Clad in such a manner as to challenge the date of any kind of fashion, he similarly escaped the evaluation of any birth certificate. Perhaps he was thirty-five. He might have been sixty—or a hundred and ten; who knows? For, since the application of the doctrines of Sieur Flourens, a philosopher of the preceding century, it was not rare to see bi- or tricentenarians.[44]

The movements of the unknown man, imprinted with an entirely spontaneous ardor had the eloquence of speech, or very nearly.

The expression on his face was one of calm resolution, benevolent irony and intermittent vivacity. With a truly unusual mobility, his features could adopt the most various physiognomies one after another. But more than anything else, what gave his face a hint of powerful originality was the gaze of two impenetrable green eyes.

Thin and angular, the unknown man would have seemed ugly to the vulgar, but he struck and interested the observer at first glance. To see him parting the ranks of the idlers, one might have supposed that he was about to intervene in the situation with an indiscreet vehemence.

He did nothing of the sort.

On the contrary, touching the brim of his hat with perfect politeness, he said to the agent of the authorities: "Would you excuse me, Monsieur?"

"Why are you sticking your oar in?" retorted the other, without taking the trouble to moderate his tone of voice.

---

[44] The physiologist Pierre Flourens, previously mentioned in a footnote to "The Merchants of Health," published *De la longévité humaine et de la quantité de vie sur le globe* in 1854; it was his most successful book and was reprinted several times.

"Because I'm astonished that all these people here haven't already done so."

"Is this dog yours?"

"That's not important."

"Be on your way, then. I have my orders."

"A thousand pardons, Monsieur; I don't know what your orders are..."

"Read the regulations."

"But what I do know," pursued the unknown man, with complete serenity, "is that if ever this dog becomes rabid, it is to your good offices that will surely owe it."

"Are you going to...?"

"I'm truly sorry to disoblige you, but permit me to tell you, nonetheless, Monsieur, that you appear to be unaware of the simplest notions of natural history. It is unprecedented that a rabid dog has ever pushed condescension to the point of obligingly allowing itself to be put into an apparatus similar to those one encounters on every street corner, but there is every chance that after repeated sojourns within such an instrument of torture, one would emerge in a state of the most perfect ferocity, and devour, by way of reprisal, all or part of its owner."

"I have my orders," the policeman repeated, while the crowd, amused by the speech, burst into noisy laughter.

"Let us take, for example, the poor griffon that you are brutalizing. You find it quite natural to abuse your strength in order to make it suffer. If its weakness used reprisals and riposted with a legitimate thrust of the teeth, you would accuse it of savagery—and yet you know as well as I do that it's inoffensive."

"Inoffensive! Inoffensive!"

"Would you give it the time to demonstrate it if it were not? Believe me, my friend, if it is necessarily the more wicked of two individuals that imprisons the other, there would be no danger that it would ever be the quadruped who would be towing the biped, locked up behind bars."

This time the crowd uttered a veritable hurrah.

The policeman, who was a novice in the profession, was troubled by the calmness of his interlocutor, whose green eyes never quit his own, but, wanting to put on a brave face, he raised his voice and repeated: "I have my orders, damn it! That's all I know. Is this dog yours?"

"Yes," replied the man with green eyes, with an impassive expression.

The dog seemed to understand, and wagged its tail, while emitting a plaintive whine..

"Oh! It's yours...."

"Certainly. Isn't that right, Médor?"

The dog approved audibly.

"Well, then, take it away...but if I find it again..."

"It's necessary to hope, my friend, than between now and then, the arguments that I have had the honor of exposing to you will have frayed a passage as far as the common sense of your superiors, and that the orders that you have mentioned to me on several occasions will have been retracted. Come on, Médor, my friend, let's be on our way. We'll take a carriage, since dogs, like people, have riding privileges."

And the unknown man, followed by the griffon, which walked respectfully between his legs, drew away from the curiosity of the audience.

V. Encounter

He had already covered some distance when he felt someone grab his arm, and a voice murmured in his ear: "I beg your pardon, Monsieur, I..."

Médor's friend turned round and found himself face to face with an individual of the most venerable appearance: white cravat, gold-rimmed spectacles and black suit.

"I beg your pardon, Monsieur," the stranger repeated, but I happened to witness the scene in which you were the principal actor."

"Ah!"

"And like everyone else, I was struck by the sagacity of your reasoning, as well as the delicacy of your heart. Permit me to congratulate you. You love your dog nobly."

"My dog!" said the man with green eyes. "But he's not mine."

"He's not yours?"

"I understood that only a lie could save him, and I adopted the poor animal until his legitimate owner comes to reclaims him."

As if he wanted to protest his gratitude, the loyal Médor stuck more tightly to his defender's legs.

"Oh, Monsieur," exclaimed the venerable stranger, "your conduct is even finer than I thought."

"It seems to me that I only did what anyone else would have done in my place."

"As modest as you are generous. Does Monsieur belong, by chance, to one of our ninety provincial branches?"

"Branches of what?"

"Those of the Animalophilic Society."

"No, Monsieur."

That's an injustice that I shall repair. Perhaps my name is not unknown to you: Baron de Tirechappe. I have the honor of being a member of the Mother Society of Paris, where my services have, I can say without vanity, conquered me a credit that I strive to justify. Put it there, Monsieur: we were born to appreciate one another. And to begin with, I beg you to give me the pleasure of coming to dine at my home."

"You're extremely kind, but..."

"I won't accept any excuses! Such a cultivated mind, and soul too! Please come..."

"If..."

"Come I beg you."

And the Baron de Tirechappe linked arms with our unknown man.

VI. The Animals' Friend

"Oh, my dear Monsieur," the Baron de Tirechappe continued, as he began to walk, "the animals, my dear Monsieur! I don't understand why there are hearts hard enough not to sympathize with the sufferings of those unfortunate and defenseless beings!"

"They are indeed worthy of interest."

"Thank you for those kind words. I was quite sure that we would understand one another. The animals! I have devoted my life to them, and I have been fortunate enough to see my efforts appreciated beyond their merits. Eleven sovereigns have deigned to grant me the crosses of their orders in recompense for the little good that I've been able to do. I swear to you that I would have been sufficiently remunerated by my conscience."

"The noblest of salaries, Monsieur; you're right."

"Isn't it true? When one has sentiments that..." The baron suddenly interrupted his dithyramb to thunder: "Damn it! Will you please leave us in peace! I don't understand why the police don't lock up such vagabonds. You're hungry? They're all hungry, to listen to them. And children! I was sure of it! Leave us alone, idler, or I'll have to arrested."

This virulent tirade was addressed to a beggar who had approached to implore the charity of the animals' friend—who, after his deeply-felt imprecation, resumed in an emotional one: "When I think, Monsieur, that natures exist in which the string of pity has never vibrated. But it must be said that, merely on seeing a poor animal limping, I feel tears coming to my eyes. You shall examine my schemes for retirement homes for dogs, hospitals for birds and crèches for kittens. Those, I dare say, and veritably humane ideas, and..."

The Baron stopped again.

This time, a traffic accident had attracted his attention. A fiacre hit by an omnibus had tipped over, and the driver had sustained two broken ribs.

The Baron ran forward with anguish, but came back almost immediately, with a smile on his lips.

"Thank God! It's nothing. For a moment I thought that the horse was injured and almost felt sick with emotion. One isn't master of oneself, isn't that right? But it's very unfortunate to be so impressionable. Oh, my dear Monsieur, those who are insensitive are worthy of envy."

"What about the coachman?" objected the Baron's interlocutor.

"Pooh! Don't talk to me about those people! He'll go to be pampered at the Company's expense. Idlers and drunks! I'll also show you the petition I'm addressing to the Prefect, with regard to the animal-tamer who is putting on a show at this very moment at the Circus. An infamy! I don't understand how such barbaric spectacles are tolerated. Also...but, damn it, I have a copy of the petition here, so, while we walk..."

The Baron took a piece of paper out of his pocket, which he began to read.

VII. An Unusual Petition

"Monsieur le Préfet,

"A theater is presently serving as accomplice to a veritably scandalous exhibition, in disharmony with the mores of the century in which we are proud to live.

"What is the point, in fact, of civilization having accomplished real progress, if it is not to leave far behind those savage epochs whose motto was: *Panem et circenses?*

"An animal-tamer whose name I do not know, and do not want to know, enters every evening into a cage with fifteen lions, on which he imposes exercises as dishonoring as they are blameworthy.

"By what right, Monsieur le Préfet, is it permissible to violate individual liberty in the person of these noble and intelligent carnivores, which have been reduced against their will to the role of acrobats?

"But that is only one aspect of the question: the moral and psychological aspect. There is another on which I must insist with an even more convinced energy.

"Can you suppose, Monsieur le Préfet, that these superb animals have voluntarily abdicated their traditional pride? No! You will not offer them that insult.

"It is, therefore, by constraint, by ill-treatment, blows and privations that their natural generous independence has been successfully tamed.

"Will modern society tolerate such abuses! Will it expose inoffensive lions to the violence of a strolling player?

"What I have to tell you, Monsieur le Préfet is not only about the ill-treatment to which these noble quadrupeds are being subjected. It is a matter of death! Yes, death! For this man, in order to excite the curiosity of the crowd, does not hesitate to enter their cage with his arms and legs naked. I ask you, is it permissible to take indecent provocation so far?

"Oh, I am shivering involuntarily. If one of those animals, carried away by a legitimate appetite, allows itself to consume the tamer, he might well be doomed—the lion, that is.

"In fact, in that profession, the man is addicted to alcoholic beverages; fatigues and old age must, in addition, have rendered his flesh tough and unhealthy. The lion might, therefore perish by virtue of an indigestion, to which he will have been treacherously provoked.

"No, Monsieur le Préfet, I repeat, by way of conclusion, your high justice cannot tolerate such a scandal, and I await, with confidence in your equity, an order that will put an end to the indignation of honest folk."

The Baron de Tirechappe folded up his manuscript and said: "Well, what do you think?"

"I think...I think that perhaps, in the case of an accident, the situation of the tamer could not be much more agreeable than that of the lion, and that..."

"Come on, my dear Monsieur—don't talk to me about those people! Trying in a cowardly fashion to provoke...never mind! Let's talk instead about your admission to the bosom of our dear Animalophilic Society. I'll propose tour candidature at the next meeting—and in order not to forget..."

The Baron took out his notebook.

"We were saying, Monsieur that your name is...?"

"Nobody," replied the man with green eyes, in the most natural tone.

"And you live?"

"Nowhere."

VIII. Monsieur Nobody

The Baron de Tirechappe started in a manner that translated the surprise caused to him by that double response eloquently.

"Nobody! Nowhere!" he repeated, with an evident hint of suspicion.

The man with green eyes did not seem to perceive it.

"I don't live anywhere, for the simple reason that I only arrived in Paris this morning. My name is Nobody because no one has wanted to call me anything else."

"But you must have..."

"Another name? Yes, once...a long time ago. A noble name. One day—it's quite funny—I learned that a schemer had taken the same name as me. It's very funny! I launched a lawsuit against him. Unfortunately, I'd lost some of the authentic documents that could have...it's very funny...could have established my rights. He, the schemer, had probably had false ones fabricated, in one of those ancestor shops that have never ceased their petty commerce, in spite of all the measures taken against them. He also had a great deal of money. I had very little. He hired the best advocates; I was obliged to content myself with the humblest. In brief, he won and I lost. He was recognized as the sole authentic possessor of the name that did not belong to him, and I was expropriated of the one that belonged to me. That's why—it's very funny, isn't it?—I

167

now call myself Monsieur Nobody. Monsieur Nobody! Ha ha ha!"

The man with green eyes burst into loud laughter.

"You've come to Paris to seek employment, then?" asked the Baron, gently disengaging his arm from that of his interlocutor.

"To seek employment, as you say."

"Oh, my God! What a scatterbrain I am! Just now, when I invited you, I'd forgotten that I'm due at seven o'clock at a meeting of the Association of the Friends sod the Porcine Race. I'm truly sorry, my dear Monsieur, but I hope that we'll meet again...that we'll run into one another again... I'm sorry, but I'm late, and I need to hurry."

"The art of protecting animals and obtaining several decorations in reward," muttered Monsieur Nobody, watching the singular Baron draw away at a rapid stride. "In fact, the Monsieur is right to cherish animals and mistreat humans. For him, it's the correct way of practicing love of his own kind..."

Médor protested against that disobliging assimilation with a growl.

IX. The Society of Saint Torquemada

After having given satisfaction to the sentiments inspired in him by the doctrine of the advocate of lions, Monsieur Nobody resumed walking.

While he walked he appeared to be reflecting, and his reflections were translated into fragments of monologue emitted every three paces or so.

"A bad start...! So, people never change... Employment... He was right...I need one. And soon...! Which? Since the time when..."

Suddenly, he stopped in front of the door of a vast house, on which was inscribed, in golden letters:

SOCIETY OF SAINT TORQUEMADA
HEADQUARTERS

In addition, to either side of that majestic entrance, pious and evangelical mottoes were inscribed.

One the right, there was:

Come to me, you who are suffering!

And to the left:

Help one another!

Finally, a poster attached to the wall addressed itself to passers-by in these terms:

SOCIETY OF SAINT TORQUEMADA

Of all the virtues, charity is the most practical and the most agreeable to the Eternal; of all the duties therefore, charity is the one whose exercise ought to be the sweetest to humans. Thus, it is exclusively for a charitable purpose that the Society of Saint Torquemada had been constituted.

In the bosom of a city like present-day Paris, which is seventy-five leagues around and has nineteen million inhabitants, poverty and needs of every sort have inevitably followed a dolorous progression. Inevitably, too, in the midst of that immense gulf, unfortunates have become more difficult to find, drowning, so to speak, in the abysms of egotism.

The Society of Saint Torquemada has devoted the intelligence and activity of all its members to the research and the relief of its brothers in humanity. It is not only by means of alms that it comes to their aid. To those who can no longer earn their daily bread, the almoner does indeed hold out an ever-open purse; but to those who can and want to work, the Society offers something even better: honorable labor for all. Disposing, by virtue of its almost infinite connections, of positions of every sort and all remunerations, it invites persons who desire it to present themselves at its offices between mid-

day and six o'clock, where more ample information will be furnished.

On behalf of the members of the Administrative Council
The Secretary.

"Damn it! That's well said and well thought!" exclaimed Monsieur Nobody. "I was wrong to speak ill of the human species, and it's my lucky star that steered me in this direction. It's strange...it seems to me that the name of Torquemada evoked memories in history quite different from those... Anyway, let's go in."

And, in conformity with his own injunction, he went into the beneficent society's house.

"What does my brother desire?" asked a porter, whose uniform was half way between those of a beadle and a sacristan, blocking his path.

"I desire to talk to the Director."

"Monsieur the Director is in Rome at present."

"With the Deputy Director, then."

"Monsieur the Deputy Director is at the church."

"The Administrators?"

"The Administrators are all at the prize-giving at Convent Number Fifty-Six of the Holy Order of the Jesuit Fathers."

"To whom, then, might one address oneself?"

"To Monsieur the Secretary General, who had just returned from the Archbishop's residence."

"Then I'd like to see Monsieur the Secretary General."

"Ninth courtyard, third stairway on the left."

X. The Devotion Bank

The house of the Society of Saint Torquemada was a veritable public administration. Everywhere, Monsieur Nobody encountered people coming and going, with mysterious and harassed expressions, who exchanged conventional signals with one another. Many of them were heading toward a wing of the building holding little pieces of paper in their hand, and soon coming out again, counting the money that they had just received.

Monsieur Nobody, struck by the strange appearance of everything he saw, arrived at the Secretary General's office with a certain apprehension.

The Secretary General, nestled comfortably in a large armchair, raised an investigative gaze toward the stranger who presented himself before him, and then, almost immediately, lowered his eyelids and resumed the meek attitude that he had initially displayed. At the same time, he bowed humbly and said: "May the peace of the Lord be with you, my brother!"

"I have the honor of saluting you, Monsieur," replied Monsieur Nobody, simply. "I am nothing and I would like to try to become something. I was passing by the door of this house just now, and I read our institution's beautiful profession of faith. You offer help to anyone who requests it, and work to anyone who desires it. I have need of both, and promise you in advance a loyal and eternal gratitude."

"You were right, my brother, to have confidence. You were right, for those who are with us grow thanks to us, and those who are against us also perish thanks to us."

At that moment, an employee came in holding some documents in his hand.

"Monsieur Secretary, these are the day's accounts.

"We have twelve hundred five-franc confession tickets, reimbursed in cash;

"Item, five hundred francs in provisions and chattels;

"We have paid out two thousand presence chips for the novena of Saint Trophime;

"Item, two thousand four hundred presence chips for the sermons of various preachers;

"Plus, nine hundred pyre premiums, for copies of works of philosophy that have been brought to us for burning.

"Finally, three thousand francs for each to our pamphleteers, for virulent responses to the latest work by an enemy of the temporal power.

Would you care to verify the total, Monsieur Secretary, and approve the inscriptions."

"That's fine. Go!"

The employee left.

Monsieur Nobody opened his eyes wide.

"As you see, my brother," said the Secretary General, returning to him, "our Devotion Bank is now a thriving enterprise."

"Pardon me, Monsieur—what bank?"

"That's true; you're not yet initiated. As I told you: with us, everything; against us, nothing. By means of the monetary currency of the confession ticket, we hold three-quarters of the families of artisans. Those tickets, redeemable at our cash-desk, each to the value of five francs, are also accepted as currency by all the suppliers of the association. Similarly the chips of presence at sermons, masses and other exercises of piety. An admirable institution, my brother! The faith was dying. We are reanimating it, and by concentrating its strength, we are making it the most powerful of political instruments. It's necessary for everyone to take account of us, for the time being. In any case, we'll initiate you fully when you've taken your place in our ranks. I'll read you the formula of the oath..."

"I don't know, Monsieur," Monsieur Nobody put in, "to what oath you're referring. I simply desire a modest position that will permit me to employ my faculties and earn my living honorably..."

"I've understood perfectly, and I'll read you the formula: 'In the name of the most holy Intolerance and the most holy Fanaticism, I swear...'"

"I'll never swear that."

"Are you a false brother, then?" exclaimed the Secretary General, with a start. "A spy? A freethinker?"

"I don't know whether I'm a freethinker, but I know that I intend to maintain the freedom to think what I please."

"Blasphemy and abomination! A Voltairean!"

"An honest man. What does the rest matter to you?"

172

"What does it matter to me? He has the audacity to mock."

"The realm of charity, so far as I know, has no State religion."

"Well, we don't care about your charity. If you think that we hand out our money for the pleasure of growing the seeds of ingratitude...! We're businessmen, you understand: serious people. Sale and purchase...giving, giving..."

"I understand now. You've invented bearer convictions and consciences at ten per cent."

"You dare to insult me! Get out!"

"I was about to solicit the favor."

"Enough, Monsieur."

"Too much, in fact..."

"Just get out!"

And, quivering with rage, the Secretary General aimed a kick at poor Médor.

"You're mistaken," said Monsieur Nobody, turning round and staring coldly at the white-faced devotee. "It's not him who's the Voltairean."

Frightened by that brazen glare, the Secretary General hastened to run into the next room.

IX. The Café Croesus

When Monsieur Nobody found himself back on the street, where the hypocritical poster of the Society of Saint Torquemada continued to beguile passers-by, night had come—and probably an appetite.

Indeed, he appeared, for a few moments, to be summoning up his memories, in order to orientate himself, and then he headed toward the Petits-Boulevards. That was the name given, in 1901, to the promenade extending from the Bastille to the Madeleine, in order to distinguish it from the other boulevards, the shortest of which was more than twenty kilometers long.

The Petits-Boulevards, which had been respected because of their ancient reputation, where then rented to a speculator who had established a café-restaurant there, known by the name of the Café Croesus.

The Café Croesus occupied all the shop-fronts on both sides of the Petits-Boulevards. Lunches and dinners were served in the rooms on the right-hand side. Wines, beer and billiards occupied the left-hand side from the old July column to the Rue Royale.

Numerous customers were sitting at the tables—so numerous that Monsieur Nobody was obliged to go all the way from the Chaussée-d'Antin to the rooms occupying the location previously known as the Boulevard Saint-Martin to find a place.

The meal that he had attested that, to the other qualities which one might already suspect, he added an exemplary sobriety: a simple soup, two modest dishes, a humble dessert and a candid half-bottle. After which, he rang for the waiter in order to ask for the bill.

"Coming, Monsieur, coming!" replied the faithful servant, hastening to go and cast a glance into the neighboring rooms.

Monsieur Nobody rang for a second time.

"Coming, Monsieur, coming."

A third.

"Coming, Monsieur, coming!"

Fortunately, the Café Croesus was a well-run business, which ensured that Monsieur Nobody did not have to wait as long as at a second-rate establishment. At his tenth appeal, the water came running.

He was holding an enormous placard at least thirty centimeters long.

"Waiter, I asked for the bill."

"Precisely, Monsieur. I've brought it. Here it is."

"What! That's it? You've made a mistake—that's evident merely by the format of the paper. My dinner only consisted of..."

"Our organization, Monsieur, never makes mistakes!"

And the waiter, drawing himself up to his full height like a majestic goose, held out the monumental account to his customer.

"Thank you, my friend, but there are no small savings, and your employer is wrong to waste so much paper for two meager dishes. It would be better to..."

Monsieur Nobody did not finish. He had just perceived the error he had made, and which the paper was utilized *in extenso*.

He read there, in fact:

ROOM 595
Table 14,863

Tablecloth....................................20 fr.
Napkin...10
Spoon..15
Fork..15
Knife...10
Glass...10
Plates..40
Salt and pepper...............................5
Mustard..5
Oil and vinegar...............................5
Toothpicks....................................5
Wine...50
Soup...15
Beefsteak.....................................35
Butter for cooking...........................15
Fried sole.....................................50
Parsley for ornamentation..................15
Cheese...15
Mouthwash...................................10
View of the Boulevard while dining,
    48 minutes at 60 fr. per hour............18
Politeness of waiter..........................15

Two smiles from lady at counter on
    Entrance and exit at 10 fr. each.........<u>20</u>
Total   398 fr.

"But, waiter...," Monsieur Nobody tried to object, on completing that terrifying list.

"If you please, Monsieur, have we forgotten to include something on Monsieur's bill?"

"Forgotten...!!!"

"In that case, if Monsieur has no error to point out, might I ask Monsieur to yield the table to a family that is waiting?"

"Pardon me, my friend: one simple observation. The wine is advertised on your menu at forty francs a bottle. I only had half a bottle and you've charged me fifty francs."

"Exactly, Monsieur; the difference is for the trouble taken in refilling the bottle."

"That's fair, waiter. One more thing. The owners must make a rapid fortune here."

"So-so, Monsieur. The one before last took a good three months, the last two."

"Two or three months is, indeed, a little long.. Well, my friend, would you care to inform your master on my behalf of a means of enriching himself more rapidly still."

"A means that..."

"Yes, my friend. My God, nothing is simpler. Tell him quite imply to take up a position in the morning at the corner of one of the busiest streets in Paris and there, with the collaboration of all his waiters, to take by force the purse of each passer-by. That same evening, he'll have enough to retire to his estates. Adieu, my friend—don't fail to carry out my commission."

After which, Monsieur Nobody paid the bill—and then, with a bow replete with urbanity, took his leave of the bewildered and open-mouthed waiter.

XII. The Giant Hotel

In the year 1901, Paris had broken overtly with the paltry traditions of the previous century, especially with regard to establishments designed to accommodate visiting provincials and foreigners.

It had been understood that for a city of seventy-five leagues around, it would be shameful to have maintained, for that purpose, the miserable small-scale hovels that were known as the Hôtel du Louvre or—probably by virtue of antiphrasis—the Grand Hotel.

Hotels of real size had, therefore, been constructed in several places. The latest, and the least unworthy of a self-respecting capital, was the Giant Hotel.

The Giant Hotel occupied, in the most central quarter of Paris, the site of what had once been the town of Versailles.

After having demolished all the buildings, felled all the trees and filled in all the water features that recalled the backward era of Louis XIV, an Anglo-Asiatic-Oceanian company had build in their stead and in their place a magnificent quadrilateral of carved stone, which numbered thirty-three thousand windows on each of its facades. The whole was divided up into furnished rooms and apartments.

In order that no comfort should be lacking the residents of the Giant Hotel, it had its own internal abattoirs, a gasplant, churches of all religions, a hospital and a cemetery. All the commodities of life, including death!

In the beginning, a railway had been constructed on each floor to transport the hotel residents to their respective domiciles, but several crashes having taken place between the guests' trains, a new system had since been adopted. The latter consisted of patented pneumatic tubes, through which, with a single thrust of a tampon, everyone could be transported almost instantaneously: a truly magnificent system whose inventor had died of poverty, but whose exploiter was in the process of banking formidable profits.

It was at the Giant Hotel that, four minutes after his exorbitant meal, a helicopter-omnibus deposited Monsieur Nobody and his companion, Médor.

A hundred gentleman in formal dress were stationed under the main porch; they were the domestics on duty. Monsieur Nobody hesitated to address himself to any of those unknowns, far better dressed than he was, whom he mistook for persons of distinction, but one of them came forward.

"An apartment for Monsieur? Something comfortable? In the six thousand francs a day range? No? A simple room, then, at a moderate price. I can see what Monsieur needs: our best bargain. Five hundred francs a day. It's sufficient… One traveler, at five hundred. Southern corridor, tenth kilometer-post, sixteenth floor…number 124395. Go! Boom!"

At the same time, the domestic in the embroidered frock-coat blew into a bagpipe similar to those employed by the employees of nineteenth-century railways. A trap-door swung open beneath Monsieur Nobody's feet, before he had time to accept or refuse, and he found himself hurled by a powerful force into a tube whose exit was situated at room 124935, sixteenth floor, southern corridor, tenth kilometer-post.

As soon as he had touched the floor of the room, engineered like the understage of a magical theater, a machine dispossessed him in the blink of an eye of his hat, umbrella, his overcoat…and, in brief, undressed him completely.

A second movement of the mechanism deposited him on his bed, a third pulled up the covers and a fourth unfurled on the ceiling a gigantic serial novel in a hundred and ten parts. It was the last word in putting someone to sleep. It was impossible to resist; it was necessary to sleep—which, sage was he was, Monsieur Nobody resigned himself to doing.

XIII. Budgeting

The following day, the mysterious hero, whom our story encountered a trifle abruptly in the middle of a Parisian street, was up at daybreak.

Briskly, he put on his clothes, which had been cleaned by an electric brusher, hurriedly patted the thickness of his jacket as if to assure himself of the presence of some object of value, slit the seam of the lining and took out a wad of paper. He sat down in front of the desk that decorated his domicile.

"A hundred thousand...two hundred thousand...three hundred thousand...five hundred thousand...a million! I am, in total, and by way of a unique resource, the possessor of one million francs, which I have in banknotes, and which I've succeeded in preserving from all searches. Given the cost of living in Paris, that's just about enough to live on for a month perhaps two, by dint of privations. After that, poverty!

"It's therefore necessary that within the next ten days I find some means of subsistence. Come on! Courage!

"And to commence economies, let's get out of this hotel and look for a mansard in some remote quarter where I can install a bed for the necessary and a chair for the superfluous. In walnut, obviously—with a million, it's necessary not to offer oneself the luxury of mahogany.

"Let's go!"

Monsieur Nobody folded his banknotes up into a packet again, replaced the packet in the lining of his jacket, paid the five hundred francs he owed for the night he had spent, plus a hundred francs for the domestic in the frock-coat, and went into the street.

Just as he set foot outside, however, he stopped. "Oh, my God! What about Médor? Médor! Médor!"

Are you looking for your dog, Monsieur?" asked the domestic, in a mocking tone.

"Yes, my friend."

"Well, it's not worth the trouble. I made a mistake and sent him with the luggage of an American visitor who has just left. By now, your pooch will already be in New York." In a lower voice, he added: "What! As if it were necessary to lavish attention to a pauper who gives you a five-louis tip. He's a good one, the man with the green eyes!"

Fortunately for the comedian, the man with the green eyes did not hear him. It was as if he were absorbed in sad reflections.

Finally, making an effort and shaking his head, he said: "Poor Médor! It's decidedly impossible to hang on to a friend in Paris...even one with four legs."

XIV. The Real Estate League

A mansard in some corner! That was easy enough to say, but infinitely more difficult to find in the Paris of 1901.

In fact, property-owners—with the sagacity that has always honored that estimable corporation—had employed the following reasoning:

"According to the most unanimous statistics, the number of citizens enjoying a mediocre ease is a thousand times greater than that of rich citizens; that of poor citizens is a hundred thousand times greater than that of citizens enjoying a mediocre ease. Therefore, we are going to fabricate all our properties as if the entire population consisted exclusively of rich citizens."

This judicious plan could not fail to produce the most fortunate results in the interest of the masses, because, seeing that they would no longer be able to find anywhere to live, the poor would be obliged to make arrangements to enrich themselves.

They had, in consequence, built palaces in which everything had been sacrificed to appearance. Thanks to the progress of industry, which, in the twentieth century, as applied uniquely to methods of falsification, they had built twenty-story houses constructed in imitation stone, with floors in imitation iron covered in imitation wood, and walls enlivened from top to bottom with imitation decorations. It was fragile, but flashy.

No more was required to serve as a pretext for the most exorbitant rents. What more could the hearts of property-owners desire?

By virtue of a natural reprisal, no one came to take up residence in these imitation palaces but imitation rentiers with imitation fortunes, who paid their rent with an imitation of regularity. The landlords, however, had not wanted to give in, and maintained their derisory prices with an obstinacy worthy of a worse fate.

To that effect, they had even formed an association known by the name of the Real Estate League, every member of which promised, by the most violent oaths, never to lower a rent, and to increase them, not only every time an opportunity presented itself, but whenever it was possible to provoke one.

The authorities—which scrupulously forbade workers to unite, even two at a time, under threat of the most severe penalties, in order to demand an increase in wages—had, by means of a decree full of solicitude, welcomed the Real Estate League as an institution of public utility.

You will not be surprised, therefore, that in such conditions, Monsieur Nobody had covered sixty leagues since the morning, as many on foot as by the means of locomotion then in usage, without being able to locate four walls and a ceiling to shelter his head.

The hazards of that research had taken him a little way out of the capital.

Fatigued and almost discouraged, he was following at a slow pace the 14,976[th] Boulevard, leading from the Étoile of the Arc de Triomphe to the suburb of Pontoise. The arrondissement of Paris bearing that name had been formed by the recent annexation of the town of the same name.

Although the extremity of the boulevard in question had only been pierced a week before, its entire extent was already fitted out, finished off and lit by gas. Sixty houses had been built there since the day before by the methods of instantaneous construction patented (without government guarantee) by an engineer. One of those houses struck Monsieur Nobody by its modest aspect relative to all those he had seen, and, resolved to make one last attempt, in despair of his cause, he accepted the invitation of a notice that said: *Apartments to Let. Apply presently to...*

XV. Monsieur the Governor

On going into the new house on the Boulevard de Pontoise, Monsieur Nobody searched in vain for an indication as to whom he ought, in the words of the notice to "apply presently."

He only perceived, in a magnificent drawing room situated on the ground floor to the right of the entrance, a liveried domestic occupied in dusting two superb Japanese vases placed on a Boulle sideboard. Guided by the livery, and naturally inferring from the costume in question that he was dealing with a well-dressed porter, he said: "Pardon me, Monsieur, are you the concierge?"

The domestic jumped as if he had been bitten by a snake, stood up straight, placing the end of his feather duster on his hip, and looked the impertinent individual who had permitted himself that blasphemy up and down.

"Who are you calling a concierge, my man? Know that my master, only last week, had a lout who had called him by that name in public imprisoned for defamation. Concierge! You're lucky he didn't hear you."

"Really?"

"Concierge!"

"Believe that I had no injurious intention..."

"Concierge!"

Would you care to inform me, then, of the title by which I ought to address the person here who has the function of talking to strangers, receiving the post and administering the necessary shocks to the exit cordon?"

"The title of governor."

"In that case, I'd like to talk to the governor."

"To Monsieur the Governor."

"To Monsieur the Governor, then!"

"He's busy—it's his Monday."

"What?"

"I said that it's his Monday. He receives visitors on that day. Is there some message that I can give him?"

"I'd like..."

"Would you prefer to speak to Monsieur the Governor's clerk?"

"It's about a tenancy."

"A tenancy. Write a request for an audience with Monsieur the Governor. I'll take it to him, and if he judges it appropriate to disturb himself, I'll take you to his study."

"A request for an audience to be allowed to visit an apartment that I want to rent?"

"The etiquette applies to everyone. There are ready-printed forms on that table, Fill one in, or else...."

"I'll fill one in, Monsieur the Valet de Chambre of Monsieur the Governor..."

After waiting for about half an hour, Monsieur the Governor's domestic came to say that his master would consent to accord him five minutes of conversation.

Monsieur Nobody was introduced into a study decorated with works of art, expensive bronzes and paintings by masters. All of that came from gifts imposed on the tenants. For the custom of the good old days that had removed in advance ten per cent of every consignment of wood had been extended, and it was now from every change of residence that Monsieur the Governor had the right to an object of his own choice.

Monsieur the Governor made his future administratee a little sign of the hand, picked up his pince-nez and whistled a tune from an operetta.

"You have the intention of being admitted to reside in my house?"

"I have the intention," replied Monsieur Nobody, "of your admitting to accommodate me."

"The first formulation is the only one in conformity with the social hierarchy, and I do not tolerate anyone trampling on my prerogatives."

"Have no fear of that, Monsieur the Governor. I would only like Your Excellency to tell me what he has for rent at present."

"On the eleventh overlooking the courtyard, three rooms, counting the cellar, plus a maid's room under the eaves. Three hundred and ninety thousand francs."

"And only taking the maid's room?" asked Monsieur Nobody.

Monsieur the Governor adjusted his pince-nez, in order to make sure that his Grandeur was not being mocked.

"And only taking the maid's room?" our friend repeated, with his imperturbable phlegm.

"You're seriously saying…?"

"That I don't have three hundred and ninety thousand livres to offer you every twelve months…all too seriously, alas."

"In fact," murmured Monsieur le Governor, "tenancies becoming so difficult…it might be as well..." He raised his voice: "For the maid's room alone, ninety thousand francs."

"That's a little dear."

"A little dear! In a quarter like ours..."

"A rather distant quarter," Monsieur Nobody objected.

"Distant! The Boulevard de Pontoise! When you're forty-eight kilometers from the Place du Palais-Royal! A mere stroll!"

"I don't deny it."

"Not to mention that a league from here you have a steam-fiacre station, and two leagues away the American electric omnibus and the aerostatic cabs."

"That is, in fact, quite convenient."

"And the air, Monsieur!"

"Is the air good?"

"Is the air good! But you're almost in the country. From the skylight of your room you can see a house eleven kilometers away that has a garden. You won't find many places in Paris from which one has such a view!"

"Are there any natural trees?" asked Monsieur Nobody, with perfect amiability.

"Certainly. If you insist, we can guarantee them in your rental agreement."

"That consideration has made up my mind. If you'll be kind enough to show me the room…"

Monsieur the Governor smiled indulgently, like a man who sees an Iroquois committing a monstrosity whose extent he does not understand, and summoned his clerk.

"Pray inform Jean that I've authorized Monsieur to be escorted by him. After that, bring me your daily report on the conduct of my tenants.

The clerk bowed profoundly and led Monsieur Nobody—who bowed to the clerk in his turn—away.

XVI. The Interrogation

"Now, sit down there," the concierge-governor instructed Monsieur Nobody, when the latter had come back down from the eaves, where the room he wanted to occupy was located. "We can say that the let suits you; now we're going to see whether you suit the let. My clerk will write down your responses."

"Damn!" remarked Monsieur Nobody. "You're treating me like a guilty party. Is it because I'm committing the sin of coming to live in your house?"

Monsieur the Governor deigned to smile at that observation, and, pursuing the interrogation, said: "You have no papers?"

"Papers? No," Monsieur Nobody replied, with a hint of embarrassment. "But since the room has none either."

"You'll have to pay three years in advance, then. You're not married?"

"No."

"You have no children?"

"No."

"Dogs?"

"No."

"Birds?"

"No."

"Flowers?"

"No."

"Furniture?"

"No."

"What, no! I meant to ask you, in fact, whether you have any personal property."

"Since I'm paying three years in advance..."

"That's not enough; you'll have to pay four."

"All right, four."

"You don't play any musical instrument?"

"No, thank God!"

"You don't sing?"

"Sometimes."

"That's a fault."

"But very quietly."

"So long as I can't hear anything! That's sufficient; having passed the oral examination, you're received as a tenant."

"Oh, Monsieur the Governor, believe in my eternal gratitude for the honor that you're granting me—payable in advance," said Monsieur Nobody, with his imperturbable mockery.

XVII. The Tenants' Code

"One moment!" exclaimed Monsieur the Governor, on seeing that his administratee was about to get to his feet.

"What now?"

"I shall have the privilege"—he took off the velvet skull-cap that he had been wearing until then—"of acquainting you, by way of conclusion, with the clauses of the Code drawn up by His Highness the owner of this house. Will you please stand up during the reading."

And the governor began:

"Code of Tenancy, revised, corrected and considerably augmented. Preface: In a tormented epoch like ours, an epoch when the most sacred principles are trampled underfoot, when al respect is unappreciated, it is important to reestablish and reconstitute the discipline of tenancy on solid foundations.

"We, Dominique Ustazade Vautour, descendant of the most illustrious and most ancient stock of property-owners, august and certified representative of the right of the riches, have decreed and decree, in the plenitude of our despotism:

"Paragraph One: Every tenant is a being physically as well as morally inferior to his proprietor, and therefore owes us veneration and obedience.

"Two: Every tenant of our house must submit beforehand to an oral examination in the presence of our delegates.

"Three: In this examination, the preliminary questions having been treated fundamentally, there is no need to return to them here, and it remains understood that our tenant is agreed to be devoid of wife, children, dogs, pianos and other domestic accessories.

"Four: Our tenant, before taking possession of the let that we have been generous enough to allow him to rent in our building, must promise by notarial deed not to contract any ulterior marriage from which infractions of the preceding paragraph might result.

"Five: As it is recognized that a death saddens a building, and might diminish its value by giving rise to suspicions of unhealthiness; and as, in addition, the placing of funereal hangings embarrasses the vicinity of the property, because the nails they necessitate damage the walls; out tenant will be obliged, before entering, to submit to the examination of one of the physician-surgeons of the United Association of Proprietors, also known as the Real Estate League, which physician will establish that his perfect state of health does not inspire any fear of imminent death.

"Six: In consequence of the considerations listed in the previous paragraph, as soon as a tenant falls ill in our house, we shall be authorized by right to have him transported to the nearest hospital.

"Seven: Any tenant who pronounces the word 'repair' or 'reduction' will be, by virtue of that fact alone, and with full entitlement, be expelled from our property.

"Eight: When it pleases us to visit our property, our tenants must, standing bare-headed, form a line in our courtyard as we enter and exit.

"Nine: Our tenants must also send us a bouquet and a gift on our saint's day and the anniversary of our birth,

"Ten: And likewise to our spouse on her feast day and birthday.

"Eleven: Likewise on the feast days and birthdays of our children, grandchildren, uncles, aunts nephews, nieces, cousins and other relatives of any degree.

"Twelve: To that effect, each of our tenants, when he enters our building, will be given a complete list, with names and addresses, of all the members of our august family.

"Thirteen: Gifts will equally due to them on New Year's Day.

"Fourteen: All these gifts will be regulated and priced in accordance with a proportional scale appended to all our tenancy agreements.

"Fifteen: We reserve the right to add, as and when we discover the necessity, new dispositions to the ones herein related.

"Sixteen: Our governor and his wife are solidly charged with supervising the strict execution of the present decree.

"Made in our residence in Paris. Dominique Ustazade Vautour."

Replacing the Tenants' Code in a drawer and replacing his velvet cap on his head, the governor-concierge added: "Now, Monsieur, you may boast of dealing with an accommodating proprietor, whose like is rarely seen any longer!"

"I'm even inclined to believe that nothing similar has ever been seen," agreed Monsieur Nobody.

"Now sign," ordered the concierge-governor, without suspecting the possibility of irony hidden in the remark. "Eh? What are you writing there?"

"Nobody."

"What, Nobody?"

"Of course; it's my name. Ha ha! It's very funny. It astonishes everyone! Of course, yes, I once had another name... a noble name... One day...it's very funny...ha ha ha...!"

And the man with green eyes repeated, with outbursts of laughter, the story that we have already heard him tell.

The memory of those misfortunes definitely had the effect of cheering him up.

XVIII. The Reign of Advertising

Faithful to his program—and as a man who had no time to waste—Monsieur Nobody, once installed, resolved to set out on campaign immediately.

But to whom should he address himself?

That question was not exactly easy to answer for someone who did not possess, as he had said himself, any other protection than his own.

Fortunately, the sun of advertising was shining for everyone in the year of grace 1901. One could not take a single step without its radiance striking your eyes in passing—not in accordance with the humdrum methods of olden times, but in the most unexpected forms.

In fact, the high price of land having erased every unutilized wall from the surface of Paris, the poster of old had been obliged to ingenuity in order to find a refuge.

It had found twenty of them.

First of all, the sidewalks had been metamorphosed into agents of publicity. A company had undertaken the colossal enterprise of Bitumen-Advertisements.

To everyone who had a need to advertise anything whatsoever, the Bitumen-Advertising Company rented a certain number of square centimeters, in which mobile and unbreakable letters were incrusted, by a special method, which proclaimed the superiority of some shop or other, or some business or other.

In that fashion, Paris was no longer paved by anything but good inventions.

Then had come Advertising Vehicles: gigantic wagons on whose external walls the most various items of information were posted.

And then many other things.

But the last resort, which had conquered fashion most completely, was the system of Human Posters.

It must be admitted that the Human Poster was an admirable combination. It provided, simultaneously, affirmation and proof, promise and demonstration.

Thus, one encountered these living posters at every step.

One was walking around carrying a piece of wood over his shoulder, terminated by a placard thus conceived:

The best chocolate is PARRON CHOCOLATE!
To convince yourself, look at me.
For ten years I have nourished myself exclusively on that precious comestible.
In that ten years I have never had a single stomach ache, nausea or indisposition!
I will give five hundred thousand francs to anyone who can prove that he is fitter and more robust than me!
Doctors, physicians and other men of the art included in the amiable society in which I move have examined me and assured themselves that his delicious aliment has given me health and strength.
The best chocolate is PARRON CHOCOLATE.

Another, elegantly dressed, was holding a notice on which one read;

STOP!!! STOP!!!

AHA! AHA! AHA!

But it's admirable! But it's incredible! But it's implausible!

Have you ever seen a man looking as good as me?
No!

It's the nec plus ultra.
Why?

Because I'm dressed by THE HOUSE OF EIGHT NA-TIONS, garments made to measure or off-the-peg, everyday suits and evening suits.

All at RIDICULOUSLY CHEAP PRICES
And don't imagine that they're shoddy gods.
No tailor has ever supplied you with such fabrics.

If you doubt it, come closer, feel the velvet of my overcoat.

Suspend yourselves from my coat-tails.

THE HOUSE OF EIGHT NATIONS will pay an annual income of fifty thousand francs, via a notary, to anyone who can rip one of my seams!

A third had his hat surmounted by an escutcheon thus formulated:

I HAVE FALSE TEETH
You'd never suspect it, but it's true.
Do they disfigure me? No.
Do they prevent me from smiling graciously? No.
Do they hinder me while eating? No.
A thousand times no.

That's because they're from the workshop of illustrious Dargentigny, the prince of dentures.

Furthermore, there were not only poster-men but also poster-women.

One was covered with advertising trimmings, all labeled like a window-display in a fashion shop—with the result that on her dress one could read: *SILK POULT by the SIX MA-*

CAQUES STORES; on her bonnet: *MADEMOISELLE EVANGELINA, Fashions and Coiffures*; etc.

Another had, above her head, a sign cleverly attached to her hat, expressing itself in the following terms:

I'M SURE OF IT!!!
On seeing me, you said to yourself: What a Lovely Blonde!
I'M NOT BLONDE
I have hair dyed with the divine TINCTURE OF PARA-DISE, by Monsieur Lavandier, a chemist endorsed by numerous crowned heads.

Every specialty had its ambulant prospectuses, whose comings and goings offered the most grotesque glances imaginable—so grotesque that Monsieur Nobody, who was decidedly not up to date with Parisian mores, turned round in amazement, his eyes widening, every time he experienced a new encounter of that sort.

Suddenly, however, he stopped dead in front of an individual who was moving in the opposite direction.

XIX. The Fortunate 100,000

The individual in question was a poster-man like all the rest, but with a different specialty. The placard he was carrying on his shoulders expressed itself in the following terms:

I'VE MADE A HUNDRED THOUSAND FORTUNES!!!
Would you like an easy and lucrative employment?
Address yourself to
ME!
THE ONLY ONE IN PARIS
Literature, finance, administration, commerce. Industry, roads-and-bridges—in general, everything that concerns the estates of others; I have them all at the cheapest prices.

By virtue of my connections in the five continents of the world, I can furnish immediately the situation that anyone might desire who has confidence in my intermediation.

Ask, and you will be served. Have no fear of addressing yourself to me.

My affability and the distinction of my manners are known advantageously throughout the world.

Emoluments from a million to a billion!

WHOSE TURN IS IT NEXT?

The wording of that hyperbolic statement and the sonorous promises that it listed emphatically had, as you will understand, attracted Monsieur Nobody's attention.

He had read it with all the more interest because that tempting claim corresponded exactly to his secret desires.

However, with the sage reserve that we know him to possess, the man with green eyes would not have dared to approach the person in question had the other not taken the initiative.

Endowed with the flair typical of that sort of businessman, the broker of the fortunate hundred thousand had divined a potential client. He was not so stupid as to let prey that was on offer escape!

Thus, full of obsequious urgency, he greeted Monsieur Nobody with an engaging smile, and bringing to bear all his resources of persuasion. He said: "Did Monsieur say something to me?"

"Not at all."

"I was mistaken—no matter! I'll wager that it's Monsieur's lucky star that has placed him in my path, and that he will have the pleasure of owing the most brilliant fortune to my intervention."

"I have no need of a brilliant fortune. The strictly necessary will suffice for my ambition."

"The strictly necessary! Modesty combined with talent! For that well-developed forehead, those intelligent eyes, and that I-don't-know-what in a physiognomy that never deceives me, all affirm that I don't have any ordinary man before me."

"It seems to me, however, that I'm absolutely similar to others."

"One never knows oneself. But will you please reply to me without circumlocutions: you're looking for a position?"

"That's true."

"I have exactly what you need."

"By you don't know my..."

"I have what you need, I tell you. My repertoire is universal. If you're a physician, I can supply you with invalids by contract!"

"I'm not a physician."

"Advocate. I'll procure you cases from the earnings of which I'll only deduct half for my honoraria."

"No more."

"What do you mean, no more? I'm the only one who contents myself with such modest fees."

"I'm not denying that, Monsieur, and that wasn't the meaning I attached to my words. They simply signified that I'm no more an advocate than a physician."

"An engineer, then?"

"No."

"Salesman?"

"No."

"Café-keeper? I have superb businesses."

"No...

"What, then, is it that you desire to do?"

"I don't know, precisely."

"What do you mean?"

"The thing is, to be scrupulously exact..."

"Of course!"

"I've made the banal studies that don't lead to anything, because they have the pretention of leading to everything."

"I'm beginning to understand."

"I'm no cleverer or more stupid than the majority of my fellows. I possess vague notions of the most various subjects, but no special aptitudes for any of them."

"That's sufficient. I know your category. Once upon a time you'd have been qualified as déclassé. Today we have a new name for that ancient malady. You're what we call a *neuter*, because you don't belong to any classification or social genre."

"Neuter—so be it. That signifies that I'm only good for..."

"Not so fast. It's necessary not to throw in the towel..."

"However..."

"From the moment that you're not particularly attached to any one career, they're all equally open to you."

"You think so?"

"It's a mathematical deduction. Neuters have been seen to become great men, and they've been seen to die of hunger. Between those two extremes there's room for all attempts. Can you spell correctly?"

"What! Of course I can spell correctly."

"Very good. The advice I have to give you, then, is to become a man of letters."

"But I've never written a line."

"Excellent! You'll have preserved the virginity of your ideas."

"There's no evidence that I have any ideas."

"If you don't have any, you'll take those of others."

"But the others will complain."

"In that case, you'll reply. The quarrel will get heated. The public will flock, and you'll be famous within six months."

"To be frank, I don't like scandal."

"You'll acquire the appetite as you eat."

"I'd rather not eat."

"Ta ta ta!"

"I swear to you..."

"Oho! You have fixed principles. Poor luggage."

195

"Your servant, Monsieur..."

"Oh no! You're not getting away from me that easily."

"Permit me..."

"Permit me yourself—to do violence to excessive scruples."

"I can't."

"Oh well, since you don't want to exploit the ideas of others at any price, you won't refuse to be exploited by them. I have a superb place working for a feuilletonist. You'll write his books and he'll sign them. Food, lodgings, laundry..."

"I don't approve of being duped any more than being a duper."

"What a character!"

"It's mine."

"I see what you need, then. Address yourself on my behalf to the newspaper *The Satisfied*. It has need of a journalist.

"What is *The Satisfied?*"

"A highly-placed newssheet. You'll do marvelously there."

"Doing what?"

"Don't worry about that. What is expected of you will be explained when you've started the job."

"But..."

"Try, damn it! It won't hurt you, and you'll retain your freedom."

"On that condition..."

"Of course. Simply present this card to the editor-in-chief on my behalf. My organization has been supplying him for years."

"And when the card has been presented..."

"You'll be part of the editorial staff, and you'll only owe me gratitude..."

"You're extremely kind, Monsieur."

"Plus sixty-five per cent of your wages."

"Ah!"

"Only for the first ten years."

"Only!"

"Those are my tariffs, approved by the Prefecture of Police."

"And these tariffs are the same everywhere?"

"No—as I told you, they're more expensive elsewhere."

"I'll go to *The Satisfied*, then," sighed Monsieur Nobody.

"Excellent! Shake my hand..." And the agent extended his hand.

"What's the point, Monsieur," said Monsieur Nobody, taking a step back, "since I have nothing to put in it?"

XX. The Steam Newspaper

The Parisian press, in the year 1901, was far from the state of infancy in which it had been seen during the first six decades of the nineteenth century. The people of the new era could scarcely believe that there had ever been a barbaric era when newspapers, of a ridiculously small format, only appeared twice a day, in the morning and the evening. Mention of those tortoises of publicity made journalists burst out laughing.

Twice a day!

Now they appeared eighteen times a day, one edition per hour from six a.m. to midnight.

Thanks to the improvements made in electric telegraphy, people were informed almost instantaneously about all events, of whatever importance, happening anywhere on the surface of the globe.

If a mandarin was crushed by a pot of flowers falling on his head while passing through the main square in Peking at twenty minutes to noon, the bourgeois of the Rue Saint-Denis would be informed of it by the midday edition.

If the great chief of the Touaregs opened the session of his parliament in the center of Africa at two o'clock, his speech would be delivered to the printing presses by quarter past two.

Every print-run had the prices on the Honolulu stock exchange, the racing results from the Madagascar hippodrome and reports on the salons of Timbuktu.

Naturally, in order to meet the necessities of promptitude imposed by these incessant print-runs, it had been necessary to improve the means of material execution enormously. In that regard, however, no other newspaper had yet gone as far as *The Satisfied*, the paper at which Monsieur Nobody was to present himself, and where he was received as we are about to see.

XXI. The Satisfied

The offices of *The Satisfied* occupied a sumptuous building in front of which a boulevard had been pierced expressly, which opened a precious direct communication link between the said offices and the Ministry of the Press. That was the name of the special Ministry of recent creation whose exclusive purpose was to supervise the world of journalism.

The Satisfied—whose title made it a mystery to no one— was the organ devoted to the Ministry and, in general, everything concerning the government. In order to render its mission clearer, it had even added an epigraph to that title, consisting of the words: *So be it!*

Monsieur Nobody—who, as we know, was not well informed on Parisian matters—was completely ignorant of the approving specialty of that printed claque. Thus, he presented himself with the greatest candor to the Editor-in-Chief.

The latter examined the card that the agent had given his protégé as a means of introduction with a surly expression, and then said: "You want to work here?"

"Yes, Monsieur."

"In the advertising section?"

"No, Monsieur."

"For the latest news, then—you want to be a traveler in accidents?"

"What did you say?"

"Traveler in accidents."

"I don't know what that means, exactly..."

"You've never worked for a newspaper before, then? A traveler in accidents is employed to roam around Paris and its surroundings incessantly, in order to discover some disaster of which he can furnish us the first details. It's not a bad métier: fifty francs for a suicide, a hundred francs for romantic details of a nature to exceed a paragraph; a hundred and fifty francs for a traffic accident with slight injuries, two hundred for serious injuries and a supplement for a fatality; for a fire it's three hundred francs and so on, in conformity with a proportionate tariff. Some days, one can make a tidy sum."

"I don't make any claim to the contrary, Monsieur, but I'd prefer another kind of work."

"Would that, perchance, be political reporting?"

"I'd prefer that."

"You should have said so right away. We need someone for that at the moment."

"I'm glad of the coincidence."

"It's agreed, then."

"Permit me, Monsieur. Don't you want to give me a trial beforehand?"

"What would be the point?"

"To assure yourself that I'm capable of fulfilling the duties that you're assigning to me."

"There's no need."

"I would have done so, because I'm anxious about my inexperience."

"All right, if you absolutely insist. Sit there."

The Editor-in-Chief of *The Satisfied* pointed to three voluminous cylinders that occupied the corner of his office.

"You want me to sit there?" asked Monsieur Nobody, surprised.

"Yes."

"In front of those wheels?"

"Evidently."

"To do what?"

"To write an article, of course!"

"An article…"

"Isn't that what you've come to do?"

"Indeed."

"Well, rotate the lower cylinder…no, the middle one!"

"You want me to turn…"

"Come on, finish it. I'm in a hurry."

"I'd like nothing better than to finish it, Monsieur, but I believe there's some misunderstanding. I'm offering myself in the capacity of journalist…"

"Precisely—and I've accepted you as such, so rotate and let's get on with it."

Monsieur Nobody did not understand at all.

"Ah!" said the Editor-in-Chief. "Is it the case, by chance, that you don't know what the functions of a journalist are here?"

"They ought, it seems to me, consist of writing…"

"What! My poor Monsieur! You're not even aware of the improvements that *The Satisfied* has had the honor of inaugurating?"

"I confess it."

The Editor-in-Chief shrugged his shoulders. "Where the devil have you come from, my boy?"

At that question, Monsieur Nobody blushed slightly.

"Not to have heard mention of…then you honestly believed that we were still cast adrift in the routine of articles laboriously extracted from the interminable and ingrate labor of the pen? That was good enough for our worthy ancestors; in those days officious journalists strove painfully every morning to execute eulogistic variations on the governmental theme. We're way past that, thank God!"

"Would it be indiscreet to enquire where you are now?"

"Nothing simpler. A technologist of genius, one may say, was struck by the futility of the trouble that our forefathers went to in order to repeat the same thoughts endlessly. He studied the question, and soon acquired the certainty that all the politics of ministerial newspapers could be summarized by a few hundred formulae indefinitely reproduced. It was a flash of enlightenment! These formulae he arranged in series, and designed a superb machine in which they're all found, grouped in different aspects—and the Mechanical Conservative was invented."

"The Mechanical Conservative," repeated Monsieur Nobody, increasingly bewildered.

"That's the apparatus in front of you," the Editor-in-Chief of *The Satisfied* went on. "One of the marvels of modern industry! To have found a means of defending the great principles of order mechanically! Isn't that wonderful? As you can see, the cylinders are three in number.

"The first one—the bottom one—is the cylinder of Simple Approval. It contains phrases of reserved admiration, such as: 'This measure proves once again all the solicitude of the authorities for...'

"The second cylinder, the one in the middle, is the cylinder of Mild Eulogy, containing warmly sympathetic adverbs and heartfelt adjectives, such as 'The generous initiative that the government has just taken will contribute powerfully to...,' or 'This decree, an efficacious protector of the interests of society, will leave a profound and durable trace in history.'

"Finally, the third cylinder, the top one, is the cylinder of Enthusiasm and Wild Polemics. That one is only used on great occasions—when a revolutionary rag has attacked an official measure too harshly, or when it's a matter of getting through a difficult act or an unpopular war. Then one brings all its metaphors to bear, and leads the rearguard assault of its pompous phrases.

"It's on third cylinder that one finds paragraphs commencing: 'It is the prerogative of those contemptuous of the family and those with obstinately closed eyes to be unable to see the benefits with which they will be heaped, etc...,' or 'Our heart, which beats in unison with the heart of France, quivered with joy on learning that...'

"I have no need to tell you that it is necessary to be sparing with the effects of the third cylinder, and that it should only be employed with caution. The other two are amply sufficient for the necessities of current politics. The two of them are able to produce a hundred and forty combinations, forming a hundred and forty types of articles. By making use of the pegs that are fitted to the right and left of the apparatus, one obtains an equal number of variants. That's more than is necessary for the public!

"To make sure that you've grasped my demonstration, I'll carry out a trial before you. Let's suppose that the government has issued a decree restricting the liberty of the press. I place a piece of paper under the bottom cylinder and I rotate it..."

The Editor-in-Chief did indeed, begin to grind away like a barrel-organ player.

"There!" he said after a few moments. And he held out the printed sheet of paper to Monsieur Nobody.

The Mechanical Conservative had written: *We can only applaud the wisdom of which proof has just been given... etc., etc.*

"Let's suppose," the Editor-in-Chief went on, "that the decree, on the contrary, extends the liberty of the press. I place another sheet of paper and turn the same cylinder—and here goes!"

The second sheet was printed in its turn. The Mechanical Conservative said: *We sincerely congratulate Monsieur the Minister of the Press once again... etc...*

Monsieur Nobody read it, dazedly.

"You see," the Editor-in-Chief of *The Satisfied* continued, "that it's no more difficult than that. Now, turn it yourself."

Monsieur Nobody did not move.

"Turn it, then, damn it!"

XXII. By the Force of the Wrist

Monsieur Nobody was about to respond to the reiterated injunction when a journalist came into the Editor-in-Chief's

202

office. He seemed to be very excited, and was holding a copy of an unfolded newspaper in his hand.

"Have you read the article directed against us in the eleventh edition of *The Progressive?*"

"No."

"A formidable broadside."

"With regard to what?"

"With regard to our Parisian news item yesterday on 'The Infallibility of Public Functionaries.'"

"Show me."

"There, in the second column."

"Ah! So that's the way it is!" exclaimed the Editor-in-Chief of *The Satisfied*, having scanned the first lines. "They're challenging us! Well, they're going to see what wood we use to warm ourselves!"

So saying he had leapt in one bound to the third cylinder, which he began to maneuver.

Then commenced a pantomime rather difficult to describe. His arm moved as the angry words passed through his lips.

"*The Progressive* doesn't realize that it's dealing with men of conviction..."

Two turns of the cylinder.

"They'll learn to their cost..."

Three turns.

"That we're not political men devoid of consistency, who don't weigh their opinions..."

Four and a half turns.

"I want all Paris to be talking about our reply, written from the heart!"

At this point, the Editor-in-Chief of *The Satisfied* produced a continuous whirling until, doubtless judging that his heart had said enough, he stopped the machine.

"Take this piece to the presses straight away," he said to the journalist. We'll soon see whether the subversive doctrines of the whole society can prevail against the energy of good men..."

As if to punctuate the word "energy," the Editor-in-Chief rubbed his shoulder, genuinely fatigued by such an eloquent refutation. Then he turned to our hero.

"As for you, Monsieur, have you decided what you want?"

"I wanted, Monsieur," the man with green eyes replied, "to try myself in a profession that I consider to be one of the most noble, but I see that I was mistaken as to my abilities."

"You'll improve with practice."

"Excuse me, Monsieur, but I'll never have sufficient..."

"Talent?"

"No, sufficient biceps, to make a right-thinking journalist."

XXIII. Theatrical Decentralization

Our friend's career was thus abruptly interrupted before even having begun. He explained his difficulty to the agent to whom he had so unfortunately addressed himself—but the latter, whose serene assurance could not be troubled, did not flinch.

"I warned you that scruples would do you a bad turn. Never mind—at ease! In that case, politics isn't your thing, and you'd act wisely by renouncing it absolutely. The more I think about it, the more certain I am that you're cut out for pure literature."

"You think so?"

"I'd put my hand in the fire. Theatrical criticism, that's what you need."

"Criticism...but I haven't set foot in a theater for twenty years."

"Then you'll find great changes, but that isn't the question. *The Impartial* has asked me for a Monday columnist. Go there on my behalf, and you'll be brought up to date with that vocation."

"I'll go."

In fact, he did.

"My dear Monsieur, said the Editor-in-Chief of *The Impartial*, "I couldn't ask for anything better than to take you on. Only permit me to assure myself that you're able to fulfill the grave and elevated functions that I'm entrusting to you."

At the same time, he approached Monsieur Nobody and took his pulse.

"Not bad. Please stick out your tongue."

"My tongue?"

"If you please."

"That's it! A nice pink...now turn round... There!"

The Editor-in-Chief of *The Impartial* applied his ear to the back of his future collaborator.

"Cough."

"But I don't have a cold."

"Cough all the same."

"Hem! Hem!"

"More forcefully."

"Hem! Hem! Hem! Hem!"

"Chest cavity good. Deep breath... The lungs are sound... Sturdy constitution. That's perfect."

Throughout the duration of that medical examination, Monsieur Nobody had seemed to be constraining himself energetically, in order to disguise a visible embarrassment. He probably had his reasons for not liking medicine.

"That's perfect," repeated the Editor-in-Chief. "You're marvelously fit."

"You think so?" said the man with green eyes, with a sigh of satisfaction.

"Marvelously. That's already one of the indispensable qualities..."

"To produce good criticism?"

"Certainly, Monsieur."

"I confess that I can't grasp, at first glance, what analogy there might be between..."

"You don't grasp it...but it's necessary to have an iron constitution, my dear Monsieur, to stand up to the fatigues of the métier of twentieth-century dramatic criticism. It's necessary to stand up to the most abrupt changes of climate, brave epidemics, laugh at the most frantic voyages. It's necessary to think, eat and work on the move. Here one moment, fifty leagues away the next...oh, we're no longer in the epoch in which the pole of Monday columnists was the Odéon!"

"Is it necessary to go further than that?" murmured Monsieur Nobody, without taking the trouble to dissimulate his terror.

"You're joking! Is it necessary to go...here! Look at this evening's theater programs. There are thirty-seven premières."

"Thirty-seven!"

"One, a drama in twenty-seven tableaux at the Gaiety in San Francisco; one, a drama in twenty-eight tableaux at the Tahiti Ambigu; one, a drama in twenty-nine tableaux at the Tehran Porte-Saint-Martin...all those by Monsieur Dennery IV, one of our authors in vogue. At theaters in Lima, Astrakhan, Melbourne and Singapore there are new comedies by Monsieur Sardou III, a fellow who made a brilliant debut. At the Siberian Bouffes of Tobolsk, there are the premières of eleven operettas by the maestro Offenbach V..."

"All of them previously unperformed?"

"So the authors assure us..."

"And one is obliged to talk about all of them?"

"Certainly! We haven't contrived dramatic decentralization for nothing. Long live decentralization! Before that, our fashionable playwrights only had a miserable dozen theaters at their disposal. Now the world belongs to them. Monsieur Dennery IV, whom I just mentioned, produces twenty-five new dramas a day for export. So do the others! Oh, decentralization is an admirable thing!"

"For them," Monsieur Nobody agreed. "But how does one take account of so many works at the same time?"

In the telegraphic style—another progress. Nothing superfluous. Twenty words for twenty acts: *Gennaro. Drama Dennery IV. Lost child. Mother's cross. Plot to kill child. Mother arrives. Recognition. Final marriage. Absurd. Great success.* After which one passes on to another."

"Indeed, I can see how that simplifies the method. But to transport oneself..."

"The critic of *The Impartial*, my dear Monsieur, has his balloon-house, with a compressed-air automotor, thanks to which one can go around the world in fifty minutes."

XXIV. In which Monsieur Nobody thinks he has a Job

The Editor-in-Chief of *The Impartial* stopped, as if to make sure that that prospect did not frighten the newcomer, who was listening without flinching.

"Better and better," he continued, after that pause. "I have an idea that you'll suit my purpose. How many men have you killed?"

"But I haven't killed anyone, thank God!"

"Impossible!"

"What do you mean, impossible? Is it necessary in order to write dramatic criticism to have..."

"Certainly. Otherwise how do you expect that your appreciations would have any weight?"

"Well...by virtue of their sincerity."

"Rub up against the self-esteem of today's actors and authors! If they learn that you haven't dispatched half a dozen stout fellows in your duels, you'll receive a hundred cards a day."

"Why, if I only tell the truth?"

"In that case you'll receive two hundred."

"I don't believe it."

"And I assure you of it..."

"Oh well," said Monsieur Nobody. "If they arrive, I'll welcome them."

"And if someone kills you?"

"I'll regret it—without much regretting what I'll leave behind me."

"That's the way to talk. You're a brave man."

"Like everyone else."

"Not at all."

"Then so much the worse for everyone else."

"Bravo! You can start today. And above all, remember that the title of our paper is *The Impartial*."

"I'll remind you of it if necessary. With which theaters should I start?"

"With those that you wish."

"If that's the case, I ask your permission to give preference to those in Paris...a matter of getting under way. The North Pole won't lose anything by waiting."

"As you wish. By the way, what's your signature?"

"Nobody."

"That's a nice pseudonym."

"It's not a pseudonym—it's my name."

"Your name!"

"It's funny, eh? Very funny. Ha ha ha! I had another once, but it was taken from me. Ha ha ha!"

When Monsieur Nobody went out, he was still prey to the fits of bizarre hilarity that the most poignant moment of his life invariably caused him.

A singular man, in truth!

XXV. Living Phenomena

Many violent surprises were in store for Monsieur Nobody in the new profession that he had just embraced, because, for a man as little up to date as he was, the theater of 1901 was a veritable mine of incessantly-renewed astonishments.

When one does not have what one loves, says a proverb of the olden days, it's necessary to love what one has.

Twentieth century dramatics had made a broad application of it.

Literature being generally lacking, it had been necessary to look elsewhere.

And then everyone fell back on whatever he could.

There was a perpetual competition between directors of every sort to substitute for the lack of theatrical talent and satisfy the depravities of French taste.

Corneille, Racine, Molière and Victor Hugo, left in lamentable forgetfulness, were sleeping side by side in the dust of libraries. The jaded palates of the Parisians of the decadence required much stronger spices!

Monsieur Nobody began to acquire proof of that right away, merely by perusing the program of spectacles that the Editor-in-Chief of *The Impartial* had given to him. The first lines that struck his gaze were expressed as follows:

THEATER OF VIOLENT EMOTIONS
The Abandoned: A Melodrama

The role of the female lead will be filled by Mademoiselle Lodoïska, the bearded lady justly appreciated in the fairgrounds of the vicinity of Paris.

THEATER OF ENTANGLED FANTASIES
The Martyrs of Love

The administration has left no stone unturned to ensure the success of this original work. To add to the illusion and better depict the sufferings and ravages of an unfortunate passion, the role of the male martyr of love will be played by a *Veritable Human Skeleton* weighing only *28 kilos*. He is the last word in scenic illusion.

THEATER OF REALISM
The Knights of the Dagger
For the debut of Monsieur Gobinard,
star attraction of the Saint-Cloud Fair

At ten-thirty, the duel scene, which concludes with M. Gobinard's brilliant exercises. In that duel, whose like has never been seen, M. Gobinard will, within the full view of the audience, *swallow his adversary's sword*. There will be no increase in the price of seats.

The list continued in the same vein. Acrobatics having, it seemed, fused with art, the entire catalogue of these phenomena was there.

One theater announced an eleven-foot giant, another a female colossus, who would pass through the audience between the second and third acts, in order that the sincerity of her calves could be verified. At another, there was a strong man who broke thirty-kilo paving stones on the stage.

"Pooh!" said Monsieur Nobody, turning the page in disgust.

XXVI. The Tenor King

The reading of the future critic of *The Impartial* was, however, interrupted by a sudden tumult.

A whole crowd of men, women, old people and children, was running around shouting: "There he is! There he is!"

Windows opened on all sides, allowing glimpses of residents of both sexes in the most various indoor costumes.

Shopkeepers were standing on their doorsteps, climbing on to chairs in order to get a better view.

At the same time, at the opposite end of the street in which Monsieur Nobody was standing, a magnificent chariot approached drawn by eight richly-caparisoned horses.

Lounging in the chariot, nonchalantly extended in a triumphantly disdainful pose, was an individual of proud and superb attitude, decked with jewelry and precious stones, surrounded by thurifers that were emitting bursts of incense every five minutes.

Fifty well-dressed gentlemen were preceding or following it, while delivering themselves to the strangest manifestations. Some were weeping, some praying. Others were on their knees, and others rolling in the dust, putting on a show of wanting to be crushed by the wheels of the triumphant quadriga.

All these contortions were accompanied by cries, lamentations and pleas:

"In the name of Heaven, Immortal Man, listen to me!"

"I implore you, Divine Man, not to reject my supplication.!

"Do you need gold? Here it is. Speak! How much do you want...?"

"Eight sovereigns are burning with desire to see you..."

"Come with me!"

"With me or I'm lost."

"With me or I'll throw myself under the hooves of your horses."

"A hundred and fifty million for a smile!"

"Two hundred!"

"Five hundred!"

In speaking thus, the well-dressed gentlemen drew handfuls from large bags and extended their arms toward the individual in the chariot—but the latter, impassive, did not even seem to hear them. He continued smiling disdainfully while looking complacently into a mirror enriched with precious stones, which a slave was holding up in front of him.

On seeing that, all the members of the crowd garnishing the sidewalks, the windows and the shops joined their voices to those of the well-dressed gentlemen.

"Immortal Man, have pity on your humble vassals."

"Immortal Man, dart a compassionate glance at your prostrate subjects."

Monsieur Nobody had absolutely no idea what was going on, so he decided to question one of the most frantic of the worshipers.

"Excuse me asking, but is the Monsieur going abroad in that chariot some kind of potentate?"

"Better than that."

"A prince of the blood?"

"Better than that."

"A monarch."

"Better that that, Monsieur."

"What is he, then?"

"He's a tenor."

Monsieur Nobody thought that he had misheard, and in order to have it repeated he said: "What did you say, if you please?"

"He's a tenor," the fanatic repeated, waving his hat as the chariot passed by. Or rather, he's the ultimate in tenors."

"What, for a mere singer, everyone…"

"Who are you calling a mere singer?" replied Monsieur Nobody's interlocutor, as if indignant at the blasphemy. "The only man alive today capable of rendering a D from his chest?" The fanatic waved his that with a redoubled passion.

"Isn't it possible to do without a D from the chest?" asked Monsieur Nobody, naively.

"Do without! Monsieur—there is the response of the most intelligent people. Look at that urgent flood, in which all the social classes are confounded…"

"I've seen that sufficiently."

"Do without a D sharp! We'd rather shed the last drop of our blood. Yes, Monsieur, when a foreign land wanted to take him away from us recently, we made it a *casus belli*."

"But you'd willing let a man of misunderstood genius go abroad."

"Certainly. Men of genius can be replaced, while tenors…"

"And who are those Messieurs gesticulating and indulging in a thousand contortions in front of the chariot?"

"Theater directors who are all appealing to the precious subject—but he knows his worth, and he only sings when it pleases him, where it pleases him, and for the price that pleases him. Recently, the sovereign of a principality offer him the cross of an officer of his order to come and be heard at a soirée that he was giving for his court. He refused, Monsieur."

"Doubtless to give the German prince a lesson in common sense."

"No, Monsieur—because he wanted the grand sash! Long live our divine tenor! Long live the D from the chest!"

"Long live the D from the chest!" the people responded. "Long live our divine tenor."

"Long live French intelligence," said Monsieur Nobody, with a snigger.

XXVII. Dramatic Courtesans

The first specimens that had passed before Monsieur Nobody's eyes were not of a nature to edify him greatly on the count of the theater in 1901. It was, however, necessary that he inaugurate his new profession that same evening.

Simultaneously taking his courage and his theater program in both hands, therefore, he resumed searching the list of the five hundred and eighty auditoria contained in Paris since theatrical liberty had been definitively established there. An entire series of singular titles struck his gaze.

In fact, the program newspaper announced:

THEATER OF THE DEMI-MONDE
This evening, for the debut of Mademoiselle Antonia
THE DIAMOND TRAVELERS
A Fantastic Vaudeville

Note: Mademoiselle Antonia is the queen of fashion who possesses the largest known diamond. She appears in the fifth act with the famous necklace given to her by one of our princes of finance.

THEATER OF SLUTS
For the Performances of Mademoiselle de Saint-Chignon
THE MARQUISE'S RUBY
A Comedy

Note: Mademoiselle de Saint-Chignon, who defies all competition and whose reputation leaves nothing to be de-

sired, has the most dazzling collection of rubies of all the no-
tabilities of the genre. In the ballroom scene she will wear one
weighing 15 carat in her diadem. The administration has had a
facsimile made by the jewelry factory, which will be on sale.

THEATER OF CUCKOLDS
Great Success
THE INFERNO OF AMOUR
A Study in Parisian Mores

The role of Amour will be played by Mademoiselle
Pichenette, also known as the Goddess of the Young Casino.
Mademoiselle Pichenette, one of the most fortunate beauties
of the gallant world, comes to the theater every evening in a
coupé whose eight springs are made of *solid gold*. During the
intervals the coupé will be exhibited in the foyer at the same
time as the rich individual who is presently paying homage to
Mademoiselle Pichenette.

THEATER OF DANDYISM

...

"No, it's impossible!" murmured Monsieur Nobody,
rubbing his eyes as if to assure himself that he was not the
victim of an illusion. The French stage could not have de-
clined to that extent!

As if to respond to that primitive doubt, *The Theater of
Cuckolds* appeared in front of *The Impartial*'s theater critic at
that very moment. He approached the colossal posters plastering the façade from the roof to the ground floor. The posters
were an exact reproduction of the note in the program-paper.
All that had been added, in order better to attract the public,
was a drawing representing the famous solid gold coupé and
the portrait of the rich protector.

Astounded, Monsieur Nobody murmured: "But that's..."

He did not have time to finish. A ticket-seller had approached.

"M'sieu," he said, "seats less expensive than the ticket office."

"I don't want one."

"With the right to touch the coupé and sit down on the cushions for a minute."

"I don't want one, I tell you...or, rather...one simple question. What is that other monument situated opposite, from which those extraordinary clamors are coming?"

XXVIII. Love in Partnership

"That monument?" replied the ticket-seller, blinking his eyes and shrugging his shoulders. "You know as well as I do, you joker!"

"If I knew, I wouldn't be asking you."

"Don't play the innocent!"

"Once again..."

"Well, it's the Heart Exchange."

"What's the Heart Exchange?"

"Oh! Where have you sprung from, fellow?"

"Where have I sprung from?" replied Monsieur Nobody, hotly, looking around anxiously. "Where have I sprung from? What's that to you?"

"It's just that, to be unaware of one of the most famous establishments in Paris, it's necessary to have come from one of the fifty planets that were only discovered yesterday, at the Observatory."

"Suppose, in fact, that I had arrived from one of those planets, and have the kindness to bring me up to date."

"It's quite simple, damn it. You know what a tart is don't you?"

"I've heard the term."

"One isn't asking for your confession, worthy apostle. It's sufficient that you know."

"Go on."

"Once, in times that are no more and will never return, those ladies had simple tastes, which permitted them to live

215

modestly on a few hundred francs a year—and because of that, an individual who could offer that privilege was in a position to win the sentiment of one of those princesses of the crinoline. When I say in a position, I'm speaking for the sake of appearances—that didn't prevent poaching, which is outside the question, isn't it?

"Well, as the price of silk always rises, and as the luxury of that society isn't disposed to decline, there came a time, quite naturally, when there was no longer any capitalist capable of holding firm. In a matter of three weeks the fattest was swallowed up, and nothing was found of him but the bones.

"Then, a luminous idea came into the head of a resourceful man, which was to apply to the subject in question the benefits of association. As soon as it was imagined, it was done. Three weeks later, a dozen limited companies had already been formed, with a capital of several million.

"It was a first rate plan. Today, shares are issued in all those ladies. A hundred shares give the holder the right to accompany her to the Bois once a month; two hundred, to appear with her once a month in the balcony of the Opéra; three hundred to take her to four-in-hand racecourses.

"Given that, in all of that, if the marionettes dance, it's only vanity that moves them; each one finds his satisfaction. He's been seen with the celebrated   —what more can he desire?

"As for the shares, their value is subject to the logical variations, in accordance with the caprices to fashion, and it's to fix the daily prices that the Heart Exchange has been set up. Listen. Today, one heard: 'Rosalinde at 119,490. Olympe at 138,000 for cash! Who wants fifty Amelias, current price?' And so on. It runs very smoothly, under the surveillance of a syndicate.

"But forgive me, bourgeois; while I'm talking to you, my business isn't making headway. You're wrong not to want my seats, but as you please—I'll go chat to that Englishman who's passing by."

And the ticket-seller launched himself toward the islander, shouting: "Here's seats for the theater. Much cheaper than the box office!"

The islander took them.

XXIX. A Performance in 1901

In despair of his cause and weary of falling between Scylla and Charybdis, the novice critic of the Impartial made a bewildered resolution.

At random—for he saw that once could only be lost for choice—he marched straight ahead, found a new theatrical establishment and, without knowing where he was going, entered intrepidly with his eyes shut. It was the Theater of Fantastic Effects, the latest to be constructed on the unused plans of an architect of the young school: something gigantic!

The auditorium could contain five hundred thousand people. One reached the orchestra stalls on horseback or in one's carriage. In addition, the Theater of Fantastic Effects had realized many other improvements.

Renouncing the pitiful and hackneyed system of chandeliers or luminous ceilings, it was illuminated by an electric sun whose glare was so powerful that the ladies were obliged to keep their umbrellas open and the men to wear green eyeshades or blue-tinted spectacles.

It was the same for the ventilation. For too long, people had been moaning about the heat and lack of aeration of the old auditoria. The architect of the new one, with the aid of a forceful pump, sent jets of air to all the seats so powerful that, if one took off one's muffler or furs momentarily, one immediately contracted a pulmonary fluxion.

In brief, every comfort had been perfected by the bold innovator.

Monsieur Nobody only just had time to pass a few of their stupefying progressive provisions in review when the curtain went up, allowing the perception of a stage five hundred meters deep. Singularly enough, however, scarcely had the actors appeared that the spectators began to chat among themselves in loud voices, without paying the slightest heed to what was happening on the boards. The majority even turned their backs ostentatiously on the spectacle, which continued nevertheless, without anyone being able to catch a single word of it.

Monsieur Nobody, who was decidedly going from one astonishment to another, waited to begin with, then grew impatient, and ended up *in extremis* turning to his neighbor in the stalls.

"Can you tell me, Monsieur, whether we shall soon be able to listen to the play?"

"Listen to the play? Why?"

"In order to hear it."

"What would be the point?"

"But it seems to me that that's generally why people come to the theater."

"To others, but not this one."

"Why, then, do people come?"

"For the railway effect."

"What effect?"

"The one in the fifth tableau. Haven't you see the poster? Ten thirty: the derailment."

"That's bizarre."

"Say full of common sense. Once, people had the patience, in order to see some piece of scenery or a fashionable effect, to consume the interminable refrains of dramatic performers; today one comes, one looks around one chats, and then the moment comes…hang on, here we go!"

Indeed, the most complete silence had just been reestablished in the auditorium, and everyone sat down.

It was the tableau of the derailment.

Two veritable railway trains came on stage, a terrible impact took place, carriages and boilers tumbled, exploding into smithereens, flying to an elevation of a hundred feet.

It was impossible to push realism any further.

Whistles, the cries of the dying, the roaring of broken boilers: everything was there.

The enthusiastic audience members clapped their hands, calling back the set-designer, the decorator and the director—and then, at the moment when the play was about to resume its course, everyone ran for the exit.

The performance concluded before the prompter and the usherettes.

XXX. No Camaraderie

"Well," said the Editor-in-Chief of *The Impartial*, on seeing his critic arrive the following day. "Have we made a start?"

"Yesterday evening."

"Perfect..."

"I wouldn't say as much about what's happening in the world in which I've taken my first steps."

"So much the better, damn it! You know what I told you: no camaraderie! Be pitiless."

"I will be, for indignation rises to my lips when I think about the sickening evidence of decadence, demoralization and depravity of taste that I bump into at every new stage."

"Superb! Print me that tirade right away."

"I'll print it."

"And you'll be right. No pity!"

"You can rely on me."

"Which doesn't prevent me from repeating to you and insisting: '*The Impartial* is the tribune of truth. Cut and thrust! Strike without mercy."

"I shall strike."

"By the way, what theater did you go to?"

"The Theater of Fantastic Effects.

"Ah!"

"Which ought rather to be called the Theater of Locomotives."

"Yes, I know...because of the...that's all right, my dear—don't be too hard on the director; he's a friend of mine, and I have dinner with him every week."

"What! I thought...just now you repeated to me..."

"Undoubtedly. I repeat it again. Except, an old college friend...that's sacred, you understand. But I leave the rest to you."

"So be it!"

"Oh, I forgot—did you notice a little blonde in the role of Salière?"

"I wasn't able to notice anything, for the excellent reason that it was impossible to perceive the slightest sound coming from the stage."

"Indeed...but it doesn't matter. The little blonde Salière is named Irma. Be kind to her. She's the mistress of a fellow at my club."

"But..."

"Oh, I abandon the others to you, ferocious fellow."

"You abandon them to me!"

"Except, however, for one fat brunette, who plays the musical snuffbox. You'll see her on the program—I can't remember her name, but I have an interest in her because she's the daughter of the porter of a lady in whose home I often have dinner."

"I understand your sympathy."

"There's also tall thin fellow who plays Curaçao, costumed as a small jug..."

"A tall thin one?"

"Yes—consult the program, and dedicate a gracious word to him.

"To him as well?"

"I know a gentleman whose nephew goes to a café where he plays billiards every evening. I promised him to instruct you."

"Is that all?"

"My God, yes. Oh., wait! Is there...? Yes exactly! That's where Chose is...a chap who talks through his nose...and the other one that lisps. Two fellows that the editor of the Artistic Reflector mentioned to me. A colleague, you understand... He met them at the funeral of the theater's auditor. Anyway, I'll give you a full list of all those it's necessary to spare."

"It would be simpler...."

"Here it is!" said the Editor-in-Chief of *The Impartial*. Write me your article quickly. And above all, don't forget that, apart from those, our motto is *No camaraderie!* Nothing but the truth. It's at that price alone that criticism is a vocation..."

"I can see that," Monsieur Nobody agreed.

XXXI. For an Adjective

Two days after the appearance of his dramatic article, in which, not without blushing at his weakness, he had sung the praises of the little blonde, the fat brunette, the tall thin one, the one who lisped and all the rest, Monsieur Nobody had just woken up.

After having, by way of innocent distraction, dreamed about the countryside while looking out of his skylight at the garden that was perceptible seven kilometers away, he prepared to get dressed, while delivering himself to painful reflections on the conditions that had been imposed on him and the adulations for which his conscience was reproaching him.

Three raps on his door snatched him out of those remorseful meditations.

He went to open up, and found two somber and solemn individuals buttoned up to the top standing before him.

"Monsieur Nobody?" enquired one of them.

"That's me."

"Good." And the orator of the duo took a piece of paper out of his pocket.

"Do you admit having written and signed this article?"

"I admit it," sighed Monsieur Nobody, humiliated on seeing that item of evidence again.

"In that case, Monsieur, it only remains for us to acquaint you with the purpose that brings us here."

"You could, without inconvenience, have commenced with that."

"We have the honor," declaimed the orator, striking a pose, "of coming on behalf of Monsieur Rocamadour, dramatic artist and our friend, to ask you the reason for the outrage committed in the article of which you declare yourself to be the author."

"What Rocamadour? What artist? What outrage?" exclaimed Monsieur Nobody, amazed.

"You are pretending in vain not to know him. The insult is too direct."

"I've insulted someone in the article I wrote, which is nothing but base flattery from beginning to end?"

"Do not add irony to insult, Monsieur. All explanation is superfluous."

"Not at all. I'd like at least to know why I'm going to be at daggers drawn with Monsieur Rocamadour. First of all, who is the gentleman in question?"

"The comedian charged with the role of Curaçao in..."

"The tall thin one!" exclaimed Monsieur Nobody, suddenly remembering.

"Monsieur, we do not appreciate the poor taste of the joke that you've just permitted yourself to make at such a moment with regard to the physical disadvantages of our friend."

"Eh? I wasn't joking."

"If the mockery is serious, the matter is all the more grave."

"Damned if I'm mocking him, any more than I've insulted him."

"Monsieur, this persistence is pitiful. We have the article here."

"I'm well aware if that, damn it, Read it."

"Since you insist…"

The majestic witness unfolded the newspaper.

"This is the passage, Monsieur, since your memory serves you so poorly: *We shall conclude*…already one can observe the wounding intention here. Why have you left Monsieur Rocamadour to the end? Evidently to offend him by refusing him one of the first places that his talent merits. But that's nothing... *We shall conclude by saying a word about Monsieur Rocamadour*... A word! It would be difficult to treat an eminent artist with more disdain. A word! That is patent malevolence! Malevolence that will overtly discard the mask in the following paragraph: *Monsieur Rocamadour, whom we do not know*... Which is to say, an unknown: a man without value, anyone at all! But let us continue: *Monsieur Rocamadour, whom we do not know, is an actor*... Why actor, and not comedian? Always the spirit of systematic denigration. Always the venom! ...*is an actor with a bright future.*"

"Well, what do you see in that?"

"What do I see? Come on, Monsieur, you really seem to be taking us for children."

"Me!"

"*An actor with a bright future!* I don't know that there's any grosser means of telling an artist that he has not, until now, had any talent, that he is nothing but an incompetent, a dullard, an imbecile..."

"It doesn't say that..."

"And you pretend that the qualifications *incompetent, dullard* and *imbecile* are not an insult...what am I saying?...are not three insults?"

"But..."

"Monsieur Rocamadour could not suffer this outrage. No, you shall not, with impunity, drag through the mud, and splash with your venomous pen, one of the glories of the French theater..."

"In the role of Curaçao?"

"Yes, Monsieur, in the role of Curaçao. The duel will take place tomorrow at six o'clock in the morning."

"Tomorrow, so be it, since you insist."

"Monsieur Rocamadour has the choice of weapons."

"And many as he pleases."

"And he has instructed me to tell you that you will be fighting with cannon-revolvers!"

XXXII. In the Queue!

The duel had taken place.

Monsieur Nobody had exchanged six rifle-shots with the insulted Rocamadour without any harm coming to anyone—after which the witnesses had declared that honor was satisfied.

However, the results of his first article were not of a nature to encourage Monsieur Nobody. So, comprehending that it was absurd to stick one's finger between the tree of editorial camaraderies and the bark of artistic self-esteems, the ephemeral critics of *The Impartial* sent in his considered resignation.

The problem of the future loomed up before him again.

What was he to do?

Our unfortunate hero had learned via the vice of publicity that a competition was to be held on the following Saturday for a vacant position in the Ministry of the Interior.

Although Monsieur Nobody did not have the appearance of feeling an irresistible vocation for bureaucracy, necessity spoke. Forcing himself to make a effort, therefore, and glad at least to see that places were awarded on the basis of a contest of merit, he left to ask that his name be entered on the list of competitors.

He was still some ten kilometers from the Ministry of the Interior when he perceived a compact mass of individuals in the distance.

Probably some army corps putting on a military parade, he thought.—and he continued going forward.

As he advanced, however, he acquired the certainty that the compact mass was completely immobile.

Soon, he was quite close and was then able to observe that what he had mistaken for an army corps was an immense column of agglomerated citizens—a file that extended as far as the eye could see.

Without paying any more heed to it, Monsieur Nobody prepared to go past. A squadron of guardsmen stopped him.

"Where are you going?""

"To the Ministry of the Interior, from which I'm still more that two leagues distant. I beg you, therefore, to let me continue my route, otherwise I'll arrive too late to put my name down."

"Oh, you're entering the competition," said an old sergeant. "In that case, join the queue."

"I beg your pardon! I repeat that I don't have time to wait; I'm going to the Ministry."

"For the competition," repeated the old sergeant. "Well, here you are. Join the queue."

"Yes, in the queue! In the queue!" vociferated the witnesses.

"What!"

"In the queue! In the queue!"

"Once again..."

"I hear you. You want to go put your name down with the aim of asking permission to enter the competition to obtain the title of candidate for the rank of aspirant to the grade of supernumerary, in order to have the right to hope to be chosen for the eleven thousandth employee position, which has just fallen vacant in the offices of the Ministry of the Interior?"

"One doesn't obtain it immediately?"

"I don't have time for joking. Take your place behind all the other postulants; as you can see, there's already a line twenty kilometers long by twenty-five applicants abreast."

"And the fortunate winner of the competition will have the joy of being able to be appointed..."

"In twenty years' time, if he has influential friends. What do you expect? Everybody clutters up the surroundings of the public administrations."

"Everyone except me," said Monsieur Nobody, drawing away at a long stride.

"He's a good one, the Chinaman," muttered the old sergeant. "Does he imagine that jobs are common?"

XXXIII. The Wisdom of a Literate Porter

That day, Monsieur Nobody went home even more bleakly than usual.

Talking to himself, and gesticulating with a strange prodigality of pantomime, he was about to climb back up the eleven flights of steps that led to his mansard when he encountered Monsieur the Governor smoking a cigar outside his door.

Monsieur the Governor was not a malevolent man. He had noticed the increasing melancholy of his new tenant some time ago, and, finding himself in a good mood for the moment, he had deigned to speak to him.

In fact, as his tenant was about to go past him, after being respectfully, he said: "Why, it's Monsieur Nobody. 'Whence comes that somber and severe attitude today?' as the poet says.[45] Have we, by chance, had a bad dream? Are we having a disastrous day?" *Nigro notanda lapillo*,[46] as Horace puts it."

Monsieur the Governor's tenant, to whom the former had not deigned to speak since the day he moved in, was surprised to hear himself addressed, and even more surprised by the literary citations with which the language of the man he had once identified as a porter was sprinkled.

But Monsieur the Governor, without paying any heed to his astonishment, and without even giving him time to reply, added: "I'll wager, my dear Monsieur Nobody, that you have some hidden chagrin: *Latet anguis in herba*.[47] Tee hee! Times are hard and fortune no longer arrives while one sleeps..."

"Indeed," sighed our hero, whom that reflection had struck full in the chest.

"Hold on—I'm sure that I've divined the cause of your sadness: 'Nourished on misfortune, I know its twists and

---

[45] The quotation is from Baudelaire's "*Semper Eadem*."

[46] Marked with a black stone.

[47] A snake in the grass.

turns.'[48] You thought that the larks would fall into your lap ready-roasted. I thought the same…but from one rung to the next... What if I told you, my poor Monsieur Nobody, that, such as you see me now, I'm a doctor of letters."

"You!"

"The very same."

"And…"

"And I pull the cord, or would if there was one. Alas, I'm not alone. Competition, competition! Today, my good Monsieur Nobody, bus conductors pass examinations at the Sorbonne. The upper crust no longer want domestics who don't have bachelors' diplomas, and there's a cleaner of the first floor apartments here who has a degree in science and a first prize in mathematics in the general competition."

"A cleaner!" murmured Monsieur Nobody. "But then, what will become of me?"

"Yes, that's the question, isn't it? To be or not to be…it's Shakespeare's alternatives more than ever. To live in privation of die of hunger. Every year the lycées throw three hundred thousand young people on to the streets of Paris, rich in hopes. What can you do? Once, I'd have advised you to set up as a photographer, but fifty of those Messieurs having attacked a passer-by in broad daylight to force him to have his portrait made, and having torn him to shreds, the police have just banned the profession as a danger to public safety."

"I approve of the authorities."

"I could tell you to try to get into the Académie."

"But I don't have any entitlement for that."

"Exactly…but you lack political antecedents."

"That's true."

"Damn, damn! Oh, but of course! Now I think of it, our proprietor…"

"Monsieur Ustazade Vautour?"

---

[48] From Racine's *Bajazet*.

"The very same, who is both one both the princes of modern finance and one of the kings of present-day commerce. If he wanted to, he could give you a job."

"Would he want to?"

"With a letter of recommendation from me, and in the capacity of a tenant in one of his properties, I hope so. It's a means of guaranteeing his rent in times to come. He'll withhold it from your wages."

"That consideration might, in fact, decide his generosity."

"Shh! As Racine says, 'These very walls, Seigneur, might have eyes.'"

"And ears."

"Precisely."

"But where might I have the honor of being introduced to Monsieur Dominique Ustazade Vautour?"

"At the Temple of the God Ingot, between noon and three o'clock. He's always three. Anyone will point you in his direction."

"What is the Temple of the God Ingot?"

"The institution that had succeeded the one that used to be called the Paris Bourse."

"Aha! Very good."

"If you don't know the Temple of the God Ingot, it will also be an opportunity for you to see one of the great curiosities of Paris and take a practical course in contemporary morality."

"I'll go."

"Very good."

"But where is this famous Temple?"

"In the Place de la Forêt-de-Bondy. Anyone will show you the way. Go—and good luck. *Macte animo, generose puer*, as the Swan of Mantua sings."[49]

---

[49] The quotation—Apollo's words to Aeneas' son in Virgil's *Aeneid*—continues *sic itur ad astra*, the whole translating as "Cheer up, youth, this is the way to the stars." Virgil was

XXXIV. The Temple of the God Ingot

The Temple of the God Ingot was, indeed, one of the great curiosities of Paris in 1901. It was there that speculation had established its general headquarters.

On penetrating into the sanctuary—which, like the cemeteries, was becoming too small from year to year, necessitating further extensions—Monsieur Nobody saw therein, with no exaggeration, almost half the population of Paris crammed together, shouting and choking, for all of the social classes had been infected with a passion for gambling. Those who did not have the means to pay in hard cash speculated in kind.

Thus, one saw a host of poor people wandering around the gigantic palace carrying their mattress, their chest of drawers or their bed on their back. When they met a speculator who offered them one or several shares to their taste, they handed over the remains of their movable property in exchange for the slip of paper that promised them a problematic gain.

In the middle of the edifice, on a sumptuously ornamented stage, the god of the place appeared: an enormous gold ingot!

Everyone, as they passed by, bent a knee before the idol. Some of them—superstitious individuals—even hung ex-votos around it, in the hope that it might bring them good luck.

Distributed throughout the building, choirs of eight hundred voices were responsible for proclaiming, at three minute intervals, the prices of various shares, and no celestial music was ever listened to with more concentration than that ritornelle of cupidity.

Then, at each new appeal, there was a frantic hubbub, and gamblers were seen going into *ad hoc* cloakrooms and taking off the garments they wore in order to emerge again, in accordance with the caprices of fate, dressed more sumptuous-

---

known as "the Swan of Mantua" because that was his birthplace.

ly or more wretchedly. For the speculation had reached such proportions that one could be ruined or enriched by single coup on the Bourse.

One thus encountered worshippers of the God Ingot who traded in their jewel-decked costumes for rags, or vice versa, twenty times a day. In view of these sudden changes of position, dwellings of princely luxury had been constructed on the four sides of the immense square that framed the Temple of the God Ingot. These dwellings, which sometimes passed into the hands of ten different owners in a matter of hours, constantly bore notices indicating that they were for sale.

As soon as a gambler had made a fortune in consequence of a shift in prices, he headed for one of these magnificent palaces and, on paying the price to the previous inhabitant, whom ruin had struck, found the table set and the horses saddled, had a good meal, rode triumphantly around the square, returned to gambling, lost, and yielded the ostentations of an hour to another player.

Nothing, moreover, had been omitted from the fixtures of the Temple of the God Ingot. In addition to the singularities just listed, one found on the left hand side after the entrance a counter for the hire of pistols. That was for the convenience of speculators who did not want to survive their disappointment. On the right hand side there as another counter selling disguises for the use of those who preferred—and they were the larger number—to escape by sudden flight from the exigencies of liquidations.

What struck Monsieur Nobody most of all, however, was the presence of a certain number of individuals who were sidling through the dense waves of the crowd, approaching people furtively and whispering in their ears: "Want to buy some false rumors? False rumors for sale!" When the client seemed disposed, the sellers of that singular commodity took him into one of the stalls established in the square and dedicated, or so it seemed, to merchandise of that particular species.

Now, it was to one of these very stalls that Monsieur Nobody was directed when he decided to ask a passer-by where he might find Monsieur Dominique Ustazade Vautour.

XXXV. An Unretouched Portrait

Monsieur Dominique Ustazade Vautour had, in fact, conquered his colossal fortune in two kinds of trading. The first consisted of spreading throughout the financial square, every day, a certain number of rumors, thanks to which he induced into temptation the imbeciles that he then robbed at his leisure.

The second aspect of his negotiations was no less extraordinary. Somewhere in Paris, he opened a shop of one kind or another—of fashionable garments, for example. After a month, notices stuck to all the windows announced:

I am ruined; there is nothing left to do but end it all. But before then, I want the public, at least, to profit from my misfortune. In consequence, from the beginning of next week, I shall liquidate at a fifty per cent discount all the merchandise that I have in the shop. Those who will have bought my madapolams at incredible discounts will bless my memory when I am no longer.

The idlers passed by, and looked as they did so, and after having looked, raced to assault the boutique of the unfortunate tradesperson—which unfortunate tradesperson was none other than Sieur Vautour, emitting abominable products, unqualifiable trash, and all the rejects of Parisian commerce...all at an enormous profit.

Oh, the honest man! The gallant man!

XXXVI. The False Rumor Shop

At the moment when Monsieur Nobody presented himself, Sieur Dominique Ustazade Vautour was in conference with a buyer. The man with green eyes was thus able to examine the shop in which he found himself at leisure.

Outside, the shop bore for a sign: IN GOOD FAITH, and for a subtitle: *News of Every Kind.*

Inside, two rows of superimposed labeled filing-cabinets were arranged along the walls: on one side, the pigeon-holes for rises; on the other, the pigeon-holes for falls. Then, on every drawer, there was a particular indication indicating the nature of the products it contained.

One read, for example:

Sudden deaths of sovereigns.

Great battles (victories or defeats).

Internal troubles.

Changes of Ministry.

Rumors related to important bankruptcies.

So-called disasters for paralyzing the response to premiums.

Etc., Etc. Etc.

In front of these filing-cabinets counters were installed occupied by clerks who were retailing the merchandise to the clientele while showing off the article.

"What, Monsieur doesn't find this rumor of a revolution in Paraguay sufficiently plausible! But it's one of the best of its kind. Take a look at what you're dealing. There isn't a single word in the news that doesn't bear a gripping seal of truth. You'll have, in consequence a considerable drop in shares in rubber mines.

"And you, Monsieur, what do you need? News of a rise…is it something well-established that you desire…yes? Have confidence in me. This is the latest thing: the announcement of a conclusion of the war between the northern States and southern States of America…will that do? Monsieur fears that it might not be sufficiently plausible? They've been fighting for fifty years, though! Well, if you prefer a news item that's less striking but more solid, we have information about the abundance of harvests, which never fails in its effect…

"Alfred, pass me the drawer of good harvests…it must be in the workshop…"

There was, in fact, a workshop; situated at the back of the shop, it was separated from it by a fluted glass window, which permitted a glimpse of some twenty individuals in attitudes of the most profound meditation. They were the manufacturers of false news, searching for ideas.

But Monsieur Nobody could not take his examination any further. Sieur Ustazade Vautour was just escorting out the client with whom he was in conference.

"That's agreed, "he said to him. "I've made a note of your order. I'll deliver your false rumors of expropriation on Thursday, in order to raise the price of your plots of land in the Rue de Fontainebleau. Don't worry, you'll be content— but it's agreed that we'll share the profits. A bientôt!"

Then he came back to the man with green eyes.

"Is it you, Monsieur, who desires to talk to me in private?"

"It's me."

"Would you care to follow me into my study."

XXXVII. Can You Laugh?

"So," said Ustazade Vautour, when he had heard his visitor's explanations and taken cognizance of the letter from the Governor of his property in the Boulevard de Pontoise, "you're one of my tenants?"

"Yes, Monsieur."

"And you desire to obtain employment under my orders?"

"Yes, Monsieur."

"Which means, in plain French, that you're at the end of your resources, and that, in consequence, that if I don't place you, I'm threatened with losing the rent payments that will be due after the deposit you've paid in advance?"

"Permit me, Monsieur…I'm an honest man…"

"Ta ta ta! No stupidities!" exclaimed Ustazade Vautour. "I've no time to waste, and I know what I'm saying…"

"I repeat to you, Monsieur, that I'm an honest man, and that I have always fulfilled my responsibilities."

"I'm not astonished that you're poor, then. But let's get straight to the point. You want to enter the world of speculation?"

"Since it's necessary."

"We'll see...we'll see," said Ustazade Vautour, passing behind the man with green eyes, hypocritically. "Will you please pick up the book that is lying on my desk."

Monsieur Nobody got up to obey the request. Scarcely had he turned his back than Sieur Vautour dropped a gold coin on the floor.

Monsieur Nobody continued walking toward the desk without turning round, and reached out a hand toward the book, but the worthy Ustazade stopped him.

"No, no, my boy. You'll never make a financier."

"Why?"

"Because I've submitted you to a conclusive trial. At the moment when, under a pretext, I sent you in this direction, I dropped that coin in the other."

"So?"

"So, it's decisive. If you had the slightest vocation for business, your first movement, on hearing the money fall, ought to have been to bend down in order to pick it up."

"In order to return it to you, you mean?" said Monsieur Nobody, loftily.

"So," the noble Vautour continued, without taking any notice of the interruption, "the matter is settled: you can't be of any use to me in that regard—but perhaps there's a means for us to reach an understanding in another way. Do you have imagination?"

"I'd try, if it were a matter of applying it to a useful purpose."

"Very useful."

"Then I'd have some."

"As useful as it could possibly be, since your daily bread would be dependent on it."

"That's not what I understood..."

"Understand what you please. Here, in brief, is the proposition I have to make to you. As you know, I'm at the head of a false news establishment—the largest in all of Paris."

"I didn't know it until a few moments ago."

"This establishment is worth a fortune to me, which had scarcely any rival. It continues to bring me satisfactory profits, but I can't hide the fact that business is becoming increasingly difficult. By virtue of having been fooled before, the marks are beginning to get suspicious. One has all the trouble in the world provoking abrupt fluctuations in prices.

"In brief, my repertoire of false news needs to be entirely rejuvenated. It's necessary to get out of the routine, to find the unexpected, the eccentric...something that, at the first stroke, will take its audience in. I'm convinced of that from the double point of view of my own interests and those of the art itself.

"You're new to the métier, you're arriving without preconceived idea and without traditions..."

"Excuse me, Monsieur," said Monsieur Nobody, "in the matter of traditions there is one that I shall never betray, and that is honesty."

"Who the devil mentioned honesty? You haven't understood me, then?"

"I fear the opposite."

"Be as honest as you like, provided that you furnish me with nice little inventions that will provoke considerable rises or falls as my whim."

"Which deprive the unfortunate."

"Fools credulous enough to let themselves be taken in. No violence is done to anyone."

"But everyone is duped."

"Hey, my boy, it seems to me that you're becoming impolite."

"You can clearly see, Monsieur, that I'll never be able to lie to others, since I can't even lie to you."

XXXVIII. *Would You Rather Cry?*

At that energetic remark, Dominique Ustazade Vautour went crimson, and his first impulse was surely to throw the imprudent moralist out—but he remembered just in time that he was a member of the committees of several benevolent societies, and that, if he manhandled the poor fellow too violently, the latter might spread the rumor of his conduct, and harm his candidature for the Institute of Social Virtue's Philanthropy Prize. He therefore repressed his anger and adopted a hypocritically honeyed tone.

"I've told you, Monsieur, that you don't understand speculation at all. If I wanted to explain its complex mechanism to you, I wouldn't have any difficulty in demonstrating that you've misunderstood my intentions and the methods of my organization, which, thank God, has an honorable reputation. Exaggerated as your scruples are, however, they depart from a natural rectitude, and I honor them.

"The best proof I can give you of that, my dear Monsieur, is that I want to make you another proposal. Don't worry—this time, it's only a matter of commercial enterprise. Commerce is the link between nations, the fecundator of public wealth, the child of work and probity..."

As he trotted out that litany of pompous qualifications, Vautour struck a superb pose. One might have thought that he was making a speech about the distribution of the recompenses of one of the eight thousand industrial expositions that took place every year in the principal cities of the world.

Monsieur Nobody gazed at him fixedly.

"Do you like commerce?" he continued, in an insinuating tone.

"I'd like it if I felt the capacities necessary for..."

"You'll acquire them over time—besides which, the functions that I have in mind for you only require a neat appearance and sincerity of expression."

236

"As regards sincerity, you have been able to see, Monsieur, that I have no lack of it."

"That's exactly what I like about you. Someone else might have taken exception to what you said just now. In me, it only inspired more esteem for your character. Listen carefully."

"I'm listening, Monsieur."

"Independently of my enterprises on the Bourse, I'm the owner of all the fashion shops in Paris, which I've centralized in my hands in order to suppress any competition."

"And to sell as dear as possible," added Monsieur Nobody.

"Well, well! You have commercial notions far more developed than I thought. But to sell as dear as possible isn't enough; it's necessary to sell a great deal, and to sell a great deal, it's necessary to keep the public incessantly in suspense. It's for that reason that I invented the liquidations cause by complete ruination for which you've probably seen the posters."

"What! That's you?"

"In person."

"And those ruinations..."

"Fictitious, with no other aim than administering a crack of the whip to sales. The crack of the whip was marvelously effective to begin with, but today, by dint of its duration, the method is threatened with wearing out. It's urgently necessary to revive it. The buyers are beginning to doubt the reality of the bankruptcies. The word 'expedient' is being pronounced. It's become necessary to impose silence upon it and reanimate faith. And that's exactly why you can render me precious help.

"In fact, the day when, on entering one of my shops liquidated by reason of bankruptcy, the buyers see the owner of the establishment, pale and bleak, with tears in his eyes, doubt will vanish, business will quintuple, and the coup will be complete! In order to convince the idlers, we'll add a family portrait, a mother—the wife of the ruined shopkeeper—

surrounded by young children. Isn't that right? That they need to be young in order to be more interesting…?"

"I confess, Monsieur, not being able to understand how my opinion can be of any importance you in all this."

"Of course! You haven't guessed! That ruined business-man will be you! You have an honest appearance…melancholy in your features. I'll find you a lady cashier who sheds tears easily… Then the brats…blond! That's much more sentimental than brown hair… I can see the ensemble from here: you in the middle, the wife to the left, the children to the right…

"We'll take amazing receipts. As for you, you'll have twenty per cent of the profits, board, lodging and heating. You'll dress in black…it's more devout…oh, I'm forgetting…"

"Indeed, Monsieur," said Monsieur Nobody, rising to his feet, pale and indignant. "You're forgetting that you have a man before you who respects poverty too much to parody it for the profit of your wealth."

XXXIX. Complications

After the further shock, in which his hopes had been dashed once again, Monsieur Nobody went home furious and exasperated.

"The rogue!" he murmured, letting himself fall on to his meager bed. "The rogue! They all seemed to have passed the word around to insult me or mystify me. Is that, then, what people are like, and ought I to envelop them in a common scorn, abandoning myself to invincible despair? After having taken everything from me, including my name!

"For I had a name once. A noble name! Ha ha ha! Whereas today, I'm Nobody. Ha ha ha! Nobody, the un-known! The abandoned! The scorned! Nobody, the…ha ha ha!"

As he spoke thus, our hero was seized by one of his heartrending fits of hilarity.

Gradually, however, he seemed to calm down.

"No!" he repeated. "No? It's impossible. I'll carry on searching. I'll make new efforts, and my perseverance is bound to be stronger than their egotism! Especially..." He paused, and went to open the widow of his mansard.

"Especially if *she* will consent to help me."

Sitting at a window of a neighboring house, a young blonde woman was embroidering.

XL. She

She was the young blonde woman.

He had seen her once without paying any attention to her. He had seen her again, and had paid attention.

He had seen her a third time, and had fallen in love with her.

She was so charming! She seemed so chaste! She blushed so modestly when her gaze met Monsieur Nobody's.

The latter had not taken long to find out about her entire life. What observers the amorous are!

He knew that she lived alone with her mother. He knew that she went out every day to collect the daily needlework from a shop that sold it. He knew that he too went downstairs at the same time, every day, that he met her, that she went past him demurely, that he had wanted to speak to her twenty times, but had never dared to do so—which betrayed his age, invisible in his features.

Monsieur Nobody was definitely still young!

That day, however, timidity was spurred by excitement- and when, the moment having arrived, he saw the young woman put on, as usual, her woolen shawl and her modest hat, he exclaimed: "Today, I shall dare! Her love will either be my last support or my last disappointment..."

XLI. Request and Response

The strategy of the preceding days was renewed, as usual.

The young blonde woman went along the sidewalk.

Monsieur Nobody advanced resolutely to meet her, and took off his hat respectfully.

"Excuse me, Mademoiselle."

The young blonde woman looked up in astonishment, but without any fear.

"Excuse me, Mademoiselle, but I need to talk to you."

"To me?" she said, ingenuously.

"Yes, Mademoiselle. For a long time, I've been observing you..."

"I know, Monsieur."

"For a long time, I've been trying to retain the secret that is ready to escape me. Mademoiselle, I love you..."

"You love me, Monsieur," the young blonde woman replied, in the most natural tone.

"Yes, Mademoiselle."

"My God, Monsieur, I'm not contradicting you."

That last phrase had been pronounced with such phlegm that our hero was momentarily stupefied, but he pulled himself together immediately.

"Believe, Mademoiselle, that my intentions are pure."

"I believe you, Monsieur."

"It's your hand that I want to have the honor of requesting; I wanted to know beforehand, however, whether such a step might...displease you in any way."

Monsieur Nobody's voice was broken by emotion.

As for the young blonde woman, without the slightest disturbance, and with the perfect good faith of a person who does not understand anything of what is happening around her, she said: "Pardon me, Monsieur, but why are you addressing yourself to me?"

That was enough to make him take twenty steps back.

"What do you mean, why?" stammered Monsieur Nobody.

"Of course. All that has nothing to do with me."

"All that has nothing to do with you? You didn't hear what I said, then? You haven't understood me? I love you, Mademoiselle."

"Indeed, Monsieur. What do you want me to do about it?"

"I want...I wanted...to solicit the honor..."

"Of marrying me?"

"Of marrying you."

"Well, Monsieur, it is precisely that subject relative to which I have just replied to you that it is nothing to do with me."

As blows go, that was crushing. Monsieur Nobody passed through all the colors of the rainbow.

The young blonde woman remained impassive.

"Who, then, does it concern?" exclaimed the man with green eyes, in a strangled voice.

"The firm of Conjugo & Co., number 171 Rue de Sèvres," replied the young blonde woman, serenely.

"You said, Mademoiselle...?"

"The firm of Conjugo & Co., 171 Rue de Sèvres, to which I've been leased since the age of five. It's therefore to that company that you ought to address yourself, in the case that you persist in your resolution."

And the young blonde woman sketched a placid gesture of farewell. "Ask for Mademoiselle Laure Dubouchet, Monsieur. It's at the back of the courtyard on the first floor. There's a plaque on the door."

XLII. Marriages to Order

In order to give the readers the key to the previous scene, it is perhaps as well to furnish them with a few items of information that were evidently unknown to Monsieur Nobody.

The latter doubtless imagined, in his ignorance, that marriage was still, as it had been in remote times, a question of sentimentality.

Marriage had become a question of business.

In the past, the parents or friends had been responsible for fixing, with covert words and under the mantelpiece, the figure of the dowry. In the eyes of the world, the fiancés, seemingly unaware of these calculations, dissimulated the speculation under an appearance of official sympathies. Soon, however, there no longer seemed to be any need to play that comedy for form's sake. Arithmetic reigned supreme.

It was then that the parents feeling that their direct intervention was too odious, resolved to put themselves in the hands of intermediaries: hence the creation of the first marriage bureaux, which went back to the previous century.

There was, however, a vast distance between those timid trials and the powerful organization and financial expertise of the establishments of 1901!

Those establishments were now as numerous as insurance companies against fire. Not a single marriage took place without their intervention.

When a poor young woman from a good family reached her fifth year, the parents went in search of one of the companies in question. An expert was charged with calculating the probabilities of the extent of beauty offered by the child's features. Those probabilities served as a basis for the contract that would link the entrepreneur to the parents. By that contract, the former promised to pay the latter a rental of varying magnitude until the young woman was grown up. It also took responsibility for giving her an education of variable brilliance, still in accordance with the degree of anticipated charm.

When the time for marriage arrived, the entrepreneur recovered all his expenditure, plus a percentage of the matrimonial contribution of the husband it had acquired. For poor young men the question was turned around. For rich young men and women, the affair was treated on bases proportional to the level of fortunes, and the unions were calculated in accordance with figures as nicely blended as the bonds of marriage.

It was, as the reader can see, a complex organization, but one that functioned with the utmost regularity.

Among the finest institutions of the kind in question could be cited The Turtle-Dove Company. The Nuptial Torch Company, the Perfect Union Company, and, above all the rest, The Agency Conjugo & Co.—the very one to which, it appeared, our hero's charming neighbor was attached.

XLIII. The Agency Conjugo & Co.

Monsieur Nobody, as has already been said, was ignorant of all these details. Thus, the conduct of Mademoiselle Dubouchet was, for him, the most exasperating of enigmas. It was necessary to obtain the key to it at any price.

Half an hour later, he made his entrance into the establishment of Conjugo & Co.

Mademoiselle Laure had not been mistaken; it was indeed number 171, Rue de Sèvres, at the back of the courtyard, on the first floor. And it had a plaque on the door! Having arrived before that plaque, Monsieur Nobody rang the bell, and a braided lackey came to open the door.

"What does Monsieur desire? Is it a project of marriage, the signature of a contract or measures for separation?"

"A project of marriage," replied the man with green eyes, privately astonished that the same administration should take charge of making ties on the one hand, and breaking them on the other.

"Very good, Monsieur. First corridor on the left, second corridor on the right, eighth door: Reception Room M.

Monsieur Nobody set off into the maze of the immense apartment.

Having arrived at the door of Reception M, he received from a second domestic the number 72, and was introduced into a vast sparsely-furnished room.

Impatiently, Monsieur Nobody began by striding back and forth for half an hour in the reception room, and then sat down. He riffled mechanically through the collections of certificates that were on the table. All the signatures attested that

Conjugo & Co. had not been mistaken by a centime with regard to the merits of their husbands or wives.

Of the happiness of the household there was not a single mention.

That examination terminated, Monsieur Nobody devoted a further half hour to counting the flowers in the ceiling rose, and then a quarter of an hour contemplating the toes of his boots.

Finally weary of the tedious wait, he decided to address a few words to his neighbor, a little old man of about sixty-five.

"Do you think, Monsieur, that we'll have to wait much longer? I have number 72."

"No, an hour at the most. There's hardly anyone here today. At my last, there were three times as many people here as this."

"Your last?"

"My last wife, of course. I've already married six times, and have had the dolor of surviving my six spouses. That's due to my particular taste for delicate women. But this time, I've resolved to try a solidly constituted Alsatian woman, because I don't like change. Is Monsieur here for an Alsatian?"

"No, Monsieur.

"Perhaps you prefer a Parisienne. Oh, Monsieur, believe me, a Parisienne is diabolically risky. Personally, I've tried the experiment twice, and I..."

"Number 72!" cried the usher's voice.

The man with green eyes hastened to leave the Bluebeard to his theories, and was introduced into Monsieur Conjugo's office.

XLIV. Current Prices

After the usual exchange of politenesses, Monsieur Conjugo was the first to speak. "Monsieur desires to marry?"

"Yes—I'd like...."

"I have exactly what Monsieur needs...a superb match. A widow with a slight limp...it's almost imperceptible."

"Pardon me, Monsieur, but my choice is made."

"Very good. Is it a blonde, brunette, chestnut or red-head?"

"A blonde.

"Aha! Blondes are much in demand at the moment, and I warn you that there's a considerable rise in price. No matter! Age?"

"Twenty, at the most."

"Very good. Blonde, young..." And Monsieur Conjugo started filling in the banks on a printed form. Then he continued: "You'll see that we have a magnificent assortment..."

He rang.

"Bring the file of blondes...medium height, isn't it? Eighteen to twenty..."

"But once again, Monsieur," our friend interjected, "my choice is made. I want to marry Mademoiselle Laure Dubouchet."

"Why didn't you say so sooner? It's a love match, then. We make so few nowadays between people who know one another...Laure Dubouchet...Laure Dubouchet..." He searched through a catalogue.

"Here it is! Laure Dubouchet, born 1881. She is, in consequence, twenty years old—you're right. Daughter of a merchant deceased in 1882; belonging to the agency since 1886. Pretty! The agency has provided her with a careful education. She has learned English by the Robertson method.[50] Character all that one might dream. Doesn't play the piano but holds a book like an angel. Has also had in the family, on the maternal side, two captains in the National Guard...

When he had finished, Monsieur Conjugo cried: "Damn! You've chosen a very dear woman there. But when one has the means to meet the price... It's a marriage that will cost you two million...in cash, of course...and the reimbursement of all our expenses. Is that all right with you?"

---

[50] The reference is to William Robertson (1721-1793), principal of Edinburgh University.

"But it's an odious bargain that you're proposing to me!"

"You think it's too much? We don't haggle here. Everything, in any case, is priced at the going rate."

"O century of traffic and mud!"

"Eh! What…? I know what it is…you haven't a sou, and you imagine that we're going to give you one of our choice items for your handsome eyes. You aren't difficult! But if you want to marry anyway, I have what you need.

"Would you like an aged Comtesse of sixty-eight? She has false teeth, one shoulder higher than the other and corns, but she can do a great many things. She'll bring you a fortune of…"

"Shut up, you old clown!" cried Monsieur Nobody. "Shut up, merchant of human flesh, abominable exploiter! If the verb *to love* has been replaced by the verb *to buy*, at least have the modesty of your abasement!"

"Oh, that's the way it is!" said Monsieur Conjugo. "Someone throw this Monsieur out."

Four tall skeletal valets hastened to carry out their master's order.

XLV. The Final Straw

When the man with green eyes presented himself that evening in order to return to his humble abode, Monsieur the Governor was standing at the door. One might have thought that he was watching out for someone. And, indeed, as soon as he saw his tenant, the said: "My poor Monsieur Nobody, you can't go in."

"Let me pass," said the latter, thinking that it was a joke. "Let me pass…I want to be alone."

"I repeat that you can't go in."

"For what reason?"

"You're no longer one of the tenants of this house," said Monsieur the Governor sadly.

"Get away!"

246

"The eviction order arrived two hours ago, and your meager property has been put outside."

"My property...but for what reason?"

"You have contravened the first paragraph of the Tenants' Code. It is, you will recall, worded thus: *Every tenant is a being physically as well as morally inferior to his proprietor, and therefore owes him veneration and obedience.*"

"Ah! Yes," said Monsieur Nobody, vehemently. "Yes, I understand...it's him, the noble, the pure, the immaculate Vautour! Him, who is superior to me morally! The great heart! Morally... Him, to whom I owe veneration and obedience... Veneration! Ha ha ha! Ha!"

And Monsieur Nobody, uttering a burst of strident and convulsive laughter, launched himself outside.

XLVI. He was...

He was obliged to run all night...

The next morning, early, there was a gang of street-urchins—hideous gnomes of the gutter—in one of the square of the fine city of Paris, who were amusing themselves in a singular fashion.

The said gang was hotly pursuing a man with haggard eyes, whose clothing was in disorder and soiled with mud, and who was making furious gestures and muttering incoherently.

"All...!" cried the man.

"Money has taken everything from me!

"It has taken my heart!

"It has taken my name!

"Isn't that funny! A man who has no name. Ha ha!

"Money has tried to take my conscience. Ha ha ha! But I haven't surrendered it...

"Then it took my reason. Ha ha ha!

"It's funny! It's funny! It's funny! Ha ha ha! I'm laughing at it, like you...

"No, I can't laugh, since I'm nobody. Ha ha!

"Since money has taken everything from me... Nobody... Ha ha ha! Laugh!"

"Nobody...! Laugh, then...! Ha ha ha!"

And, indeed, at every fragmentary phrase the unfortunate spoke, there was laughter, gibes and jeers—when, all of a sudden, an agent of the authority, cleaving a path through the derisory cortege, stared at the man who was occasioning all that scandal.

"I'm not mistaken! It's Nobody, the man escaped from Charenton, for whom we've been searching for six months!"

At the same time, his hand fell upon the other's collar.

At that contact, it seemed that the unfortunate recovered his self-possession.

Impassively, he paraded his profound gaze around, and then halted it on the policeman who had apprehended him.

"Yes, it's me," he said, in a firm voice.

"A lunatic!" howled the urchins. "Hey! The crackpot! Hey!"

One of them pulled on the tails of his coat, knocking him over and throwing him into the mud.

And while the human mob bayed at the man in that fashion, a poor dog was seen crawling forward, ugly, dirty and unrecognizable, which began licking the unfortunate's hand timidly.

"Médor!" the latter murmured. "You've come back too late, my poor friend..."

Then, furtively wiping away a tear that was trembling on the rim of his eyelid. Monsieur Nobody stood up and addressing the policeman who was still holding his collar, said in a firm voice: "Where are you taking me?"

"To Charenton, from which you've escaped!"

"To Charenton—so be it. I'll swear an oath not to try and get out again. I've seen enough of all these madmen."

THE AERIAL OMNIBUS

All the newspapers have been talking for some time about the projected balloon-omnibus traveling between the Place de la Concorde and the gate of the Bois de Boulogne.[51]

At the moment when we are permitted to place ourselves on the scene, that omnibus-balloon has already been operating for a fortnight with a regularity that is beginning to encourage travelers. Thus, the nacelle is encumbered by a crowd as numerous as it is varied—which is all the more easily explained because it is Sunday morning.

The Conductor (three hundred feet above the Obelisk). All aboard for the Bois de Boulogne! All aboard! All aboard!

A Bourgeois (to this wife): When I think that cuckoos once stationed themselves in this same spot, summoning people to different practices in different voices. A gripping example of the progress that humankind realizes in its quotidian march.

His Wife (contemptuous of new ideas): A fine progress—to risk breaking one's neck!

The Bourgeois: Madame Glucôsin, he who risks nothing, has nothing. Aerial navigation is one of the great problems of the nineteenth century, and the duty of good citizens is to encourage its indefatigable pioneers by bringing them their modest obol. (To the kiosk attendant selling tickets to the omnibus-balloon) What is the price of a seat, Monsieur.

The Kiosk Attendant: Fifty centimes, payable in advance.

---

[51] The idea of a "*ballon-omnibus*" discussed—usually as a joke—in the French press appears to have first mentioned in the pages of *L'Illustration* in 1852. The term was further popularized by Alfred Assollant in his humorous novelette "Les Amours de Quaterquem" (1860; tr. as "The Amours of Quaterquem").

The Bourgeois: Do you hear that, Madame Glucôsin? It is the prerogative of our epoch of civilization to bring the conquests of science within the range of all purses. Will you let me have two tickets please, Monsieur?

The Lady: What! You want to get into that machine?

The Bourgeois: Yes, Madame. If I have no other heritage to transit to our son, I desire to leave him the glory of having had a father who was one of the first experimenters to travel the aerial plains. Follow me.

His Wife: But...

The Bourgeois: Madame Glucôsin, you have, I am pleased to render you the justice, fulfilled your duties as a spouse thus far. The law orders you to accompany me, and...

The Conductor: Climb aboard down there; or I'll leave.

The Bourgeois: Here I am, noble descendant of Icarus. (He drags his reluctant wife with him.)

Clampinet (a young Parisian lout arriving breathless, with a colleague): Ahoy the balloon! Hang on a tick. Here are two young folk of good family who want to play Nadar. Are you coming, Boireau?

Boireau: All right, if you pay for the ticket.

Clampinet: When I invite someone, I have a principle of not lacking delicacy. Here's twenty sous, my dear controller. Hand me two boarding passes.

The Conductor: We're full.

Clampinet: What do you mean, full? Where there's room for a hundred, there's room for a hundred and two. Just time to wipe our feet and we're yours. Forward ho, Boireau!

Boireau: What if we have an accident?

Clampinet: So what? You can't be afraid of causing your parents grief, since they've never given you their address. Give me a leg up, and look lively.

The two friends climb up rapidly and fray a route through the crowd of passengers.

A Dandy: Look out, you clumsy oaf.

Clampinet: What? Is it perhaps necessary to walk on one's hands so as not to indispose Monsieur's varnish?

Boireau: Throw him overboard if he's not content.

Clampinet: Follow in my wake, while I get to the balustrade. I want a view for my money.

Boireau: Damn it! We're casting off. Can you hear the balloon sliding on its pulleys?

Clampinet: Music that reminds me of the overtures of the orchestra of the Petit-Laz![52]

The Bourgeois: Madame Glucôsin, doesn't our situation remind you of anything?

His Wife: Oh, my God! That creaking!

"I was asking you whether our situation doesn't remind you..."

"It's abominable. The wires are going to break!"

"Personally, Madame, I'm thinking about the ballad we heard sung the other night at the Alcazar, Nadar's *Aerial Voyage*."[53]

"I urge you to have the decency not to sing."

The Bourgeois (singing): And in the immensity I floa...oa...oat...

Clampinet: Oh la la! Will you look at that, Boireau. There's a real swarm of Parisians.

---

[52] The Théâtre du Petit Lazary was a marionette theater named after its Italian founder, initially specializing in harlequinades, but run in its heyday, in the 1840s, by a Monsieur d'Auvigney. By 1860 it was regarded nostalgically as a relic of Old Paris and a declining tradition.

[53] Nadar (Gaspard-Félix Tournachon, 1820-1910) is nowadays remembering primarily as a pioneer of photography whose portraits of the personalities of the late 19th century are still widely reproduced, but he was also an intrepid aeronaut, journalist, caricaturist (for *Le Charivari* among other periodicals) and one of the most prominent Parisian socialites of the 1850s and 1860s.

Boireau: It's funny, all the same, the capital as a cockchafer sees it!

"When one thinks that in the drawers of all those sideboards, thousands and thousands of people are amusing themselves snatching the bread from one another's mouths."

"Well, thanks! Philosophy!"

"If you think it doesn't make one reflect, to see oneself above the tops of lightning-conductors! Eh, Boireau?"

"What's that?"

"Look at the Panthéon! The domicile of the great men. From here, they look as if they're all grouped around a country oven. Cures you of the temperament for running after glory."

"And the Sorbonne to the right."

"The apartment of science. It takes up hardly any space on the surface of the globe."

"What's that further away?"

"Where?"

"That grape-pip on the edge of the water."

"The Institut, of course! The fatherland of Messieurs the Academicians."

"I've seen anthills that looked more consequential."

"And where a lot more work gets done—the ants are flattered by it."

A Joker: Great God, we're doomed! The balloon's running away.

The Bourgeois (going pale): Great God! Did you hear that, Madame Glucôsin? My days are in danger because I pushed conjugal condescension to the point of waning you to enjoy the spectacle...

His Wife: But it was you that wanted...

Clampinet: Don't make life so hard. There's no more danger than in a sedan chair. Eh, Boireau?

"What?"

"Look at the Butte Montmartre. One might think it was a Strasbourg pâté."

"And the Seine!"

"A reduction of the gutter in the Place Maubert."

"Clampinet!"

"Go on. I'm following your reasoning."

"Do you know what that square of spiced bread is that one can see in the direction of my index finger?"

"Down there? You no longer know your geography, then? That's the Bourse, my prince."

"Where they shift the millions with a spade?"

"Yes, precisely. The millions, the millionaires, the contents and the container—it seems so me that I could pick it all up in my hand like a basket to take to the market."

"Fortunately, I don't have millions myself—otherwise, I'd feel humiliated on their behalf!"

"The fact is that..."

A Rich Man (looking through a lorgnon and talking to his companion): My dear, I believe that I've just recognized Adèle going to the Bois in her victoria."

Clampinet: That's true. Hey, Boireau, can you make out that little black dot that seems to be moving?"

"Just about."

"The Avenue des Champs-Élysées, my lad. All that there is of high society, apart from us, circulating for the quarter of an hour on that ribbon. It's not voluminous, seen from here.

"And seen at close range..."

"No sarcasm, Boireau. Al the same, when one thinks that each of those microscopic flies probably represents one of those beautiful ladies for whom we have the weakness to commit follies!"

"Speak for yourself!"

"Thanks very much! I'm speaking for them—the ones that are amused by it."

The Conductor: Mesdames et Messieurs...

The Bourgeois: "What is it now? A new danger! Why are we stopping. Oh, you won't catch me trying to realize Monsieur Nadar's ballads again.

The Conductor: "We've arrived.

Clampinet: Arrived! Arrived! I haven't had a laugh for my money.

Boireau: I'd rather have twenty sous' worth of galette—it lasts longer.

The Conductor: Get down, Mesdames et Messieurs. Get down!

Boireau: Is he in a hurry, that one? Is he afraid that someone will drink the gas from his aerostat?

Clampinet: If that's it, I want to be searched first.

The Conductor: Get off, or pay for the return trip.

Clampinet: The return?

Boireau: That's an idea.

"What! I don't think so. At the price you put on your emotions, you'll take another turn, would you?"

"Right!"

"Well, me, I've had enough."

"Because you don't have any more money."

"It's not that at all—but aerial navigation gives me too bad an idea of our fellows."

"Pooh!"

"There's no pooh about it! If I continue to see Parisians so small and paltry, it'll offend my dignity in future to pick up their cigar butts!"

SECOND SIGHT

I had just finished reading about the trial of the latest somnambulist hauled up before the correctional police.

As I finished, I began to think that it would, in fact, be a very precious faculty for a man to be exceptionally endowed that way, with the second sight of which one so often hears mention, but which, unfortunately, has remained thus far in the state of a fantastic hypothesis.

I had scarcely sketched that mental commentary when my door opened and I saw an unknown man come in of strange appearance. He was, feature for feature, the individual once described by Frédéric Soulié in his prologue to *Les Mémoires du Diable*: the same sardonic face, the same sarcastic gaze.[54]

Also as in *Les Mémoires du Diable*, my bizarre visitor sat down without even waiting until I had offered him a chair, nonchalantly picked an ardent coal out of the fireplace with his crooked finger, and, having lit his cigar, said: "Pardon me, my dear Monsieur, for that unceremonious entrance, but I never make any other kind. Just now, I was strolling in the vicinity and, my gaze having chanced to pass through the walls of the house in which you live, I caught you in the process of formulating a regret and a desire..."

"What does this signify?" I stammered, slightly troubled. "Do you have the pretention of making me believe that you're...?"

---

[54] *Les Mémoires du Diable* (1837-38) was one of the classic feuilleton melodramas, which remained popular throughout the century and beyond; it describes the adventures of an amorously-inclined young aristocrat who obtains assistance from the Devil in plumbing the mysteries of the fickle female heart.

"Astaroth, Satan, Beelzebub...the name doesn't matter. What ought to matter to you is that the second sight, after which you seemed to me to be sighing only a moment ago, I'm in a position to give you."

"You."

"Me."

"I'd be curious, of course..."

"Be careful—I warn you that it's not a very brilliant gift that I'll be making you!"

"You're joking! To be able to decipher thought through skulls, to unearth all secrets, lift all veils? If nature hadn't made us as wretched and as impotent as we are, and didn't feel obliged to give us that indispensable power, is it...?

"You want it—that's understood. I won't insist; your wish is granted."

My unknown had scarcely finished that sentence than a revolution immediately seemed to take place within me. My eyes were no longer the limited organ that I had known thus far. They traversed space; they overcame all obstacles; it seemed to me that they entire world was displayed before me like a panorama.

Carried away my enthusiasm, I cried: "But that's admirable! That's sublime! That's..."

My speech was interrupted by the arrival of my domestic, affable and smiling who said: "Here are the monthly accounts, Monsieur. If Monsieur will cast an eye over them...I've followed his prescriptions, and I'm happy to observe that I've been able to realize a considerable saving on the expenses of my predecessor. I hope that..."

While he was speaking, my eyes went back and forth between the page he was showing me and his face. Beneath the figures of the account, the true figures immediately appeared to me, and I was able to convinced myself that I was being robbed by a good third. At the same time, I read his thoughts like an open book:

Imbecile! I'll soften you up. I've stolen a bit less than the other for the first month, and as you have the habit of being duped, you'll take me for an honest man. Triple idiot! He thinks he's cleverer than us and is scornful of us because we don't have an education. We know enough, nevertheless, to keep you in the dark.

I didn't feel the need to decipher any more. In a thunderous tone, I said: "Here's your week's notice, and do me the pleasure of decamping immediately, crook that you are!"

"My God, what's the matter? Whence comes that distraught expression? On what grass have you been walking this morning?"

That was my friend Paul, who came in a few minutes after the execution that I had just carried out.

My friend Paul! The cream of friends, a Pylades!

"Can you imagine, my dear chap, that I've just sacked that wretch Joseph?"

"Has he done you a bad turn? That doesn't astonish me; the best are worthless. But let's talk about more serious things. I ran into the Minister yesterday in the Comtesse de B 's salon. He talked about you a great deal. He likes your paintings. As you can imagine I agreed with him. You'll be decorated at the next Salon. And I can say without boasting that I'll have had something to do with that..."

I looked my friend Paul straight in the eyes, and while the words pressed upon his lips, I read through his pupils: *You know my friend, that charity begins with oneself: I had myself introduced to the Minister and used your influence for that position I covet. As for your decoration, I'm damned if I have any desire to get mixed up in it. You don't deserve it as much as all that, anyway, and you can easily wait, my lad.*

Meanwhile, he was still speaking: "No, it's unworthy!" I exclaimed, suddenly. "One doesn't lie with that impudence."

"What do you mean?"

"That you're a scoundrel, and that I've been stupid to have the slightest confidence in you—and you'll do me the pleasure of going downstairs at the double."

"You're insolent, Monsieur, and my seconds will visit you this evening."

He had scarcely gone out when the doorbell rang.

"Who's that now? Damn! That rich collector who's supposed to be buying my last two paintings. Monsieur le Baron, do come in..."

The Baron came in, his lorgnon in his hand.

"Delightful, those two canvases, utterly delightful—that's the kind of paining I like, No, without compliments, it's quite remarkable."

Meanwhile, the satanic second sight read:

Personally, I find it frightful, but you're fashionable, my lad, and as I only have a gallery in order to pose, I have to feature you in it. Besides, you're going up, and I can probably make a profit reselling you, taking care to hurry, for your renown won't last. You're too superficial. In ten years, your daubs will no longer be selling.

"Well, what's your latest price, my friend?" said the Baron, terminating his little speech.

"None. I don't sell to idiots of our species. I'm not a grocer to haggle over the cinnamon. I don't want people just to buy my paintings, but to appreciate them. Go to all the devils."

"You're a boor or a lunatic, Monsieur. I'll tell all my friends about this, and if you receive the scrap of a commission again, I'll eat my hat."

I was suffocating. I needed air, and also consolation.

I ran downstairs after the stupid Baron. *Let's go see her*, I thought. *The sight of her will do me good.*

"Her" was an adorable creature, an ideal young woman to whom I was engaged. We were only waiting to complete the formalities before getting married.

I went in. She welcomed me with her angelic smile.

"How nice it is of you to surprise me! I didn't hope to see you during the day."

"Dear Berthe!"

"But I was talking about you with my mother. How can one forget you?"

Abomination! The second sight read:

Maman was explaining to me just now that this marriage is an excellent affair. I understand. You displease me horribly; you're too old for me, fat, gauche and disagreeable. But we're five girls in the family. Anyway, one will have consolers later. First, let's make sure of the income...

"Berthe!" I exclaimed, in a voice strangled by wrath. "That's infamous! Look elsewhere for a dupe; you'll never see me again."

After having run around like a madman, I found myself, I don't know how, in my armchair by my fireside.

I was weeping hot tears.

A finger was placed on my shoulder; it was the stranger from that morning.

"I told you that your wish was insensate."

"It's you! A curse upon your deadly present! I'm all alone now. In one day I've lost my best friend, the woman I loved, and my clientele; I don't even have a domestic on whom to take out my anger. All that by the fault of that infernal second sight, which..."

"It was you who asked for it, my dear."

"I was nothing but an imbecile."

"I don't say any different."

"Impertinent"! You'll give me satisfaction!"

After you've crossed swords with your friend Paul."

"That's true—I forgot about that. That's another one of the felicities I owe you. Triple brute that I was to want to undo nature. But I want to avenge myself on you, at least, and you're going..."

So saying, I had pounced on the fire-tongs. I brandished them, and...

And I awoke with a start.

All of that was no more than a frightful nightmare caused by the somnambulist's trial.

The *Gazette des Tribunaux* had fallen at my feet while I was asleep. I had not lost my fiancée or my friend. I was still the painter in fashion. My domestic, more obsequious than ever, announced that my lunch was served.

I had finally recovered that precious ignorance without which life would be impossible. And I went into the dining room singing, to the tune of *Galathée*:

"Oh, how sweet it is to see nothing!"

THE BRAIN-MENDER

One morning in the year 199 , the walls of Paris were suddenly plastered with colossal posters.

These posters expressed themselves in the following terms:

CONSULTATIONS
WITH DOCTOR MYSTERY
Supernatural surgeon
Every day from noon to four p.m.
452 Rue de Rivoli

Dr. Mystery! Supernatural surgeon! That was already enough to catch the eye of passers-by, so it did not take long for crowds to gather in front of the multicolored placards.

Who was this unknown scholar who claimed to be ally-ing science with miracle? Where had he come from? What did he do?

All these questions, the posters took it upon themselves to answer in detail, for they expressed themselves thus:

"After long and patient research, Dr. Mystery, who has made the human brain the object of a special and sustained study, has finally contrived to discover the secret of thought.

"As a result of countless experiments, he has succeeded in locating every human faculty, thought and passion.

"He has classified vices and virtues with a mathematical certainty.

"He has been able to draw up a kind of Cerebral Atlas, in which the exact location of everyone is noted.

"Each lobe has its function. Every circumvolution corre-sponds to a modulation of our character and temperament.

"The discovery, which has been the object of several re-ports to the Academies of the two worlds, was already sufficiently important to place the author in the first rank of physiological psychologists, but he did not stop there.

"With a new ardor, he returned to work, and his efforts have been crowned with success: a success that, it can be said without vanity, extends almost to prodigy and challenges incredulity.

"By means of a system of his invention, he makes an opening in the skull, without danger as without pain, after which he operates with a sure hand on the lobes, still without pain as without danger, making the modifications necessary to correct completely or to attenuate the work of nature.

"Let him be put to the proof: not words but deeds.

"For further information apply to the office of DR. MYSTERY, 452 Rue de Rivoli."

Two days later, people were fighting to get to the doctor's door. They had come to consult the prodigious surgeon, all desirous of asking him, on their own behalf or that of their loved ones, for the revision of their constitution.

Among the most determined was a charming young lady dressed entirely in black and discreetly veiled, who, after waiting for seven hours, was finally admitted into the innovator's office.

The latter made a majestic hand gesture, which signified: "Sit down."

Then he waited.

"Doctor..." the veiled young woman began. She stopped, as if it were impossible to overcome her timidity.

Doctor Mystery, dignified in his stance, adjusted his gold-rimmed spectacles, looked at the visitor and decided to throw her a lifeline.

"Madame has come for me to revise her? What are the faculties that Madame desires to modify?"

"None, Monsieur. I find myself perfectly adequate as I am."

The veiled young woman blushed on perceiving that; the confession had peeled away her modesty.

"But in that case, Madame, why have you come?"

"The thing is, Doctor..." The client made a supreme effort and, doing her best to steady her voice, said: "I'm married, Doctor. Married to a man who is deceiving me shamefully."

"The case is not uncommon, Madame," the Doctor opined, "but it is inexcusable when one is dealing with a woman as..."

"Isn't it, Doctor? It's an indignity. To run after just anyone! Because it is just anyone, Monsieur. Before having read your prospectus, I imagined that there was no remedy, but when I discovered your theory, I said to myself, perhaps there's something to be done—and I came in haste."

"Pardon me, Madame, but would you are to explain more clearly what you want me to do?"

"But can't you guess, Doctor? The passion for...how shall I put it?...libertinage..." The veiled young woman blushed again, but she was in full flow now and did not stop. "The passion for libertinage must be localized, according to what you say, in a lobe of the brain."

"Indeed, Madame."

"Well, I've come to ask you to operate on my husband. Render him calmer, I implore you. Let him be content with his wife."

"I should like nothing better, Madame. Nothing is simpler."

"It seems to me that I can be quite sufficient for him."

"It seems so to me too. Except, would your husband want to submit himself to the necessary operation?"

"I'll see to that. He's subject to terrible headaches, of which he wants to be rid at any price. I'll tell him that your treatment is infallible against headaches too. You'll confirm what I say, and he'll consent to the operation. But you'll promise me that Alfred won't be in any danger, won't you?"

"None, Madame, absolutely none. Oh, the old surgery never fails. I trepan a man, I manipulate his brain, and I stick it all back together painlessly. It only takes ten minutes."

"How grateful I am, Doctor! For it was frightful to think of Alfred deceiving me all day long. Yes, Doctor, all day long."

"Don't worry; we'll temper him. I'll take care of everything."

"That's admirable."

"Admirable indeed, Madame. Bring him to me on Monday, at two o'clock."

"Two o'clock, doctor. Understood."

And the veiled young woman left, with a light step.

The following Monday, at the appointed hour, as agreed, she came back with Alfred: a hearty fellow, in truth, whose appearances justified the information furnished by his wife.

The crowd in Doctor Mystery's reception room was as numerous as ever—to the extent that the concierge had been obliged to close the coaching entrance and only let people in on presentation of a visiting card. As the doctor had taken care to give his client an appointment, however, she got in without difficulty.

When she and Alfred had been introduced into the study, she said: "Doctor, I've brought you my husband. You know...for his frightful headaches."

She winked at the same time—a signal that he understood. He was a cunning fellow, untroubled in the midst of the improbable influx of visitors attracted by his marvelous discovery.

"Would you like to sit down in his armchair," he said to Alfred. "You won't feel a thing..."

The veiled young woman's husband sat down.

The doctor proceeded.

After a quarter of an hour, at the most, everything was back in place.

"It's done," said the strange practitioner.

And Alfred got to is feet, smiling, paid the bill, and left with his wife, who seemed delighted.

Meanwhile, Doctor Mystery's discovery had continued to make a great deal of noise in Paris.

Although the beginning of the twentieth century was accustomed to such prodigies, the new method surpassed in strangeness everything that had been seen thus far to such an extent that the excitement was at its peak.

To correct the work of nature, as the Doctor put it himself in his prospectus—to erase, so to speak, the human brain—was, it is necessary to agree, the most audacious of improbabilities.

Lively polemics were, therefore, engaged throughout the press. As usual in such cases, while some proclaimed that the bold experimenter was a man of genius, others accused him of being a bold charlatan.

For their part, the Académie des Sciences and the Académie de Médecine could not remain indifferent. Each of them had devoted an entire session to the examination of the doctrines and methods advocated by the innovator.

As always, the discussion had been as confused as it was sterile. The leading lights of the two Academies had pulled out one another's hair with their customary petulance. An investigation had been voted, but when the time came to elect the delegates, no one wanted to serve on the committee charged with reaching peremptory conclusions—and the public, with nothing to guide their incompetence, continued to rush intemperately to Dr. Mystery's consultations.

The evidence was there, anyway. One could not deny the materiality of the facts.

The doctor operated exactly as his prospectus indicated. He had already opened a considerable number of skulls in that fashion. He had carried out the stipulated ablations and readjustments in the brains.

It was truly miraculous. It only remained to see what ultimate results the method produced. For the practitioner had declared himself that it required a delay of three months before the faculties revised by him would recover their equilibrium and begin to function normally.

That three-month delay had just expired for the first subjects of the operation—and now, bizarre rumors were suddenly running through Paris. It was said at first covertly, that the operations had produced the strangest results.

Soon, there was a formidable crescendo: jeers from some, imprecations from others.

What had happened?

Something curiously ludicrous had happened.

As he had affirmed in his advertisements, Doctor Mystery really had found a means of scalping people for good reasons, and also a means of carrying out variations of brains without danger.

He had only forgotten one thing—the most important of all, alas: it was impossible for him to measure the dosage precisely.

You can understand, therefore, what extraordinary consequences, comical for the gallery, terrible for the interested parties, the hazard of the fork produced.

Astonishing stories circulated on that subject.

One gentleman had taken his son to the doctor, whose quarrelsome temperament made him fear for the future, for he had already fought three duels at twenty-two. The supernatural surgeon had plied the scalpel, and the young man had been metamorphosed, but to excess.

The surgeon had removed too much of his combativeness—to the extent that the unfortunate fellow had become a shameful coward, frightened of everything, trembling at the slightest gesture and allowing anyone who cares to do so to administer slaps to his face.

Then again, Doctor Mystery had treated a wastrel who threw money around recklessly—and the prodigality had given way to a hideous stinginess that made everyone bitterly regret the original fault.

No dosage, no dosage! All the harm came from that—and unfortunately, it as irreparable.

No dosage! That was what caused Dr. Mystery to see, one morning, at his consultation time, a young woman suddenly come into his study like a whirlwind. It was the veiled young woman whose husband he had treated in the circumstances described above.

On perceiving that abrupt visitor, and seeing on her face an expression of irrepressible anger, the physician guessed straight away that he was about to face a furious protest.

Alas, he had already seen so many in the last ten days.

"You recognize me, don't you, Monsieur?" the angry woman suddenly shouted.

"Madam, I…that is to say…I'm very conscious of having seen you, but I don't know in exactly what circumstances…"

"But I know only too well. Oh, I know only too well!"

She collapsed into an armchair. Then, suddenly, she leapt up again under the spur of indignation.

"But this won't do…no, it won't do at all…you have to put it right…"

"I would be obliged, Madame, if you would remind me in what circumstances…"

"I'm married, Monsieur; married to a husband whose escapades were driving me to despair."

"Ah! I remember now."

"You remember? That's very good. I came to find you on the strength of your brazen posters."

"Excuse me…"

"Yes, brazen—and even that word is too mild. I told you about Alfred's case, begging you to moderate it."

"I agreed to do that Madam, at your request. What complaint do you have to make?"

"You ask what complaint I have to make! Don't you know what you've done, wretch?"

And the veiled young woman drew nearer to the doctor, as if she wanted to scratch out his eyes.

"Please calm down," said the latter, genuinely frightened.

"I have enough calm; I have too much. Alfred has wearied of me, permanently. Oh, I complained before that he was

too high-spirited... I any case, Monsieur, if you have any conscience... What did we agree? That you would temper Alfred,
so that I would be sufficient henceforth for his happiness."

"I don't deny it."

"You don't deny it, but the facts are there. It was agreed,
I repeat, that you would temper him. Instead of that, you've
wiped him out, Monsieur! Completely wiped him out. He's no
longer a man."

"You must be exaggerating. I might have been mistaken
to a certain extent, and removed a little too much of the sensu-
al lobe, but..."

"But it's as I tell you, do you hear? Nothing left, nothing
left, nothing left!"

"Believe, then, that I'm very sorry."

"I don't care how sorry you are. You're going to restore
part of what you've taken away immediately...better all of it
than leave him in the state he's in."

"Unfortunately, Madame, that's impossible. I can't put
back what I've removed."

"But that's abominable! What do you expect me to do
with a husband in that condition? Oh, my God, my God, how
unhappy I am!"

She melted into tears.

"Please, Madame..."

"No, no, I don't want to weep, I want to avenge myself.
We'll take you to court, Alfred and I. You're a wretch, a thief.
Yes, a thief! See you soon..."

She went out, spreading imprecations through the apartment and the stairway, with which the crowd joined in chorus.

The veiled young woman kept her word. She instituted a
lawsuit. But when the day came for the hearing, Doctor Mystery had fled in order to escape the angry mob.

The young woman's lawyer then advised her to get a di-
vorce, and in the meantime, offered her his consolations.

She accepted the consolations and followed his advice.

As for the unfortunate Alfred, the victim of the intra-cerebral procedure, it's said that he has left for Constantinople, where he has become a Muslim and has been promised a position in accord with his lack of aptitude.

THE END OF THE WORLD AGAIN

Science is good for us.

It never neglects an opportunity to make some disagreeable prophecy. It is a first class alarmist.

In order not to get out of the habit, a gentleman from England who works in astronomy and physics has thought it appropriate to predict the end of the world for us.

It is about the five hundredth time that that gracious prognosis has been launched into circulation by various tricksters, but Mr. Thompson has the pretention of not being a trickster. He takes himself seriously and intends everyone else to do the same.[55]

At the last scientific meeting of the Royal Institution of London, he opened his heart, and allowed the heart-rending verity to escape that the world would come to an end.

The excellent Thompson has his reasons for being convinced of that. Do you absolutely insist on knowing what they are? Try to comprehend.

He supposes, like Helmholtz, that the sun is a vast sphere in the process of cooling—which is to say that it is contracting, by virtue of the effect of gravity on its mass as the cooling occurs, with the result that the temperature remains reasonably constant.

Solar heat, the savant Mr. Thompson adds, is equal to that which would be necessary to develop a force of

---

[55] Sir William Thomson, later Lord Kelvin, published a classic article "On the Age of the Sun's Heat" in *Macmillan's Magazine* in 1862. He reiterated its argument and conclusions in a lecture on the topic at the Royal Institution in 1887, subsequently reprinted in *Good Words* as "On the Sun's Heat." The essay helped to inspire several works of far-futuristic fantasy, including H. G. Wells' *The Time Machine*.

476,000,000,000 horsepower, which is about 78,000 horsepower per square meter of the surface of the photosphere.

Enormous as these figures seem to us, the dynamic theory of heat shows that a retraction of 35 meters a year ought to be sufficient for the sun to continue to emit the same quantity of calories in that time.

In these conditions, the radius of the photosphere would diminish by one per cent every two thousand years.

Oh, *zut!* I shall leave the excellent Thompson, whose calculations are becoming boring. I shall restrict myself to his total: ten million years!

I shall not hide it from you that that colossal figure made me think, and I started thinking:

My God, before arriving at that supreme landing-stage, through what stages will poor humanity have passed? What might have been, during those ten million years that remain to humans to live, the evolution of their politics, their letters and their arts?

And then, launching myself on the track of those hypotheses, I asked myself a heap of questions to which, in truth, I made myself very strange responses.

Politics first.

How many revolutions do you think it will have engendered between then and now? How many civil wars? How many regimes acclaimed and then demolished? How many problems solved one day and called into question again the next? How much bloodshed and sterile quarrels? How many frauds exploiting dupes? How many simpletons allowing themselves to be maddened by big words mistaken for great remedies? How many orators growing fat at the expense of the people? How many sovereigns dying in exile?

O Penelope of the perpetual recommencements! O human squirrel turning the utopian treadmill in its cage and mistaking its rotation on the spot for progress!

After politics, letters.

What might well be, in only five million years—I shall stop half way—the new idea of we use will be made for the fabrication of novels and plays?

We are already at the end of our tether, and have been for a long time. Everything has been said, everything has been done. Everything has been said again and done again.

And we scarcely date at present, historically, a few million years. Trivial!

When, on top of that, hundreds and hundreds of thousands of years have passed, I wonder where an unfortunate vaudevillian will be able to go in search of an unused pretext to marry Josephine to Albert. I wonder where the Ohnets and the Dumases will find material for plays that are not tiresomely repetitive, and where the Dennerys will obtain a professional accessory to replace "my mother's cross."

And the books—merciful Heaven! What library will be able to accommodate them? The surface of the Earth will be insufficient, only supposing that production continues in the same proportions as today—but it increasing; it is increasing frightfully, and there is no reason why it should not keep on increasing forever. In which case, we shall be obliged to adopt coercive and repressive measures.

In the same way that prefects are now obliged to publish a decree every year on the clearance of caterpillars, we shall see—or, rather, others will see—that a time will come it will be necessary to publish annual ordinances requiring the destruction of all unnecessary books. And in that category will be ninety-nine point nine percent of the intellectual production.

And the same elsewhere.

Thus, for the arts, there will be annual sessions of artistic cremation, in which five hundred thousand paintings will be destroyed in one go.

Oof! What a relief that will be.

But the excellent Thompson's prediction goes much further.

Go there yourself.

Launch yourself through those two million years that are the future of our old Earth, already so worn out, and our race, already degenerate.

I can assure you that, for evenings when one is idling by the fireside, it is more recreative than dominoes, or even Chinese bezique.

SF & FANTASY

Adolphe Alhaiza. *Cybele*
Alphonse Allais. *The Adventures of Captain Cap*
Henri Allorge. *The Great Cataclysm*
Guy d'Armen. *Doc Ardan: The City of Gold and Lepers*
G.-J. Arnaud. *The Ice Company*
Charles Asselineau. *The Double Life*
Henri Austruy. *The Eupantophone; The Olotelepan; The Petitpaon Era*
Barillet-Lagargousse. *The Final War*
Cyprien Bérard. *The Vampire Lord Ruthwen*
S. Henry Berthoud. *Martyrs of Science*
Aloysius Bertrand. *Gaspard de la Nuit*
Richard Bessière. *The Gardens of the Apocalypse; The Masters of Silence*
Albert Bleunard. *Ever Smaller*
Félix Bodin. *The Novel of the Future*
Louis Boussenard. *Monsieur Synthesis*
Alphonse Brown. *City of Glass; The Conquest of the Air*
Emile Calvet. *In a Thousand Years*
André Caroff. *The Terror of Madame Atomos; Miss Atomos; The Return of Madame Atomos; The Mistake of Madame Atomos; The Monsters of Madame Atomos; The Revenge of Madame Atomos; The Resurrection of Madame Atomos; The Mark of Madame Atomos; The Spheres of Madame Atomos; The Wrath of Madame Atomos* (w/M. & Sylvie Stéphan)
Félicien Champsaur. *The Human Arrow; Ouha, King of the Apes; Pharaoh's Wife; Homo-Deus*
Didier de Chousy. *Ignis*
Jules Clarétie. *Obsession*
Michel Corday. *The Eternal Flame*
André Couvreur. *The Necessary Evil*; *Caresco, Superman; The Exploits of Professor Tornada* (3 vols.)
Captain Danrit. *Undersea Odyssey*
C. I. Defontenay. *Star (Psi Cassiopeia)*
Charles Derennes. *The People of the Pole*
Georges Dodds (anthologist). *The Missing Link*
Charles Dodeman. *The Silent Bomb*
Harry Dickson. *The Heir of Dracula; Harry Dickson vs. The Spider*

Jules Dornay. *Lord Ruthven Begins*
Alfred Driou. *The Adventures of a Parisian Aeronaut*
Sâr Dubnotal *vs. Jack the Ripper*
Alexandre Dumas. *The Return of Lord Ruthven*
Renée Dunan. *Baal*
J.-C. Dunyach. *The Night Orchid; The Thieves of Silence*
Henri Duvernois. *The Man Who Found Himself*
Achille Eyraud. *Voyage to Venus*
Henri Falk. *The Age of Lead*
Paul Féval. *Anne of the Isles; Knightshade; Revenants; Vampire City;*
The Vampire Countess; The Wandering Jew's Daughter
Paul Féval, *fils. Felifax, the Tiger-Man*
Charles de Fieux. *Lamékis*
Louis Forest. *Someone is Stealing Children in Paris*
Arnould Galopin. *Doctor Omega; Doctor Omega and the*
Shadowmen (anthology)
Judith Gautier. *Isoline and the Serpent-Flower*
H. Gayar. *The Marvelous Adventures of Serge Myrandhal on Mars*
G.L. Gick. *Harry Dickson and the Werewolf of Rutherford Grange*
Delphine de Girardin. *Balzac's Cane*
Léon Gozlan. *The Vampire of the Val-de-Grâce*
Edmond Haraucourt. *Illusions of Immortality; Daah, the First Human*
Nathalie Henneberg. *The Green Gods*
Eugène Hennebert. *The Enchanted City*
V. Hugo, P. Foucher & P. Meurice. *The Hunchback of Notre-Dame*
Romain d'Huissier. *Hexagon: Dark Matter*
Jules Janin. *The Magnetized Corpse*
Michel Jeury. *Chronolysis*
Gustave Kahn. *The Tale of Gold and Silence*
Gérard Klein. *The Mote in Time's Eye*
Fernand Kolney. *Love in 5000 Years*
Paul Lacroix. *Danse Macabre*
Louis-Guillaume de La Follie. *The Unpretentious Philosopher*
Jean de La Hire. *Enter the Nyctalope; The Nyctalope on Mars; The*
Nyctalope vs. Lucifer; The Nyctalope Steps In; Night of the
Nyctalope; Return of the Nyctalope; The Fiery Wheel
Etienne-Léon de Lamothe-Langon. *The Virgin Vampire*
André Laurie. *Spiridon*
Gabriel de Lautrec. *The Vengeance of the Oval Portrait*
Alain le Drimeur. *The Future City*

Georges Le Faure & Henri de Graffigny. *The Extraordinary Adventures of a Russian Scientist Across the Solar System* (2 vols.)

Gustave Le Rouge. *The Mysterious Doctor Cornelius* (3 vols.); *The Vampires of Mars; The Dominion of the World* (w/Gustave Guitton) (4 vols.)

Jules Lermina. *Mysteryville; Panic in Paris; To-Ho and the Gold Destroyers; The Secret of Zippeliu; The Battle of Strasbourg*

André Lichtenberger. *The Centaurs; The Children of the Crab*

Listonai. *The Philosophical Voyager*

Jean-Marc & Randy Lofficier. *Edgar Allan Poe on Mars; The Katrina Protocol; Pacifica; Robonocchio; Return of the Nyctalope;* (anthologists) *Tales of the Shadowmen 1-11*

Xavier Mauméjean. *The League of Heroes*

Joseph Méry. *The Tower of Destiny*

Hippolyte Mettais. *The Year 5865; Paris Before the Deluge*

Louise Michel. *The Human Microbes; The New World*

Tony Moilin. *Paris in the Year 2000*

José Moselli. *Illa's End*

John-Antoine Nau. *Enemy Force*

Marie Nizet. *Captain Vampire*

C. Nodier, A. Beraud & Toussaint-Merle. *Frankenstein*

Henri de Parville. *An Inhabitant of the Planet Mars*

Gaston de Pawlowski. *Journey to the Land of the 4th Dimension*

Georges Pellerin. *The World in 2000 Years*

Ernest Pérochon. *The Frenetic People*

Pierre Pelot. *The Child Who Walked on the Sky*

J. Polidori, C. Nodier, E. Scribe. *Lord Ruthven the Vampire*

P.-A. Ponson du Terrail. *The Vampire and the Devil's Son; The Immortal Woman*

Edgar Quinet. *Ahasuerus; The Enchanter Merlin*

Henri de Régnier. *A Surfeit of Mirrors*

Maurice Renard. *The Blue Peril; Doctor Lerne; The Doctored Man; A Man Among the Microbes; The Master of Light*

Jean Richepin. *The Wing; The Crazy Corner*

Albert Robida. *The Adventures of Saturnin Farandoul; The Clock of the Centuries; Chalet in the Sky; The Electric Life*

J.-H. Rosny Aîné. *Helgvor of the Blue River; The Givreuse Enigma; The Mysterious Force; The Navigators of Space; Vamireh; The World of the Variants; The Young Vampire*

Marcel Rouff. *Journey to the Inverted World*

Léonie Rouzade. *The World Turned Upside Down*

Han Ryner. *The Superhumans; The Human Ant*
Pierre de Selenes: *An Unknown World*
Angelo de Sorr. *The Vampires of London*
Brian Stableford. *The New Faust at the Tragicomique;The Empire of the Necromancers (The Shadow of Frankenstein; Frankenstein and the Vampire Countess; Frankenstein in London); Sherlock Holmes & The Vampires of Eternity; The Stones of Camelot; The Wayward Muse.* (anthologist) *News from the Moon; The Germans on Venus; The Supreme Progress; The World Above the World; Nemoville; Investigations of the Future; The Conqueror of Death; The Revolt of the Machines*
Jacques Spitz. *The Eye of Purgatory*
Kurt Steiner. *Ortog*
Eugène Thébault. *Radio-Terror*
C.-F. Tiphaigne de La Roche. *Amilec*
Louis Ulbach. *Prince Bonifacio*
Théo Varlet. *The Golden Rock. The Xenobiotic Invasion; The Castaways of Eros; Timeslip Troopers* (w/André Blandin); *The Martian Epic* (w/Octave Joncquel)
Paul Vibert. *The Mysterious Fluid*
Villiers de l'Isle-Adam. *The Scaffold; The Vampire Soul*
Philippe Ward. *Artahe ; The Song of Montségur* (w/Sylvie Miller) *Manhattan Ghost* (w/Mickael Laguerre)

MYSTERIES & THRILLERS

M. Allain & P. Souvestre. *The Daughter of Fantômas*
A. Anicet-Bourgeois, Lucien Dabril. *Rocambole*
A. Bernède. *Belphegor; Judex* (w/Louis Feuillade); *The Return of Judex* (w/Louis Feuillade); *The Shadow of Judex*
A. Bisson & G. Livet. *Nick Carter vs. Fantômas*
V. Darlay & H. de Gorsse. *Arsène Lupin vs. Sherlock Holmes: The Stage Play*
Séamas Duffy. *Sherlock Holmes in Paris*
Paul Féval. *Gentlemen of the Night; John Devil; The Black Coats ('Salem Street; The Invisible Weapon; The Parisian Jungle; The Companions of the Treasure; Heart of Steel; The Cadet Gang; The Sword-Swallower)*
Emile Gaboriau. *Monsieur Lecoq*
Goron & Emile Gautier. *Spawn of the Penitentiary*
Paul d'Ivoi. *Around the World on Five sous* (w/Henri Chabrillat)

Rick Lai. *Shadows of the Opera: Retribution in Blood; Sisters of the Shadows: The Curse of Cagliostro*

Steve Leadley. *Sherlock Holmes: The Circle of Blood*

Maurice Leblanc. *Arsène Lupin vs. Countess Cagliostro; Arsène Lupin vs. Sherlock Holmes (The Blonde Phantom; The Hollow Needle); The Many Faces of Arsène Lupin; The Island of the Thirty Coffins*

Gaston Leroux. *Chéri-Bibi; The Phantom of the Opera; Rouletabille & the Mystery of the Yellow Room; Rouletabille at Krupp's*

Richard Marsh. *The Complete Adventures of Judith Lee*

William Patrick Maynard. *The Terror of Fu Manchu; The Destiny of Fu Manchu*

Frank J. Morlock. *Sherlock Holmes: The Grand Horizontals; Sherlock Holmes vs Jack the Ripper*

Jean Petithuguenin. *The Adventures of Ethel King*

Antonin Reschal. *The Adventures of Miss Boston*

P. de Wattyne & Y. Walter. *Sherlock Holmes vs. Fantômas*

David White. *Fantômas in America*

Pierre Yrondy. *The Adventures of Thérèse Arnaud*

Victor Margueritte. *The Bacheloress; The Companion; The Couple*

SCREENPLAYS

Mike Baron. *The Iron Triangle*

Emma Bull & Will Shetterly. *Nightspeeder; War for the Oaks*

Gerry Conway & Roy Thomas. *Doc Dynamo*

Steve Englehart. *Majorca*

James Hudnall. *The Devastator*

Jean-Marc & Randy Lofficier. *Royal Flush*

J.-M. & R. Lofficier & Marc Agapit. *Despair*

J.-M. & R. Lofficier & Joël Houssin. *City*

Andrew Paquette. *Peripheral Vision*

Robert L. Robinson, Jr. *Judex*

R. Thomas, J. Hendler & L. Sprague de Camp. *Rivers of Time*

NON-FICTION

Stephen R. Bissette. *Blur 1-5. Green Mountain Cinema 1; Teen Angels*

Win Scott Eckert. *Crossovers* (2 vols.)

Jean-Marc & Randy Lofficier. *Shadowmen* (2 vols.)
Randy Lofficier. *Over Here*